CONRAD PHILLIPS

KV-029-025

Walk in the Dark

**MUSEUM
STREET
THRILLER**

LONDON
ARTHUR BARKER
LIMITED

First published in Great Britain 1955

For

CONRAD, JEAN

and

MASTER PATRICK HAVORD . . .

MADE AND PRINTED IN GREAT BRITAIN BY
MORRISON AND GIBB LIMITED, LONDON AND EDINBURGH

AUTHOR'S NOTE

Walk in the Dark really began for me in that scruffy café I popped into to get out of the rain in West Berlin in 1946. I was over there looking for a story. It was a harsh cold day. Opposite me in the café, a tall, blond young man with strange opaque blue eyes and a gaunt scarred high-arched face, drank black coffee. He had a twitch and an out-of-this-world look about him. He could have been a character out of something by Edgar Alan Poe.

We got talking. He said he'd just come from behind the Iron Curtain, where grey masses of humanity drifted aimlessly in search of bread and potatoes. He told me about the forced labour battalions. The back-street hovels in Moscow and the vivid greenness he'd seen in Culture Square. His stories of brain-washing—how it killed a fellow's soul and made the victim both ready and eager to confess that he was a traitor, a creature unfit to live—were fantastic and fascinating. Then he got around to the Hoffman Twins, which gave me the germ of an idea for *Walk in the Dark*.

It was a story of the great love an identical twin had for his twin brother. How he took his brother's place in Lubianka prison, where the brother awaited a brain-washing after being arrested as a spy. The brother escaped with his secret information.

What happened to those twins afterwards, I don't know. It didn't matter, because I had no intention of using the story. It seemed too fantastic to be true. But in those days I knew nothing of abreactive drug techniques and other shock treatments used to destroy behaviour patterns in the nervous system.

It wasn't until five years later when I read a paper by Mr. W. Sargant, F.R.C.P., in the *British Medical Journal*, on the mechanism of 'Conversion' that I realised that the character I'd met in Berlin was telling the truth.

One paragraph in Mr. Sargant's paper sufficed to convince

3

me of this. It was: 'There is also the bewilderment with which people witness the preparation of a person for his trial behind the "iron curtain" by a method which makes him not only believe but proclaim to the world that his past actions and ideas have been wrong and worthy of death, though shortly before he had thought them to be both right and honest. . . .'

I am also grateful to Dr. Phillips, Mr. Sargant's assistant at the Department of Psychological Medicine, St. Thomas's Hospital, London, for his kind help in explaining some of the modern methods by which conversion is achieved.

CONRAD PHILLIPS.

HOVE, SUSSEX.

1

IT all began the day Nina sent me that cable from Paris telling me Rick was dead. When I saw her name, I thought, Nina? Who's Nina? Then I remembered how Rick had mentioned her name in his last letter to me. It was some time after this I got that strange feeling Rick wasn't dead. And had I acted on this hunch instead of making that impetuous journey to Paris, this walk in the dark I want to tell you about would never have happened.

It was funny—I mean the mood I was in when that cable arrived. Everything was so normal, except possibly the weather. It was one of those bright blustery days we usually get in January. I remember how I'd arranged to take the afternoon off and watch Surrey play Yorkshire at the Oval.

I was in light training for my fight with Big Jim Hanslip, the southpaw, who'd made quite a name for himself up in Bruce Woodcock's country. I hadn't a clue what was waiting for me in the offing. I wasn't even thinking of Rick at the time. I'd got used to our separation by now. All that worried me was this fight. The articles weren't signed yet. Motty, my manager, was still haggling with the promoter 'to up' the lolly. And boy, we certainly needed that dough! At least, I did. For I hadn't had a fight since I K.O.'d Battersea Boy Boyd in January.

I had a long way to go in the fight game. I couldn't afford to be choosey about opponents. I was still fighting for peanuts. But my first big chance was in September—that was of course if Motty got what he wanted from the promoter. This was July. . . .

At this time Joan's tragic death still haunted me. I was feeling so lonely—so lost without her. When she was killed by that lorry we'd been married less than a year and I was struggling like hell to get used to living without her. It wasn't easy—acquiring new habits and everything. . . .

I'd got to the gym early that morning it all began, feeling somewhat lethargic, due I guess to the fact that I hadn't slept well the night before.

Nina's cable came while I was sparring with Golden Boy Sparrow, a young heavyweight from the Elephant and Castle. We were lamming into each other, when Motty yelled, 'Here's a cable for you, Harry.'

'Cable?' I said, breaking away from Sparrow and leaning on the ropes. I'd never had one before. Who the hell would send me a cable? I thought, sucking in an acre of air.

'Let's have a decko at that,' I said, jumping down from the ring.

'Here, kid,' Motty said, looking curious.

I took off my gloves and opened the cable. It said: 'Rick killed believed murdered stop Ring Hotel Sylvia Rue Norious Montmartre Paris stop Nina Dupont.'

It was like a kidney punch. I must have wobbled at the knees or something.

'What's wrong, kid?' Motty said, peeping over my shoulder.

A coloured boy was beating a tattoo on one of the small balls near the window. Sparrow leaned on the ropes, staring at me in that oafish vacuous way of his.

'It says Rick's been killed, believed murdered!' I mumbled, handing Motty the cable.

Before he read it he threw my dressing gown over my shoulders and then put on his horn-rim specs.

'I can't believe it,' he said, staring at me incredulously. 'Old Rick killed? It don't make sense, Harry.'

He was telling *me* it didn't. I just stood there, gaping at the window unable to believe it.

Motty re-read the cable. Suddenly everybody in the gym became concerned. First the coloured boy stopped punching. Then the whine of a skipping rope ceased. I looked round. The coloured boy was staring at me quizzically. But he didn't know Rick. None of these scrappers did. Rick hadn't been around since they'd been here. They were the new bunch Motty had collected from the Micawbers, who specialise in spotting potential Rocky Marcianos.

While Motty was perusing the cable I got to thinking how

long it had been since I'd last seen Rick. Over a year? It must have been that. I remembered how he'd dropped in to see me on his way to the States. Now he's dead! I thought. Dead!

I could'nt believe it. I remember how I shook my head and said, 'No, no,' aloud. Then I saw Sparrow staring at me. . . .

'Anything bad, Harry boy?' Sparrow called from the ring.

'Yeh,' I said. 'My brother's been killed.'

'Killed!' he blinked.

Sparrow wasn't very quick on the uptake—a good scrapper but not a very bright boy. Very few pugs are. Being socked isn't exactly conducive to being bright.

'That's right,' Motty called, holding up the cable and walking back to me. 'It says so here.' He glanced at the boys in turn. 'You didn't know him, did you?'

They wagged their heads, solemn-eyed.

'I heard about him,' Sparrow said, sliding through the ropes. Motty stared at me.

'Know something, Harry,' he said. 'Might not be as bad as it sounds.' He knew Rick well. They got on together like a house afire.

It was curious. I didn't feel Rick's death either. But I should have done—I was his identical twin. We were like two peas in a pod. If our mother was alive she'd tell you the same. Before even she could tell us apart she'd have to peep at Rick's mole. Another thing, when Rick felt down in the dumps, I was the same. If I were in trouble, he'd know it. That's how it was between us, so why was I getting no reaction now?

I stared at Motty.

'Tell me something,' I said. 'If Rick's dead, why don't I feel it? I have every other time he's been in trouble. But nothing ticks—nothing at all.'

He never said anything. I knew why. There were tears in my eyes. Is it any wonder? I'd had the lot—first it was Mum who died, then Dad, then Joan. Now Rick. . . .

While Sparrow took off his gloves, Joan's death flashed through my mind. One minute she was pulling my leg about something. The next she was a mangled corpse. It happened just like that. It wouldn't happen that way again in a million years. We were in Piccadilly, going towards Hyde Park Corner.

7

I didn't see it—that big yellow lorry which killed her. Joan didn't even scream. Never had a chance to. . . . One second she was smiling at me, the next she was a mangled corpse. This was what? Less than three months ago. . . .

'Tell you what,' Motty said, linking my arm and walking me to my dressing room. 'Go get your things on and leave everything to me. I'll do all the necessary.'

What a pal! I'd gone to Motty soon after Rick went to Tangier. He'd been like a father to me. From a crude slugger, he'd made me into a useful heavyweight. When Joan died, he handled all the funeral arrangements, the insurance—everything.

John P. Mott, was a short, wide man, with a broad, high check-boned face and a nose broken at the bridge. He'd captained the Golden Gloves team we sent to the States in the early 'thirties. In 1935 he went the distance with Kid Johnson for the lightweight title.

On the way to my dressing room, he stopped at his office and yelled, 'Hey, Jo.'

The kid appeared in the doorway.

'Will you check this address,' Motty added, giving him the cable, 'and see if they're on the blower.'

Jo was a dark boy—thin and dark, with a sad broken face. He'd once been in the running for a title too. But young Danny Peters of Bethnal Green, stopped him in the eighth round of the eliminating bout. He nearly killed Jo.

He blinked at the cable. He'd never been the same after that fight with Peters. Motty stared at him as he might at a kid.

'Well?' he said.

Jo glanced up, puzzled.

'This is Paris!' he said.

'So what?'

'What do I do?'

'Do?' Motty said, talking to him like a patient teacher to a backward scholar. 'There's nothing to it. Just dial O. . . . Get it? Do that, Jo, then when the operator says "Hello," ask her for continental directory enquiries. . . . And when you get them, you just ask for the Hotel Sylvia's number.'

While Motty was talking, Sparrow was showing off with the skipping rope—doing a lot of fancy stuff.

'O.K.' Jo looked at me. 'How's it going?'

'So-so,' I said.

'O.K.,' Motty said. 'Let's go.'

He pushed the swing door and we walked through to the passage leading to my dressing room.

2

A FLY sunning itself on the dusty window, was scrubbing its hind legs. I stood watching it for a minute or so. Nervousness I guess it was. I was like that—always scared to look ugly things in the face. But I couldn't ignore Rick's death.

Sitting on the chair, I unlaced my shoes and thought—Paris! I was going to Paris. I'd never been there before. I'd been to Belgium and Holland but not to France. At school both Rick and I were good at French and German. Although I still spoke good French, my German wasn't so hot.

Dad wanted me to teach languages. Just before he died I was all set to go to college. I'd have probably made a better teacher than I did a pug. But Rick didn't like the idea. There was no dough in teaching. 'If I could hit as hard as you,' he told me one day, 'I'd go in for the fight game.'

A couple of weeks after this we gate-crashed Motty's gym and Rick talked him into giving me a try-out. I was lucky. The boy they put me against thought he was in for a joy-ride. In the second round he got careless and dropped his guard. He'd belted me a couple of times under the heart and as we broke, I saw my chance and let him have it on the chin. He fell like a sack of spuds.

After that it was work, work, work. . . . I had to forget all I ever knew about the game.

The fly on the window flashed into a yellow blade of light and disappeared. I stripped off, picked up a towel and had a shower.

While I was soaping myself, I recalled that last letter Rick had sent me from Paris—how optimistic he was—how he hoped soon to hit the jackpot. But it was all so vague. His letters were like that. . . .

Rick went abroad soon after I started in the fight game. He craved adventure—always did, even as a kid. He went from job to job. I understood his inability to settle down. He liked to gamble. It was all or nothing with Rick. Routine bored him stiff. Just what he did abroad, I didn't know. I never bothered about it. Whatever it was, he was O.K. by me.

Rick and I were the best of pals. As kids we'd been inseparable—played the same games, shared the same mischief. We never rowed. We'd have arguments. But we never rowed. Once we got heated, we'd automatically cool off.

I dried myself. Then returned to the dressing room. While slipping on my trousers, I remembered that Rick's last letter was in my jacket pocket. I'd have to read it again. The sun had gone behind a cloud-bank. Looking out of the window, I watched a solitary butterfly vacillating between the blooms of flowers out there in the garden.

After I'd put my shoes on, I re-read Rick's letter. He mentioned this Nina Dupont. I'd ignored the name before. Rick had plenty of girls. There was that one in Rome—Gina Costello. Another one he used to rave about was a red-head—Charmaine somebody. Judy Drake was his favourite before he went abroad. There were so many of them. . . .

I took the letter to the window and read it carefully. After saying he hoped to hit the jackpot, he went on: 'Did I tell you about Nina? We met some weeks ago in the South of France. I'm doing a job for her father. That's why I'm in Paris. It's the sort of job you can't talk about. But it yields the potatoes. Maybe it will yield more than I dream of. You never can tell in this game what might happen. One day you're eating peanuts, the next caviare. But it is always dicey, boy. You never know when you're going to get the kidney punch.'

I hadn't taken much notice of these hints of danger. All of his letters were the same. He was forever trying to put himself over as a tough guy. But that was Rick . . . as much a part of him as his curly black hair. He'd posted this letter a couple of days ago.

As I knotted my tie, the sun came out again. The wind appeared to have dropped and the sky was almost clear of clouds. I listened to one of the boys out there in the gym beating a tattoo with the small ball. Sparrow, I guessed it was. . . . He liked to show off with his fancy stuff. Why not? It was the one thing at which he really excelled.

Well, I thought, we'll soon see what's what—whether Rick has been killed accidentally or murdered. Staring at my face in the mirror over the washbasin, I was alarmed by the pallor and those dark half-moons under the eyes.

I sighed a couple of times, then I wondered what the real gen about Rick was—what was in the bag for me.

Had I known half of what it contained, I'd never have left England. . . .

3

THERE was that fly again. It was back on the window scrubbing its hind legs. Why did I notice it? It was unlike me. I wasn't an observant type. So it must have been nerves.

I was feeling worse than ever now. A lump of concrete lay in my stomach. The inside of my hands were weeping. I hated the idea of going to Paris. When Motty burst into the room, I almost hit the ceiling.

'Say!' he drawled, staring at me incredulously. 'What's the matter, kid?' He came over, quizzical, alarmed. He had never seen me quite so overwrought.

'Blessed if I know,' I sighed. 'Nerves, I guess. . . . Any joy with that Paris number?'

'They're on the blower. But it's out of order.'

'So what's the drill?' I brushed my hair and Motty lit a fag. He looked as bad as I did.

'You're flying over to Paris,' he said.

'Me,' I said, glaring at him in the mirror. 'What, alone?'

'Afraid so,' he said. 'I'd like to come with you, Harry. Nothing would please me better. But you know how it is.

I've got all this—the boys to look after, the thieving promoters to watch—all that stuff, Harry boy.'

'I've never been there before.'

'There's no need to worry. A coach takes you to Paris from the airport. All you have to do then is to get a cab. It's as easy as that. You speak French, don't you?'

'Sure, but——'

'Look,' he cut in. 'All you do is to tell the taxi driver where to take you. That's after you're in Paris. It's no different there than it is here.'

Later, while walking back to the gym, I thought of Rick and me as kids—Harry and Ricky Hammond—the Hammond twins, they used to call us. How proud Mum and Dad were of us. We were up to all sorts of larks. . . .

'You see this Nina,' Motty said, pushing the gym door. 'Get the lowdown from her. She's bound to have all the gen. Give me a tinkle. When I know the strength, I'll advise you what to do.'

We entered the gym—a hive of activity now. All the boys were doing their stuff—sparring, shadow boxing, skipping and thumping the balls.

'O.K.,' I said to Motty. 'I'll do that.' It seemed simple, so straightforward. 'What do I do now?'

'Go home. Pack a bag. Collect your passport and leave the rest to me. . . . Jo will drive you down to London Airport. You'll need travellers' cheques. You get these at the airport. Anybody will tell you where. . . . Show your passport and they'll enter at the back how much money you're taking.'

He gave me a wad of notes. 'Another thing, you're not allowed to take more than five quid English money out of the country.' He faced the boys. 'Listen, fellers,' he shouted. 'Harry's off.'

They stopped working and looked at me.

'So long,' they chorused. 'And all the best.'

'So long, boys. Be seeing you.'

On the way to the car Motty said, 'If you're in any trouble just give me a buzz.'

Trouble? It seemed ridiculous. What trouble could I get in? That's how ignorant I was of Rick's set-up.

12

'Don't worry about me,' I said. 'I'll be O.K.'

Jo was standing by the Buick, the sun on his broken face. Before he drove off, I took one last look at this old pub where I'd done all my training. Something was hitting me now—a feeling of impending doom. But I hadn't a clue of what awaited me in Paris.

I got in beside Jo. Motty came round to the window and grabbed my hand.

'So long,' he said eagerly. 'Best of luck.'

'So long. And thanks a million.' Beyond him on the other side of the road, a woman was cleaning her front step. As we drove off, she rose and shaded her eyes. A white dog with a black patch over its eye trotted past on three legs, its nose to the ground. Jo swung the Buick into Marston Street and we shot past the blitzed site as far as Janson Street. What a mad driver that kid was!

I was thinking of my passport, how I'd only renewed it a couple of weeks before. The last time I'd been abroad was in June the year before. Motty and I had popped over to Ostend to watch the Belgium heavyweight fight young Henriques.

I was living in Shepherds Market—in the same flat poor Joan had furnished. It wasn't far from The Running Horse pub. We had four rooms—two bedrooms, living room and a big kitchen.

Jo and I never spoke till we were in Piccadilly. He was like that. He never spoke unless you said something first. That beating he took from young Peters had done something to him —had destroyed his confidence.

'Motty told you about Rick?' I said.

'Pretty bad, huh?' he nodded.

'Yeh,' I drawled. 'It couldn't be worse, Jo.'

'Wish I were coming with you, Harry. Always wanted to see Paris. Nearly did once. . . .' He stared sadly and reminiscently. The traffic was piling up ahead. 'That was before my do with Peters,' he added. 'Some town, they say. Nude shows and everything.'

'I've never been there.'

'Ask Johnny Miller. He'll tell you. Him and Sarah were over there in the spring. Nude shows and everything he said there was.' He licked his lips and wagged his head obscenely, a dreamy look in his eyes.

We stopped at the lights near the Ritz. Then I saw how I had to get used to the idea of Rick being dead, the same as I had to about Joan's death. But I was sure I'd never be quite the same again. It was like a part of me had died and I'd never, never be quite the same again.

What was holding us up? I came to earth and stared at the road-makers—at them and that tar-boiler from which all the wretched smoke was curling. Glancing at Jo, I saw he was even more impatient than I.

'Can you imagine it,' he said. 'Working here on a day like this. Why the hell don't they do these jobs at night when there's no traffic about?'

Suddenly the jam broke. The cars scattered like so many scalded cats. Jo swerved past a taxi, almost lifting its nearside fender off. He raced a couple of Morrises and then turned right into Shepherds Market.

It didn't take long to pack. While I was doing so Motty gave me a buzz. Everything was laid on for me at the airport, he said.

'All you do is get your travellers' cheques, your francs and then collect your ticket from the B.E.A. office.'

'Thanks,' I said.

4

I DIDN'T know it then but I'd been shadowed right from the time I left Motty's gym. . . . I wasn't looking for it. It was the last thing I'd have thought of. I'd been living too long in dear old England to look for this cloak and dagger stuff old Rick was mixed up in.

Jo parked the car in the yard near the departure building at the airport. When we got out a cop said it would be O.K. there for about ten minutes. 'No more,' he warned. A plane was just taking off. Another one was coming in to land, swooping down like a giant bird. The noise was pumping me up like a

14

balloon and creating a feeling that I was going to bust any moment.

Passengers leaving the Customs shed were clambering into one of those grey B.E.A. coaches, parked near the exit.

'I'm very sorry about Rick,' Jo said.

'There it is,' I said. 'If he's gone there's nothing anybody can do about it.'

'He had a lot of guts—a lot of guts and he was a nice fellow, Harry. One of the best.'

We entered the departure building and walked through to the B.E.A. counter. Settees in front of the other airline desks were crowded with passengers and groups of tourists returning to the Continent gossiped in the foyer.

'Look at the way they stare at you, Harry—all these people,' Jo went on. 'Know why? I'll tell you. You're somebody, Harry. You give something—something these people feel—something that tells them you're somebody important. They never look at nobodies. When I was going to the top, I got the ganders too.'

I wondered what all this was in aid of. Jo spoke such utter nonsense at times. Anyway, at that moment I wasn't interested in him—it was the bloke who'd jumped up from a settee in the foyer and had followed us, that interested me. He kept right behind us. He was a humpback—a strange, sinister little cove with a check suit and a grey Anthony Eden hat sitting precariously on the side of his long head. The cigar slanting across his receding chin was well chewed at one end and he kept stroking his crescent-moon nose with his right index finger.

Jo was still talking. I collected a few francs and travellers' cheques. Then we went to the girl behind the B.E.A. counter and asked her about my flight. She told me where to go.

I said good-bye to Jo. Then joined the other passengers of my flight. We were told to have our passports ready.

As we walked down to the Customs tables, a trim blonde number gave me the eye. Then as I lifted my bag on to the table, this humpback stopped behind me. . . . That was the last I saw of him till we got to Paris.

As we followed the pretty hostess in charge of us to the

15

plane, I noticed that the blonde kept staring at me. Then when I was about to sit down in the plane, I saw her standing next to me, smiling.

'Would you like the inside seat?' I asked the blonde.

'That's very sweet of you,' she smiled. She sat down, putting her shiny black bag on her lap. 'Not much of a day for flying, is it?'

'No,' I agreed. 'It's been pretty lousy all day.'

The 'fasten-your-safety-belts-no-smoking' sign flashed on the screen ahead. Then the plane taxi-ed to the runway. A few minutes later it was roaring and I somehow shared its desperation to become airborne. It was always the same when I was flying. I always participated with the engine as it strained to leave the ground.

'Do you like flying?' the blonde smiled.

'Quite frankly, I don't,' I said.

'That's funny,' she said. 'I'm the same. It always gives me the willies.'

We yapped a lot of small talk. Then I fell to thinking about Rick—how he'd come to get himself killed. . . .

The flight was uneventful. At Le Bourget Airport we were escorted to a coach. The blonde was still with me.

'Staying long in Paris?' she asked, as we entered the coach. The humpback chose the seat behind us.

'I don't know,' I said. 'It all depends. . . .'

'Been here before?'

'No.'

'You'll love it,' she smiled. 'It's a wonderful city.'

'I don't think I shall,' I said, as the other passengers piled in.

'Oh, why?'

I told her about Rick.

'How terrible,' she said. 'I'm—I'm so sorry.'

The coach left the airfield and turned right into that straight road that leads to Paris. I was still nervous, still full of strange foreboding. When we got to Paris the blonde and I each changed a travellers' cheque.

'It looks an awful lot of money,' I said.

'It won't go far in this town.'

We shook hands. She said she was staying with friends on the Left Bank.

'Probably see you again,' I said.

'Let's hope so.'

Then I was alone. A flunkey got me a cab. As I went out, I passed the humpback, who stood on the front step of the B.E.A. office. He didn't even look at me this time.

I told the driver where to go and then got in the cab and tried to relax.

Paris! I thought, as we went along. What a city! The spacious boulevards, the mad traffic and the crowds of people flocking the pavements were all so entrancing, so exciting.

The driver was crazy. At least that's what I deduced from the way he drove. He would have done well as a driver in one of those old Keystone Kops' films. I thought I was a fast driver. But this boy was at the top of the class. It wasn't until we reached the curving Rue Custine that I relaxed. The traffic fell away. The cab, groaning like an old woman, slowed, and I was able to see something of the cafés and the people on the terraces.

The Hotel Sylvia was at the far end of a little square up there in Montmartre. Artists painted in the sun. People sat under red umbrellas sipping beer and wine. Tourists were shepherded into the square by a roguish-looking French-woman. We had to stop to let them go by.

An artist in a black beret, stood at the end of the square, rocking with laughter. An urchin stared up at him in wonder.

The Hotel Sylvia was a scruffy, yellow building with cracked walls. Paint on the woodwork was blistered and the name painted in white was so badly faded you had to look twice at it before you could read it.

It looked like a private house to me. I paid off the cab. Then I climbed a couple of steps and tried the front door. While I did so somebody in the square played an accordion. The door was locked. A dirty bell-push on the left looked as if it had never been used. I stabbed it. A bell rang inside. A white cat meowed and ran in front of me. The door opened.

'Bon soir, Monsieur.' He was a tall, scruffy character in a black beret. He wore a broad satin bow and a black velvet jacket.

'Is this the Hotel Sylvia?' I said.

'Oui,' he frowned. Then he suddenly stiffened, blinking at me as he might at the man in the moon. 'Why—why—why,' he stuttered. 'Monsieur Rick!'

'No, I'm his twin brother,' I explained.

'Ah, oui,' he sighed emotionally. 'I remember. Nina she say you were 'phoning her from London.'

'I was going to. But your 'phone's out of order.'

'I'm afraid so. . . . You want Nina, yes?'

'Is she in?'

'No. But please come in.' He opened the door wide. Beyond him was a flight of stairs. The floor was bare. On the left was a little office. 'Nina has a studio up in Olympus.' He grinned. 'That is our little joke.'

'Will she be long?'

He glanced at my suitcase and shrugged. 'No, Monsieur. She's in the Rue Lamarck, near the steps, I think. Should be back in ten minutes, maybe. She pop out for some food. You like to go and wait in her apartment, oui?'

'Think she'd mind?'

He grinned.

'Mind, Monsieur? Oh, no, why should she? She'll be happy to see you, Monsieur. What trouble!' He raised his hands. 'The poor girl. Only a few weeks ago it was her brother, Pierre. Now it's your brother.' He broke off and stared at me. 'It happened so suddenly, Monsieur—so—so swiftly. The night before last.'

'How?'

'I really don't know, Monsieur. You had better see Nina. She tell you all about it. . . . Will you come this way?' He turned and I followed him up the stairs.

On the top landing, he stopped and looked round, breathing hard. 'These stairs will kill me,' he said, unlocking Nina's studio.

It was large—a studio-cum-kitchen affair. A skylight formed the west side of the ceiling. On an easel near the door stood the partly painted canvas of a girl in the nude.

'Nina's an artist?' I said.

'Ah, oui, Monsieur,' he grinned. 'A very clever one too.

"The Genius" we call her. That of course is an exaggeration. But she is good, Monsieur. Very good indeed.'

Seeing Rick's school blazer on a hanger, I said, 'Did my brother stay here?'

'No, Monsieur. He live in the Latin Quarter, I think. He came here sometimes to see Nina. Rick was a friend of Pierre.'

'I see.' Beneath the blazer were two zip-bags. 'And those things?'

'Nina got them today from his lodgings.'

He turned to go.

'Perhaps,' I said, 'you could help me. My brother—he was shot?'

'Shot! Oh, no, Monsieur. It was in the Rue Lamarck. They found him run over.'

'Run over!'

He nodded, looking surprised at my incredulity.

'But Rick—why, Rick wouldn't get run over. . . .'

He hunched his shoulders and then dropped them.

'Maybe he'd too much wine, Monsieur,' he suggested. 'It happens all the time—just enough to blur judgment, and woomph! It's all over. Happens in a matter of seconds.'

'Did Rick drink much?'

'Much? I don't know. Nina, she'll tell you.' He went out to the landing. As he turned to go downstairs, I said, 'Excuse me. But where's my brother's body?'

'In the mortuary.'

'Where's that?'

'Rue Benard.'

'Nina's been there, of course?'

'Oui.'

He went downstairs. I sat in an easy chair. The little girl smiled winsomely at me from the canvas. The shadow of a bird on the skylight had me staring up. Night was advancing. It would soon be dark.

What had existed between Nina and Rick? Were they lovers? What was Rick doing with her brother, Pierre? These were a few of the questions I asked myself while I awaited Nina's return.

A loose floorboard on the stairs creaked. It sounded as if somebody was taking pains not to be heard. I stood up, stepped over my bag and tiptoed to the door.

'Who's that?' a girl called.

'Henri.'

'What are you doing up there?'

'You've a visitor, my dear.'

'Visitor?'

I opened the door and stepped through to the landing. The old man was hurrying downstairs. Why was he still there? I saw him stop to let Nina pass. She was carrying a shabby basket from which protruded a long, crusty french loaf. She looked up. Our eyes met. So—so you're Nina, I thought. What a strange, tragic face! Its beauty was awe-inspiring—a classical pallid beauty. The long, lank, chestnut hair hung listlessly over her shoulders. The face—high arched and oval, was dominated by deep-set amber eyes. You scarcely noticed the nose, straight with small marbled lobes which were now flared. She was staring at me as she might at an apparition, the eyes bulging and incredulous. Mounting the last flight of stairs, she still stared, her pace increased with each step. Then, just before she reached the top, she cried, 'Harry!'

'Nina?'

She dropped her basket and then fell on to me, whimpering like a child.

'You, you scared me,' she managed to say. 'I—I thought at first you, you were Rick come back to life.' She stood back and stared at me afresh. 'Why—why didn't you say you were coming?'

'Your 'phone's out of order.'

'Ah, well. Rick said you'd come, cherie, if he were in trouble. He said, "Don't forget—if I'm in a bad way, send for Harry."' She picked up her basket and led the way into the studio.

5

NINA's ability to cool rapidly after an emotional outburst amazed me. It seemed contradictory. It left me wondering—wondering whether she was sincere or just a phoney. Perhaps it's the French temperament, I concluded. Having come all the way from London, I expected her to give me the gen about Rick's death right away. But after this emotional outburst she suddenly went off the boil and settled down. I watched her unpack her shopping. She took her time. When she'd finished, she went to the kitchen. I heard water squirting into something. A couple of saucepans banged against something hard. She coughed. Then I saw her framed in the doorway, a cigarette between her lips. Our eyes met. She looked very sad and troubled now.

'What happened?' I asked.

She came over, her head bowed, her eyes loaded with woe, and sat opposite me on a straight-backed wooden chair. After coughing, she crushed her cigarette in a glass ashtray on the table.

'They killed him,' she said, twisting a handkerchief. 'That's what happened. He knew they'd have a try. He told me so. He said, "You wait. They'll try to do to me what they did to Pierre." They must have known that Rick had found them somewhere on Pierre's body—that Pierre had told him where he would find them in the event of anything happening to him.'

I blinked at her in bewilderment.

'Who are *they*?' I asked.

'Didn't you know—didn't Rick tell you where he'd put them?' She reached over and picked up a blue pack of cigarettes.

'I don't know what you're talking about,' I said.

She shook a cigarette from the pack, poked it between her thick lips and then asked me for a match.

'I don't smoke,' I said. She got up and walked to the gas stove. While she lit the cigarette I had an uneasy feeling Nina

21

wasn't all she appeared to be; that she was playing poker with all the skill of a professional gambler.

'Excuse me.'

'Yes.' She snatched the cigarette from her lips and sat down again, apparently eager to listen to what I had to say.

'Would you put me in the picture? I gather somebody was mixed up with Rick because he had taken something from your brother's body. Who are they?'

'Red agents,' she said, swallowing a mouthful of smoke. 'Rick never told you?'

'Never mentioned it.'

'Really?' She looked as if she doubted my word.

'Don't you believe me?'

'I can understand your reluctance to admit anything about it to anybody. I'd be the same in your place. The game they were playing wasn't for peanuts. The boys from Moscow were desperate. They had to get the micro-film Rick took from my brother's body before Washington saw it.'

'What was photographed?'

She shrugged.

'I don't know. That was the trouble. Neither Rick nor Pierre told me anything. All I know is that Pierre had been in Moscow. Rick told me. He'd come into possession of this micro-film. Rick found Pierre hanging from the banister in the house in which they both had a room. Rick told me. It was the first I knew my brother was in Paris. We hadn't seen each other for years.'

'Would the agents murder your brother if they found the film?'

'I never said they murdered him.'

'Where did Rick find the film?'

'He never told me.'

'But he did tell you he found it?'

'Yes.'

'And that he had it in his possession?'

'Not exactly.' She shrugged. 'It's all so complicated. It's a long, long story. I've been terrified. How do I know what they'll do next?'

'When was Rick killed?'

22

'The night before last.' She dragged hungrily at her cigarette, her eyes heavy with trouble.

'How did it happen?' I said.

She got up and lit the gas.

'He was run over,' she said, glancing at me over her shoulder.

'Run over! Rick! Are you absolutely sure?'

'Of course I am.'

'Where's his body?'

'In the morgue, of course.'

'You've identified it?'

'Yes, yes. I identified it the same night.'

'You said you'd been out with him?'

'Yes. . . . We were celebrating in Le Café Noir. It was getting on. We were having a wonderful time. We'd been drinking in the cafés before. We weren't exactly plastered, but we'd had a few. Just merry. It was the first time in weeks I'd been this way. You can guess why. Pierre. His death had upset me. I was all pent up inside. Anyway, Rick took me to Le Café Noir. He liked it there. He'd just come from the South of France. He was doing a job for my father.'

'But you said he lived with your brother.'

'He had a room there. This was weeks before.'

'I see. As long as I get it right.'

'Rick told me about you.'

'What did he say?'

'Not much. He looked scared. I knew why too. He was scared of the Reds. Anyway, Le Café Noir was packed with writers, artists, professional bohemians, you know the type. Rick and I danced a couple of times. Then I went out to powder my nose. I wasn't gone five minutes. When I returned, Rick had vanished. Nobody remembered seeing him leave—the hat-check girl, the doorman, nobody had seen him leave I rang his digs later. There was no reply. In view of what he'd told me about being followed, I contacted the police. They asked for a full description of Rick and for me to ring them back.'

'You did that, of course?'

Nina nodded.

'Yes. They said a man answering Rick's description had been

23

run over and killed. He was in the mortuary. Would I go along and identify him? I did that.'

'Are you sure it's Rick?'

'Positive.'

My heart sank.

'Was he badly injured?'

She heaved a profound sigh and glanced the other way.

'You'll see for yourself.'

'Tell me—did you recognise him?'

'His face was crushed—unrecognisable. But it's Rick all right—his suit, letters from you, me and other friends were in his pockets. The colour of hair, eyes, the build—everything is like Rick.'

'Except the face!' I broke in excitedly.

'That's crushed.'

'I thought so,' I said.

'What do you mean?'

'I've got a feeling it's not Rick. Had it been, I would have felt it.'

A tiny smile played around her mouth.

'I hope you're right. Go and see for yourself.'

'Before I go, tell me: how did Rick come to know your brother?'

Nina had to think about that. Dragging her cigarette she stared speculatively at the skylight. It was dark now. The noise in the square outside had increased. People were singing and shouting.

Rick met Pierre a few weeks before Pierre died, Nina said. He was leaving a café in the Rue la Fayette one night and saw Pierre involved in what he thought was a brawl. Three men were pushing Pierre into a car. Actually they were trying to kidnap him. Rick waded into them and a fight followed. The gendarmes arrived and the kidnappers fled.

Nina squashed her butt in the ashtray.

'Pierre,' she went on, 'was so secretive, so aloof from me. He made a friend of Rick. And I presume he told him all about himself. I don't know. They never disclosed their business to me.'

'Did Rick tell you how Pierre got hold of the film?'

'No. But he must have got it in Moscow.'

I was anxious to see the body which was supposed to be Rick's. What she'd said about the face being crushed, excited me. I wasn't interested in the face. I could tell whether or not it was Rick without even looking at it.

'Did Rick have the film on him the night you celebrated at Le Café Noir?'

'I think so.' She lit another cigarette.

'Did you find it afterwards?'

'No.'

'So someone must have stolen it?'

'If he had it on him.' She stared at me under her long, curly lashes.

'You're not sure whether he had it?'

'No. But it was nowhere in his things—I searched for it. I never asked him about it.'

'Why?'

She shrugged.

'Because he might have suspected that I was specially interested.'

'What do you mean—specially interested?'

She glanced away, dragging her cigarette furiously.

'I might as well be frank with you. Pierre had told him I was once a member of the Communist Party.'

'I see. So that's why your brother never confided in you what he was up to?'

'I suppose so. But it was a long time ago. I was only a probationer. Nothing more than that.'

'How did you know Pierre didn't trust you?'

'Rick told me.'

'Do you believe your brother was murdered?'

She shrugged.

'I have no evidence that he was. Why should they murder him?'

'They may have known that he had the film on him.'

'How do you know that?'

'It's just a guess. Anyway, Rick was sure Pierre was murdered.'

She laughed.

'You know Rick—he had such a romantic imagination.'

'Do you think he was murdered?'

'I can't be sure. Maybe. He wouldn't have left without saying something to me. Anyway, I've got to get hold of the film. It's my property.' Her eyes went cold.

'It wasn't on Rick's body?'

'No.' She stared at me. 'Maybe you'll get a letter. Maybe before they took him, he posted one to you in which he told you where the film is.'

'He said nothing about it in his last one.'

'He wrote another. But he never posted it. When I went to the mortuary, they said it wasn't in his pockets.'

All the time I'd been with her, I had a growing conviction that she wasn't a hundred per cent sincere with me. Moreover, I grew more and more optimistic about Rick. I had a sneaking feeling that she had got me to Paris for some ulterior motive. It was her demeanour. She kept glancing away from me, avoiding my eyes like the plague.

She sat now staring at the smoke crinkling from her cigarette, her eyes blind with troubled speculation. The ticking of the clock on the mantelpiece grew louder.

'What business was my brother in?'

She stared at me in surprise.

'Don't you know?'

'No.'

She shrugged.

'Neither do I,' she said. 'All I know is that he lived with my brother.'

'But didn't he give you a hint about what he was doing?'

'Me? Why should he? I was nothing to him.'

'You say you can't find the film?'

'Yes, I say that,' she snapped.

'The only explanation is that it was taken from him before he was run over.'

'I wonder. He may have lied about it.'

I'd had enough of this. I had to see the body. Until I did, I'd get no peace.

'I'll pop along to the morgue,' I said, standing up and reaching for my hat on the table. She stood up too, looking very thoughtful.

'You coming?' I asked.

She shook her head.

'Tell me, did Rick not say what he was doing in Paris?'

'No.'

'But he was supposed to be doing something for your father. He said so in his last letter to me.'

'Daddy's like Pierre. They're all the same. Never say a word to me or to Mamma.'

I gave up. She was too much of a wriggler for my liking.

'Will my things be O.K. here till I return?'

'Sure—sure. You'll come straight back, of course?'

'Just as soon as I've seen——'

'I'd come with you,' she broke in, 'but I'm expecting a 'phone call.'

'Isn't your 'phone out of order?'

She smiled, showing her teeth for the first time.

'Yes—yes. I'm getting mine at Susan's. That's the café I use. . . . Come, I'll get you a cab.'

She opened the door. We walked through to the landing and then hurried down the stairs. Henri was eavesdropping. As we entered the hall, he pulled his head back into his room and closed the door.

'Nosey Parker,' Nina said, as the dirty white cat I'd seen when I came in, ran in front of us, its tail up, meowing.

Nina opened the front door. The cat ran out. Standing in front of me, Nina stared across the road at a man leaving a ragged shadow of a tree. We watched him hurry through the square. He was tall and lank and wore a cap and raincoat, the collar of which was upturned.

6

You'D have thought Nina would have come to the mortuary with me. After all, I was a stranger in Paris. Besides, had there been any doubt about the body's identity we would have been able to discuss it on the spot.

'I'll get the cab,' she said.

'Thanks.' I watched her run to the end of the square. She was gone several minutes. When she returned, she seemed less agitated and preoccupied than before. As she got out of the cab the driver said something to her.

'You won't be too long?' she said, as I got in.

'No. . . . I'll be back as soon as I can.'

She smiled and waved. I wondered what she'd got to be happy about.

The morgue was ten minutes' ride away from Nina's place—a drab, grey building standing in the shadows of some huge plane trees. It had a forlorn eerie look about it. Perhaps it was just my imagination. Paris did this to me. After what Nina had told me about Red agents, I felt that anything could happen here.

The cab stopped at the front entrance. I wondered what to do—whether to pay it off or to keep it. I got out and stared at the shadowed swing doors at the top of a flight of stone steps.

'Could you wait?' I asked the driver, who was staring at something on the other side of the road.

'Oui, Monsieur,' he said, without looking at me. I thought nothing of this. That's how naïve I was at this time. But I wasn't so indifferent when I saw the man standing in the fat shadow at the top of the steps—a squat, stunted little fellow with a black hat over his eyes. He looked like the humpback I'd come over with. As I drew level with him, he glanced the other way. I remember thinking how I'd probably been followed from England.

The cold, marble-floored foyer, with its mean lighting and panelled walls, was empty. I went in and walked to a small office facing the door—a mean little fleapit of a place, in which a scruffy, bald-headed official was sitting at a desk, studying what looked like sweepstake numbers through his thick-lensed, steel-rimmed spectacles.

'Bonsoir, Monsieur,' I said.

'Bonsoir.'

I explained who I was and what I'd come about.

'Ah, oui, Monsieur,' he said, pressing a white button on his desk. 'I'll get the porter to take you downstairs to the mortuary.'

28

I waited a couple of minutes. Then a skinny little man in a grubby blue uniform piloted me down a long curving flight of marble stairs to the basement.

'You come to identify somebody?' he asked.

'My brother.'

He tutted, sighed and shook his head.

'That is sad,' he said. 'This is a sad job, Monsieur. Every day we see tragedies of life—mothers, fathers, brothers, sisters, sweethearts—they all come here to see their dead.'

We went through some swing doors and entered a big, dimly lit smelly room.

'Jacques,' the porter called. 'I've got a customer for you.'

The mortuary keeper, a huge sad man, with a heavy black moustache and a thick red bottom lip, took off his leather apron and threw it on a marble slab. I told him who I was.

'Oh, yes,' he sighed. 'Please come this way. . . You come from England?'

'Yes,' I said.

'You think him maybe your brother?'

'I shan't know till I see him.'

I saw the first body—an emaciated old man lying naked on a marble slab, his eyes staring starkly at the murky ceiling.

'They found him dead in a cellar,' the mortuary keeper said.

'Poor man.'

'Oh, I don't know, Monsieur. If he could talk he'd probably say of us—"Ah, the poor devils are still living." '

A bent old man with a watching black patch over his eye met us as we entered another room.

'The Englishman,' the mortuary keeper said. Then turning to me, he added, 'It's not a pretty sight.'

The other man pulled out a drawer.

'Is that your brother?' the mortuary keeper asked.

I looked.

'The lorry wheels went right over his face,' the keeper grunted, glancing at me over his lumpy shoulder. They had crushed it beyond recognition. But I wasn't interested in that. It was the chest that fascinated me. I bent down. There was an ugly wound on the right side of the ribs.

'Well?' said the mortuary keeper.

I stood up, wagged my head. Boy, was I feeling happy!

'It's not him,' I said dramatically.

The keeper was flabbergasted.

'What makes you so sure?' he blurted.

I pointed to the left pectoral muscle.

'My brother has a strawberry mole no bigger than a pin's head just there.'

He bent down, squinted, closed one eye and said, 'You're right. There's no mole there. But I don't understand. A lady identified the corpse as Monsieur Rick Hammond. The papers in the pockets—they're all to do with Rick Hammond.'

He took me to see his chief. But he wasn't in.

'I don't know what to do.' He looked positively bewildered. 'We've never had one like this before.'

'I couldn't care less,' I said, bubbling over with joy.

'You'll have to see the police. They say he's Rick Hammond.'

'And I say he's not.'

'It must be wonderful to find it wasn't your brother,' he added.

He was telling me. . . .

7

ON the way out, I thought of Motty—how happy he'd be when he heard the good news. But it wouldn't surprise him. Like me, he knew Rick wasn't the type that gets himself killed. But elation over the discovery that it wasn't Rick's body, was, however, short-lived when I started to reflect.

There were questions. Who put Rick's clothes and letters on the corpse? Where was Rick? Was he dead? If not, where was he? Where was I to start looking for him?

There was nothing I could do about it at the moment. I'd discuss it with Nina. She might have some ideas. Then I'd ring Motty in London. After that, I'd consult the police.

Perhaps Rick was O.K. Perhaps he'd suspected Nina and had done a bunk. Or he might have decided while she was away to give his 'tails' the slip. There were no flies on Rick. If he were playing a dangerous game, he'd know all the snags.

Outside, I sucked in the warm night air, and stared up thankfully at the winking stars. A breeze had got up. It was playing games with bits of paper in the road. Where was my cab? I looked each way for it. Why had it moved off? From where I stood it was scarcely visible in the black shadow bulging from the gaunt building. What was it doing there? I hurried over the cobbles and past puddles, reflecting trembling street lamps. Where were all the people? The only living thing I could see was the skinny black cat that ran across my path and into a fat ragged shadow of a tree.

'Sorry I was so long,' I said, as the driver reached back and opened the door for me. I wondered why he never turned; never said anything. I didn't have to wait long to find out. Just as I was about to sit down, the humpback whom I'd seen on the plane coming over, said, 'O.K., Mac. Sit down and make yourself at home.'

The automatic in his right hand had a stunted black barrel.

Swallowing hard, I wondered what to do.

'Who are you?'

'Just sit down like a good boy,' he said in a gruff American voice.

I sat down.

'Now put your hands behind your neck.'

When I hesitated, he thumped my ribs with the gun and murmured, 'Up—put them up, Mac.'

The car shot forward, forcing me to roll away from the gunman. For a fraction of a second I was tempted to grab him. On second thoughts, I decided it would be a most unwise thing to do; that before I could lower my hands to grab him, he could squeeze the trigger and blow a hole in my ribs. So I sat up with my hands laced behind my sweating neck and said, 'What's the lark?' or something like that.

'Look, Mac,' he purred, 'suppose you leave the quizzing to me. Tell you for why? I'm not the sort of guy who answers questions.'

Lights were flying past the windows and now and then I had glimpses of rumpled faces, of houses standing shapeless in dark shadows, of lighted windows and wet cobbles running under the cab's bonnet.

'You've got the wrong man,' I said, after a pause.

'That's what I like about you, Mac,' he crooned, 'your inferences. . . . So cocksure, aren't they?' He chuckled to himself. 'Know what I'd do in your place? Just sit tight and wait and see what it's all about. It won't be long. Just a few minutes, then the whole mystery will be cleared up.'

'Would you answer me one question?'

He chuckled again.

'I'll try. What is it, Mac?'

'Who are you?'

'Me. . . . Why, I'm—I'm Little Bo-Peep.'

He was quite a character. Despite the fact that his gun was hurting my ribs, I couldn't dislike the fellow. Apart from what he was doing, there seemed to be nothing dangerous about the man. I got the impression he was doing it as a bit of fun.

The cab squealed round innumerable corners. Then it shot up a steep hill.

'Would it be too much to ask where you're taking me?' I said.

'Much, much too much.'

I felt a fool, sitting there in that cab with my hands behind my neck. It reminded me of my school days—when we played cops and robbers and used toy repeating pistols to stick up our chums. If they got tough, we squeezed the trigger and the cap would explode and the kid would fall down and pretend to be dead. But I wasn't daring this boy to squeeze his trigger. I had a hunch I'd been mistaken for Rick and I hoped that once I'd seen the people who'd sent for me, I could explain who I was to their satisfaction.

The cab turned into a dark gateway and roared up a winding gravel path. The driver switched on the headlights and there on either side bunchy laurel bushes crouched like beasts of prey waiting to spring on a victim. The house silhouetted against the starry sky, looked like something out a spook novel. Standing like a sentinel on top of a hill, its windows stared down at a sloping lawn. As we drew nearer, the shape became more clearly defined—the slit windows, the turrets—it looked like something in mediaeval Spain.

The cab went round what was apparently a circular garden in front of the house and stopped at the foot of a flight of steps which ran up to a porch and the front door. The only lights were two thin yellow rods on either side of the curtains in one of the ground floor windows.

'Here we are, Mac,' the humpback said. 'You'll soon know what it's all about.'

I got up and stepped out into the drive. The house loomed darkly against the stars. It was quite a mansion. Somewhere at the back a dog barked.

'Mind if I put my hands down?' I asked, turning to the humpback.

'Any moment now, Mac,' he said.

'I'm off to the garage,' the driver called. 'If they want me tell 'em to give me a buzz.'

'O.K.' My captor pushed the gun gently in my ribs and whispered, 'Make for the steps.' The cab drove off, its lights raking the laurel bushes, and left us in the dark. Grains of gravel cracking under my feet as I mounted the steps sounded like machine-gun fire. The front door opened. An avalanche of bright light overwhelmed us. I blinked. Then I saw him standing in the doorway—tall, dapper, with a long English face. The dazzling light came from a magnificent chandelier in the spacious foyer.

'You Harry Hammond?' the man said.

Stopping on the threshold, I said, 'That's me.'

'Put your hands down.' I did that. He spoke to the humpback. 'You can blow now. Thanks for bringing him along.'

The humpback turned and walked down the steps.

'Excuse me for being nosey, but, but who are you?' I asked the man in the doorway.

'I'm Stanley,' he said in perfect English. 'Will you come this way please.'

He was older than his figure suggested—about fifty, I should say, with a lean frame and one of those high angular British-officer type of faces.

'I'm sorry about the way we had to get you here,' he apologised, as we walked to the double white doors at the foot of a broad staircase. 'I was against it personally. But there it is. It's done now.' The walls were draped with exquisite tapestry. Covering bald spaces were ancient shields and crossed lances.

'Who'm I seeing?'

'Marc Lamond,' Stanley smiled.

'Who's he?'

'Ah, you'd better let him tell you, don't you think?'

He opened the left door. As he did so blue cigar smoke limped out over the top of the air which rushed in the room. What a sumptuous drawing room! What exquisite furniture! Everything in the room blended—the pictures, brasses, carpets, everything.

Marc Lamond stood near the open fireplace, tall, wide, debonair. With him was an attractive blonde of forty, wearing a red off-the-shoulder evening gown and smoking a cigarette in a red holder. She had all the poise and dignity of a queen. But as soon as our eyes met, she drooped perceptibly. I wondered why. The man's face expanded in surprise.

'Good God!' he cried. 'I'd never have believed it.' He turned to the woman. 'Look at him. Isn't it incredible! Did you ever see anything quite so fantastic?'

Dragging at her long holder, the woman still stared at me in that rather sad repressed way of a wife whose man has crushed her.

'This is Mrs. Lamond,' Stanley said, presenting the woman. 'And this, this is Marc Lamond I told you about.'

'You gave me quite a shock, young fellow,' Lamond said, pumping my hand. 'I'm not fooling either. Believe me. It has to be seen to be believed. I must have looked surprised, huh. You're telling me. . . . Then of course I realised that it couldn't be Rick—that you were his brother.'

His sparkling forget-me-not blue eyes spaced wide apart under exquisitely arched black brows, were never without a smile. The nose, retroussé and feminine, had something very provocative about it. Here was a character who could have played a diplomat in any film.

'Kathie,' he added, clearing his throat.

'Yes, dear?'

34

'Ask our guest what he'd like to drink. After all, you are the hostess, you know.'

She turned slowly towards me smiling winsomely, still dragging at that holder.

'What will it be?'

She had expressive dark eyes and a very thin nose. But her beauty was already fading.

'Suppose you tell me why I've been brought here?' I glanced at them each in turn.

'It's about Rick,' Lamond said. 'And before I forget it, I must apologise for the way I got you here. You see, I didn't want to risk any fisticuffs. Rick has often told me what a hitter you are.'

'So far so good,' I said.

'Please have a drink,' Kathie Lamond said.

'Sorry, I don't drink,' I smiled.

'Of course he doesn't,' Lamond cooed, grinning affably at his thoughts. 'He's a pug, aren't you—a pro. Yeh, old Rick told me all about you—how sure he was you'd get that world title one day.'

'I hate to be rude,' I said. 'But I *would* like to know exactly where my brother is.'

'Perhaps Mr. Harry would like a ginger ale?' his wife said, her dark eyes expanding, smiling.

I liked her. Why, I didn't know. Something in her clicked with something in me—something nice, I like to think. Looking back it might have been a premonition of some sort—something which told us that our lives were inextricably mixed up; that we were destined to play such a vital part in each other's lives.

'No, thanks just the same,' I said.

'One of my contacts in the cable and wireless business,' Lamond said, 'told me you got a cable from a Commie called Nina Dupont. We flew somebody over to see you were O.K.'

'The humpback?'

'You see, we didn't want what happened to poor Rick to happen to you. You can't be too careful these days.'

Stanley went to a tray and helped himself to a Scotch. Then he picked up a syphon and squirted soda into the glass. I watched it bubble up to a foam and then stole a glance at Lamond's wife, who was smiling her approval of me.

'What happened to my brother?'

'I'm coming to that,' Lamond said. 'I'm glad you decided to come over of your own volition. Actually it was a Commie trick. Had Nina not sent you that cable I'd have got you over here somehow. Anyway, the set-up is so fantastic I don't know how to begin.' Pausing, he cleared his throat and added, 'Look, I might as well come straight to the point. Your brother's behind the Iron Curtain.'

I laughed.

'What, Rick!'

'Yes, Rick,' he drawled. 'We know that to be absolutely true. We got it straight from our agents in Prague. I spoke to Rick on the 'phone the night he was snatched. I'd just returned with him to Paris. It was just a bit of luck that I spoke to him then. He left me a 'phone number. I had a queer feeling about him that night. I don't know what it was—one of those things, I guess. The number was Le Café Noir's. I actually spoke to him. He sounded plastered. You see, he hadn't really expected me to ring until the day after. He said he was with Nina Dupont. I saw it all then—that the Commies would probably snatch him. So I asked him to leave and meet me at the Hotel Scribe.'

'Let's get this right,' I said. 'Pierre and Nina were brother and sister. Nina is a Commie. But her brother wasn't?'

'That's right.'

'What sort of work was Rick supposed to do for Pierre's father?'

'I'll tell you that later.'

'Darling,' Kathie Lamond said. 'Mr. Harry's obviously confused. He probably doesn't know the first thing about the film.'

'Oh, yes,' I smiled. 'Nina Dupont told me about it.'

Stanley took Kathie Lamond's glass and gave her another drink.

'So you rang Rick at the Café whatever-it-was,' I said.

'I told him to meet me. He said he would, in twenty minutes. When he didn't turn up I sent a man round to Le Café Noir

36

to get him. But it was too late. Rick had disappeared. Nina Dupont was still there. My man tailed her to a café. Here she was joined by a man—a man named Josef Mueller, a Red agent. They left and went to the mortuary together.'

'Excuse me,' I said, 'but who exactly are you?'

Lamond pouted.

'I'll tell you that when I've finished what I'm going to say. My man rang me and I went straight to the morgue. As soon as I saw the body I knew it wasn't Rick's.'

'Who's is it, then?'

'Who cares?'

'What was the idea of them trying to establish it as Rick's? It doesn't make sense to me.'

'They had to have something to show you,' he said. 'Then again they might have wanted to pull wool over my eyes.'

'How?'

'It's easy,' Lamond said. 'They'd know that if we believed the body was Rick's, we'd conclude they had the film. In that event we wouldn't bother to hunt for it any more.'

'Surely they'd realise that I'd know it wasn't Rick's body. After all we are identical twins.'

'That may be. But the fact remains that they got you here. And having done that, they had to have a body for you to see. Moreover, they allowed you to go to the mortuary alone. What they didn't anticipate was that we knew you were here and would snatch you away from them.'

'But why did they go to all the trouble to get me here?'

'The only reason I could think is that they might have thought you knew where the film was or to hold you as a bargaining counter with Rick.'

'But he's behind the Iron Curtain, you say.'

'Yes. Anyway, I can't read their minds.'

'For what reason did they kidnap him?'

'Now you're right up my street. To force him to tell them where the film is.'

'How can they do that?'

'By giving him the brain-washing treatment. It's shock therapy. When they're through, Rick will be pleased to tell them were the film is.'

'This is what will happen,' Stanley said. 'After forcing Rick to tell them where the film is, they'll check. If Rick's told the truth, he'll be liquidated. If he's lied then they try new treatment.'

It was like a crazy dream—my being here and listening to all this stuff. It was all so alien to my way of life.

'What do you want me to do?' I said.

'Let me explain who I am first,' Lamond said. 'I'm known as the fixer—he's a sort of middleman. My clients are people like Pierre—freelance agents who specialise in stealing valuable plans and secrets. I finance them. But don't get me wrong. Your brother wasn't in the racket. His meeting with Pierre Dupont was purely fortuitous. Pierre had got the film of top secret Soviet plans. It was given to him in Moscow by a man named Roper. This poor devil knew he had no hope of escape. The Secret Police were on his tail. Pierre was promised £40,000 if he delivered the film to a certain man in Paris. Before he arrived here Roper was caught and given the treatment. . . . Then he told them everything about Pierre.'

'What was Pierre doing in Moscow?' I asked.

'He went there for the Americans. But the man he went to see disappeared before he could contact him. So he stayed. He had to—at least until after he'd contacted those who make a business of getting people out of there. Meanwhile, he met this unfortunate Roper. Pierre went first to Berlin. It was from there that Red agents traced him to Paris. Nina told you what happened to her brother?'

'Yes.'

'Now, this is the truth. Never mind about Nina. This is the truth. Rick and Pierre became friendly. Then Pierre dies— suicide or murder—who knows? It doesn't matter. What does matter is that the Reds believe that either (a) Rick has the film, or (b) he knows where it is. They're after him. So he goes to the South of France to Pierre's old man—just to get away. We search high and low for him. Then one of our boys hears that Nina has gone to the South of France. He follows her there and reports to me. Meanwhile, I have evidence that the Reds are still hunting for the film Pierre had. So I see Rick on the train. I tell him who I am. But he doesn't admit having the film. Moreover, he naturally wanted absolute proof that I was the man Pierre had to see in Paris.'

'Yes. But what was Rick doing in Paris for Nina's father?'

'That was Nina's doing. At least that's what we think. He told me he had some business to do for Pierre's father and he had to see Nina that same night to discuss things. I warned him to watch his step with her. You know the rest. He gets plastered at Le Café Noir.'

I wasn't satisfied.

'Did Rick talk about money on the way to Paris?'

'Yes.'

'Then what?'

'The appointment was fixed for the following day. I told Rick I'd have a representative of the U.S. Embassy there. He agreed.'

'This was when?'

'Three days ago.'

That checked with Rick's letter to me.

'The next you know is that he is with Nina Dupont at the Café Noir?'

'Yes.'

'Were you sure Rick had the film?'

'Positive.'

'How?'

'Because Pierre sent me a coded message to that effect.'

'Were you in contact with him?'

'Only the day before he died.'

'Why didn't you tackle Rick before?'

'We didn't know where he was till Nina was followed.'

'All this fuss over a strip of film,' Kathie grinned.

'Please don't be facetious, dear,' Lamond said. He looked at me. 'Is it all clear now? Your brother didn't keep the appointment. I sent a man round to Le Café Noir.'

'Briefly,' I said, trying to get the thing clear in my mind, 'Pierre should have delivered the film to you. But he's scared to because he fears the Reds will kidnap him.'

'Actually I wasn't in Paris,' Lamond said. 'And we didn't know he was in Paris until we had certain information.'

'I see. So Pierre had to stay put.'

'Yes. . . .'

'Meanwhile, the Commies had caught up with him—they tried to kidnap him?'

'That's how he met Rick,' Stanley said.

'Exactly. Pierre dies and Rick goes to his father in the South of France. You intercept him on the way back because by this time one of your men has found him by following Nina.'

'That's it exactly.'

'You kidnap me and bring me here. What for?'

'To help us.'

They all sighed.

'Why should I help you?'

'Why? You don't suppose we'd ask you unless we had a good reason. And believe me, it is the best in the world. We want you to help us save your brother's life.'

'Really!' I didn't believe him at first. I thought they were kidding me about Rick's life being in danger. 'What do you want me to do exactly?'

'Rick's in a hospital near Prague,' Lamond went on. 'We want you to take his place.'

'Me! Me take his place! Are you crazy?'

Lamond picked up his drink, wiggling it nervously. Then he stared at me. 'Listen carefully,' he went on. 'It's not so crazy as it sounds. We've made arrangements to rescue Rick. But we can't carry them out unless you take his place.' He put his glass on the table. 'He mustn't be missed. If he is, the balloon goes up—the Q-plan goes into operation. Once that happens the fugitive has little chance of making good his escape.'

I felt like laughing.

'What's the point of rescuing him?' I said. 'If he's had the treatment, he'd have told them where the film is.'

'But he hasn't. We know that for sure. He's due to get it the day after tomorrow. That's why we want you there.'

Want me there! It sounded so ludicrous.

'Are you trying to tell me that you know exactly what's going on behind the Iron Curtain?'

'As far as Rick is concerned, yes,' Lamond said. 'Don't treat this lightly. You either believe what we say or dismiss it as piffle.' He was looking very grave and earnest.

'So I take Rick's place. And then what?'

'He'll be brought back here and the secret plans will go to the Western Powers.'

'And poor little me. What happens?'

He shrugged.

'Don't worry. We'll get you out of the hospital.'

'That's where Rick is?'

'Yes.'

'What about the Q-plan?'

'Let me be more explicit. If we rescue Rick now, he'll be missed. And his chances of getting over here will be practically nil. But if he's not missed, he'll have little trouble in getting here.'

'I got that,' I said. 'What about me? How do I fare with the Q-plan?'

'It won't matter. You tell them who you are. How you came to be there and they won't bother with you.'

'All they'll do,' I said sarcastically, 'is to pick me up and kiss me.'

'This is not a joke,' Lamond said. 'You don't have to do it. You're a free agent. And we don't intend to force you to, either. Quite frankly, I'm in this purely for cash. If you turn it down, O.K. That's the end of it. Rick gets the treatment. The Reds will get their film back and your brother will ultimately be liquidated. It's as simple as that, chum.'

'And you?'

They all glanced at each other.

'I told you. We get no potatoes. The Western Powers lose the film which might well contain plans that will ensure peace for a century.'

'You really expect me to say yes, don't you?' I said.

'Nothing of the sort,' Lamond said in his most charming way. 'Why should we be so optimistic? After all you've only our word that Rick's on the other side. It's like I told you before, you either trust us absolutely or dismiss what I've said as so much piffle.'

'What's the set-up in Prague?' I asked, feeling that maybe I was misjudging them.

He gave me the lot then. He said Rick was in the ward of a

mental hospital outside Prague—at a place called Slany. He'd probably know what to expect, that he'd get the treatment. He was no fool. Pierre had obviously given him the gen on what operated if they caught you. Lamond said he had the organisation to get me into the hospital.

'If you decide to play ball with us,' he said, 'we'd like you to go to Slany tonight.'

'What! At this hour!' I said.

'Yes. We have a plane standing by to take you to a place in Germany near the border.' He glanced at his watch. It was just 9.35 p.m.

'Let's be sensible,' I said. 'O.K. I'm Rick's brother. I'd do all in my power to save his life. But how do I know you're not Commies? How do I know you're not going to use me as bargaining bait with Rick?'

'I told you,' Lamond gestured. 'You can turn us down flat. There's the door.' He pointed to it. 'You're free to go when you like.'

I had to believe them. But I couldn't leave tonight. Nina expected me. I told them that. 'Being a Red agent, she'd naturally suspect something—something she could pass on to her Moscow bosses. Suppose she tells them I'm missing——'

'Forget her,' Stanley said. 'She's already been taken care of —so has the bloke downstairs. We've planned this like a military operation. Time, as Mr. Lamond explained, is a vital factor.'

Lamond cleared his throat.

'Have you any other points?' he asked.

'I promised to ring my manager,' I said. 'If he misses me, he'd start the ball rolling.'

Kathie Lamond smiled and said, 'We can take care of that.'

'Please, dear,' Lamond snapped. 'Let me do the talking. After all I'm supposed to be the——'

'All this aside,' I cut in. 'Can you give me one good reason why I should risk almost certain death?'

'I can,' Kathie Lamond said. 'Your brother's life. Another is that the film might be vital to the Western Powers. Don't you see? You'll—why, you'll be doing something very, very noble.'

'Aw—chuck it, Kathie,' Lamond cut in. 'Harry's not a fool. He's not influenced by slush like that.'

'I'm sorry,' she said, lowering her eyes.

They sold me the story—hook, line and sinker. The big test was that I could have walked out of there and done what I liked. This was true. Had I been unwilling to co-operate I'd have been useless to them. Moreover, Lamond had given me the worst possible picture of what I'd be up against. I was no hero. I loved life. I had ambition. There was indeed so much I wanted to do before I died. Rick was my twin. O.K. But would he give his life so that I could live? Maybe. But I doubted it. This wasn't the case of somebody jumping into the water to save his drowning brother. There was no apparent drama. What had been put to me was a cold proposition—as cold as death itself. Had I irrefutable evidence that Rick was where they said he was, I wouldn't have hesitated.

Sighing, I looked at them each in turn and said, 'Had some-body asked either of you to do what you've asked me to do, would you have done it?'

'I don't think I would,' Lamond said. 'I'm no hero. In fact, I'm very cowardly in some things. But let's be logical. You'll be risking very little more than you would as a front-line soldier.'

'But I'm not a soldier,' I said. 'Even if I were I wouldn't be a one-man army. If I agree to what you say, I shall be. If I'm got out of that hospital it will be the whole of the Soviet Republics versus yours truly.'

They never said anything; just shrugged and looked sheepish. They couldn't argue. There was no reply to what I'd said.

I quizzed Lamond further about Prague. He said he had a first-class set-up there. 'When I say we, I'm lying,' he said. 'I mean we are in contact with a first-class set-up there. People who specialise in smuggling refugees through the Iron Curtain. They are, of course, unscrupulous. Rogues and vagabonds. They'll cheat you if they can. I wouldn't trust them as far as I could see them. But our ace in the hole is that they are as much dependent on us this side as we are on them their side. If they double-crossed us, we could double-cross them. But it is most unlikely. Such a situation would finish them for good, and they know it.'

43

I was about to say something but Lamond stopped me.

'Just a minute,' he said. 'This is all I have to say. . . . After I've said it you can please yourself what you do. You've got to know that I'm inherently honest even in my dishonesty. It sounds paradoxical, I know. But it's true. You see, I could never face your brother again unless I told you the truth, the whole truth and nothing but the truth. This is not a game of ping-pong. I realise your life is all you've got.' His eyes moistened. I liked the way Lamond held my eyes. He looked so inherently honest. But I still wasn't happy. There were so many ifs and buts in this set-up. So much that seemed fantastic and untrue. Yet compared with the cloak and dagger stuff that had been going on in Berlin since 1945, it wasn't perhaps so fantastic after all.

'Apart from death,' I said. 'What's the worst I can expect?'

'Life imprisonment in a slave camp,' Lamond said. 'But don't be so pessimistic. There's always the chance that you might get away.'

'Can you guarantee once Rick is free and you've got the film, to rescue me?'

'From the hospital, yes,' Lamond said.

'We're probably exaggerating,' Stanley explained. 'You'll have an hour's start on your pursuers. It takes that time for the Q-plan to get going.'

'But I'll be on my own?' I said.

'Not necessarily,' Lamond said. 'A lot will depend on what Big Francis decides. He's the boss. But I must warn you. Have no illusions. He's not the type to risk anything. Even if it means your losing your life, he'll play a safe game.'

'But you might make it,' Kathie Lamond broke in. 'Others have.'

'Please, Kathie.' Lamond looked pained. 'Stop building up his hopes.'

'I'm sorry,' she said, lowering her eyes.

I felt sorry for her. Why was Lamond always bitching her— trying to reduce her to the least common multiple? What had he got against her? She didn't look the type he'd marry. She was too—too subdued, I thought.

Taking a cigar from a box on the sideboard, Lamond broke

the band and pierced the end of it with a metal gadget he carried in his waistcoat pocket. Moving a step nearer to him, Stanley, who was obviously a yes-man, snapped a Ronson and held the flame at the end of the cigar. Lamond puffed vigorously. Smoke billowed up around his head. While it was doing so, Kathie Lamond stared at me, her eyes sad. I hadn't made up my mind about her. She had something—something that was difficult to define—a sort of awareness which made you feel she wasn't as supine as she looked.

'Well, what's it to be?' Lamond said, smiling at me.

I thought about it.

'O.K.,' I said. 'You've got yourself a boy.' That hit them for six. There was no fuss, no honeyed words. Just a forthright expression of pleasure at my decision in their faces.

There was no turning back. I was in this thing right up to the neck. Brushing past Stanley, I went to the sideboard and picked up a bottle of Scotch. They stared at me in wonder. Grabbing a glass I poured myself out the first alcoholic drink I've ever had.

'That's right,' Kathie said, smiling her approval. 'It will do you good.'

'Please,' Lamond winced.

'What about my manager?' I said, before I made a beast of myself. 'Who rings him and when?'

'He'll be rung just as soon as we've got that film,' Lamond said. 'We don't want any panic——.'

'But he expects me to ring.'

'I'll attend to that later,' Lamond said. 'There are things to be done.'

I squirted soda in my glass. Then I smelt the Scotch. What did it taste like? I threw back my head. They were all watching, amused, smiling. The liquor hit my throat. It didn't burn as much as I'd anticipated, possibly because I'd drowned it with soda.

'You forgot to say Cheerio,' Kathie smiled.

8

You make a grave decision. Then you play bo-peep with your critical faculties. You don't think about it for—oh, it may be minutes or may be hours afterwards. Then you get the kidney punch. Suddenly your mind's a snake-pit—full of dangerous thoughts that writhe and hiss for as long as you allow them to.

Mine mainly concerned what I agreed to do. Perhaps when Lamond had told me what I'd be up against behind the Iron Curtain, I had allowed it to go in one ear and out of the other. This might have been my way of rationalising the danger portents. I don't know. I'm no psychologist. All I know is that I'd either been playing bo-peep with my critical faculties or I'd deliberately refused to think about the dangers. Now I was thinking of death for the first time since I'd been a kid—since those terrible days when we were given gas-masks and attaché cases and marched to railway stations to be evacuated.

I'd been sipping my Scotch for some time. The others had been busy, yapping and 'phoning. I kept on saying to myself —Where do we go from here—doing this and wondering how much longer I'd be alive. What got me down was being in the dark. What were the details of my journey to Slany? I didn't know. But I wanted to know them. If you're going to your doom it's only natural you're curious about the route you're to take.

I could hear Lamond on the 'phone. Stanley was told to lay on transport for me. Suddenly, I came to and saw Kathie Lamond sitting in front of me, smiling.

'How you feeling now?' she asked.

'Fine—just fine,' I said, slapping the air with my hand.

She started to talk then—to tell me about luck. What a line she had! The lucky people she'd known! She told stories about sole survivors of air crashes; about millionaires who by cancelling train journeys had avoided death in rail disasters. She'd known soldiers whose lives had been saved by prayer books,

cigarette cases and other things which bullets had partly pene-
trated. She spoke of big-game hunters who'd survived maulings
from lions and tigers. And she herself had survived a most
virulent attack of pneumonia by luck.

'That week,' she said, 'the sulpha drugs were available for
the first time.'

I myself never subscribed to this fatalistic philosophy. That's
why when crossing roads, I watched vehicles instead of the
pretty girls. So what? To have argued with Kathie Lamond
would have been easy. Indeed, it was most tempting to do so.
But as I was about to embark on the most perilous journey of
my life, what she said was music to my ears.

'Drink up,' she said.

I did that. She poured me out another.

'Do you like me?'

I nodded and grinned. She glanced over her shoulder at the
other room in which her husband was 'phoning.

I felt more than ever that I was dreaming all this. And no
wonder. In England we pooh-poohed this stuff. It just couldn't
happen to us.

Kathie raised her glass and stared at me rather sadly, I
thought. Perhaps she sensed what was going on inside me. I
was feeling as most soldiers must have felt the first time they
went into battle—optimistic about my chances of survival but
not blind to the grim realities that loomed ahead of me. I was
full of prickly restlessness—anxious to get started—to plunge
into this unknown adventure and get it over with.

The door opened. Kathie put her glass on the table, and
smiled as her husband joined us. But he ignored her.

'Well, old boy,' he said, slapping my back affectionately.
'It's all fixed. You'll be leaving here at midnight. You'll be
flown to Germany. There you'll pick up a guide who will take
you to Slany. Once you're there, you'll be smuggled into the
room occupied by your brother.'

'And after that?' I said, feeling a little tipsy.

He glanced away, frowning, pouting reflectively.

'Who knows,' said Kathie, 'it might turn out to be——'

'Now, please, darling,' Lamond said, sarcastically, 'please
don't buoy up his hopes too much.'

'Oh, why not?' I said. 'It's jolly decent of her.'

He heaved as if to say something, but changed his mind.

'About your manager?' he said, after the hesitation.

'Motty? What about him?'

'Do you want me to tell him the truth?'

'I'll leave that to Rick,' I said.

'Oh, but Rick won't know—about you, I mean.'

'Won't know?'

'Not until after the film is safe in Washington.'

'But Motty will be bound to report me missing long before that.'

'That's what I was afraid of. . . . So would—would you mind just giving him a tinkle before you go? Tell him you've arrived O.K., that it's not Rick in the morgue and that you're staying a few days until he returns.'

'And I say nothing about what's really happening?'

'Good God, no! Not a word. He'd probably think you were mad or tight.'

'He undoubtedly would. Where's the blower?'

He looked at his wife.

'Would you mind, dear? Use the one upstairs. I'm expecting a call on the other.'

She looked at me, her face flushed, her eyes bright and said, 'This way.'

I followed her through the doorway and up the wide staircase to a bedroom schemed in blue. She stood near the door. As I entered the bedroom, she looked to the left and then closed the door.

'Before you 'phone,' she said, coming close to me. 'Do you mind if I kiss you—I'll tell you why. I think you're the bravest man I know.'

She was high. There was no doubt about that. Her eyes were misty. There was a flush on her neck.

'I don't mind at all,' I said.

She came to me. I took her in my arms. She held up her face. Our lips touched. Then she went suddenly limp and for the next few seconds it felt as if the top of my scalp was going to blow off. I hadn't expected it. I merely expected a chaste kiss. But she gave me the works. I'd never experienced any-

48

thing like it. But there was nothing dirty about it—nothing I could recriminate myself for later on. It was just an impulse on her part. I didn't know the woman. I didn't know what pent-up longings or emotions that poor creature had. All I know was that as soon as I touched her lips something exploded inside her. It was all over in a few seconds. She broke away from me—pale, frightened, ashamed perhaps and panted, 'It's over there.'

I nodded. It was a white instrument.

'Who do I ask for?'

'You'd better let me get it for you.'

No sooner had she dialled the number than the door burst open. Lamond's face was for a fraction of a second livid with rage. But when he saw what his wife was doing, his ire collapsed like a parachute when the jumper hits the ground.

'What are you doing, darling?'

I couldn't look at him. But she never batted an eyelid—looked as cool and as composed as a turtle.

'Just getting him through to London,' she said.

'Why shut the door?'

She looked at me.

'It must have blown shut,' I said. 'I didn't notice.' What worried me was the thought that my mouth was smudged with lipstick. But I needn't have worried. When Lamond left us, Kathie told me she used a special kind—a type that stays put. She seemed happier in herself, as though she'd done something of which she was proud. I no longer mattered to her. That was obvious.

When she left me, she squeezed my hand and then hurried away looking so palpably female. I stood for a minute confused by my thoughts. Joan, who was dead, had always been so frankly feminine. She had none of the female subtleties that characterised Kathie, no capacity to impart secret promises of future delight as Kathie had.

I felt so remote from London, Motty and everything that Harry Hammond was or had been. Even when I spoke to Motty and heard his voice, I felt as alien to that old Harry as the devil is to virtue.

Motty was emotional—emotional and overjoyed by the news

that Rick was still alive. I told him I was with Nina; that Rick was out of town and would be back in a few days.

'You'll be O.K.?'

'Sure—sure.'

'You're all right for cash?'

'Fine—fine thanks,' I said.

'Look after yourself, kid,' he said.

They were all smiling and relaxed when I entered the drawing room. Kathie didn't even look at me. When I came in she was relating an anecdote to the others. She seemed to be much more composed and less subdued than she had before. She was talking to Lamond as though she wore the trousers. I couldn't believe my ears. It was good to see. The other fellow was frowning at her. As I closed the door, she suddenly changed to her former self, looking subdued, a nagged and unloved woman.

I coughed. They all stared at me.

'Why, hello, Harry,' Lamond said, killing his wife's story. He came over to me and took my arm. 'Everything will be explained to you as you go along. You won't need any things. When you get to Germany, they'll fix you up.'

Just before I was due to depart I was introduced to the man who was to escort me on the first part of the walk in the dark. He came into the room looking like a fierce mongrel.

'This is Maurice,' Lamond said.

The man bowed. He was short, squat, thick-set with a round swarthy aggressive face and kinky pomaded black hair. He wore a leather jacket and black trousers.

'How do you do,' I said in French.

Kathie Lamond was still ignoring me.

'You speak pretty good French,' Stanley said.

'I wouldn't say that.'

'Know any German?' Lamond asked.

'Enough to get by on.'

Maurice asked if I were ready to leave. I said I was. He turned to Lamond. 'Is it O.K.?'

'Sure—sure,' Lamond said.

Now came the big good-byes. First Kathie.

'You'll be all right,' she said. 'I feel it in my bones.' She still didn't look at me. One of her top teeth was scraping her bottom lip. I tried once more to catch her eye. But it was no dice.

Lamond winked as much as to say, 'Ignore the silly bitch.' He wished me the best of luck and then told Stanley to escort me to the car.

'So long, feller,' Stanley said, as I sat beside Maurice.

'So long.'

'I wish you all you wish yourself.'

Suddenly we were away—the sound of crunching gravel in my ears, the black smudges of laurel bushes were on either side, a solitary star winked at us through the ragged silhouettes of overhanging foliage.

Paris was quite still that night—so uncannily quiet. And that sky—gosh, it was like those I'd seen in nightmares—full of swirling, sooty clouds. The promise of a full moon was implicit in everything I saw up there.

We jogged along, over the cobbles, through those meanly lit streets that formed the bowels of this gay city. I felt so alone, so impotent to grapple with the fates that had plucked me out of the sanity and tranquillity of England. The shadows of my new world were intensifying, lengthening. Soon it would be dark . . . soon I must start walking.

'How's the weather for flying?' I asked.

'Good.' Maurice's voice reassured me—I wasn't alone. . . .

'It doesn't look so good to me,' I said, screwing up my nose and staring at the cloudy sky again.

'Nor me,' said Maurice, his voice tinged with sarcasm. 'But the experts all agree it will be good for flying. So who are we to make inferences?'

That was all. . . . We sank into our respective inner worlds —there to browse over the things most dear to our hearts at this time. Rick was uppermost in my mind. Never before had I felt quite so close to him. Something in me was rejoicing at this chance to help him. Never before had I really put myself out for anybody. Reflecting on my past, I saw that most of my actions had been actuated by selfish motives. This was different. I was embarking on a journey into the unknown. I only hoped if I emerged, to be a better person than I was before I undertook it.

A match cracked and exploded, the flash from it painting Maurice's nose and chin a bright yellow. Then there was the glow of the cigarette. It winked at me like a friendly eye as much as to say, 'Don't worry, Harry. Perhaps things aren't going to be as bad as you imagine.' Then I was suddenly calm and conscious of an inner strength, of a spiritual might and I felt equal to tackling anything. . . .

9

I GOT out of the car and Maurice told me to open the gate. We'd run up an incline at the end of a rough stony track between lofty hedges. I opened the gate. He drove the car through to a field, stopped and pushed the nearside door. I got in. Then we drove without lights across the open fields to a squat farmhouse, slowly, now wobbling, now bumping over ruts and mole hills. As we stopped in the farmyard, two men emerged from a bulky shadow slanting from a barn. They whispered something to Maurice in German. He reached back and opened the rear door. They got in. We moved on, crossing more fields.

I only saw the men in silhouette. One was stunted and powerfully built; the other, a tall gangling fellow, was about six feet three inches tall.

Nobody had spoken all the way over to the hangar, disguised as a barn. It was hidden in the shadows of a wood and was on a plateau. The two men got out.

'O.K. Let's go,' Maurice said.

The door squeaked open. I jumped out and looked at the dark sky.

After opening the double doors of the hangar the two men pushed out a biplane on to what was apparently a runway. The stocky man returned to the hangar. A few minutes later he appeared with a short gangway which he propped against the plane. Maurice went up first. I followed. There were only four slotted seats on the port side of the plane. The tall gangling fellow went to the pilot's seat in the nose of the aircraft and switched on the instrument-lights.

'Don't they warm it up first?' I asked Maurice, as the pilot yelled something to a man standing in the field by the propellor.

'It was warmed up before we got here,' Maurice said. 'That's part of the set-up. That hangar back there is sound-proof.'

The pilot twiddled some gadgets above his head. Then he yelled something to the man outside. The engine croaked and spluttered. Then she broke into a loud roar. We taxied into the black breeze. Suddenly the engine seemed to be straining desperately to leave the earth. Its noise became part of me. We were off now, bumping over that field and between opposing rows of cunningly concealed lights which had been mysteriously switched on.

Then at last tension fell away like the earth and we were soaring into the dark unknown. Way over in the west Paris was a mass of glittering lights.

'Often do this trip?' I asked Maurice.

He shrugged, pressed his index finger to his lips and said in English, 'No names, no pack-drill.'

I was snubbed. Surprising how a little crack like that can nark you almost to a point of hatred.

The effects of the alcohol I'd had in Lamond's place had left me with a thirst. I looked at Maurice. He sat staring sombrely at his button boots.

'Anything to drink?' I snapped.

'What would you like?'

'Coffee?'

'Certainly,' said Maurice. He got up and moved towards the cockpit, returning later with a flask of coffee.

'For me,' he said, sitting down, 'I love the cognac.' He carried a flask of it on his hip. He was happier now we were airborne. Below was the black countryside, pricked here and there with lights. The plane buzzed, now bumping, now wobbling like the car had over those fields. I fell into a reverie. This is it, boy! I thought. This is where the journey into the dark begins. It was, too. I'll never forget it—how I first faced up to the fact that I was really taking Rick's place. . . .

What they intended to do to him, they would now do to me. What was the treatment. . . ? Something of which I had no conception. This was just as well. Lamond had wisely omitted to describe it to me. What you don't know, you can't brood about. The question which intrigued me most was—Would I see Rick? The next in order was—How would they smuggle me into the hospital? It seemed fantastic that anybody could do this. Who were the people concerned in this smuggling? Looking back, I'm glad I knew nothing of the set-up.

The plane droned on. After a while I got bored with the journey. For the most part there was little or nothing to see below—just the lights and when the moon peeped through the clouds an occasional glimpse of water.

Maurice was dead to the world. I think he was drunk. He'd sipped the cognac for over half an hour. Then his head became top-heavy. It waggled. It swayed. Finally his chin sank into his chest.

The pilot sat there at the controls, immutably rigid, a tower of strength in this little world. . . .

Maurice began to snore. I tolerated the noise for sometime. Then I gave him a sly kick. It paid dividends. He suddenly stopped. He shuddered out of some troubled dream, snorted and stared about him, potentially aggressive. Squeezing his eyes, he shook his head, yawned a couple of times and afterwards peered out of the window.

'Five minutes,' he mumbled.

The engine's tempo had already changed. You felt its petulance. You could also feel its antagonism to the earth. Little fears started to creep into my mind as we came down.

'What's the drill?' I asked.

'From now on,' Maurice replied, 'you're Captain Rumbold's pigeon.'

'What sort of bloke's Rumbold?'

He winced and hunched his shoulders.

'Rumbold? A Boche.'

'Yes, but what——'

'To add to that would be superfluous.'

Suddenly we were bumping and passing cats' eyes on the runway. It was still dark and little of the surrounding country was visible. We stopped near a hangar like the one near Paris. Maurice opened the door. The gangway was already there. Maurice picked up an attaché case and led the way out.

'Have a good trip?' a man asked him in German.

The pilot remained behind. Maurice escorted me across fields to a farmhouse. The cats' eyes went out. The moon was now behind clouds. I heard the pilot and the German hurrying to catch up with us. Walking in single file under the cover of a hedge, we all listened to a dog barking on the same monotonous note.

As we reached the farmyard, a pig grunted. The smell of new mown hay mingling with manure reminded me of those long summer vacations Rick and I spent in Bucks during our boyhood.

Mind how you go,' Maurice whispered. 'There are holes in the concrete.'

We passed manure heaps. Sometimes when the moon came out behind the clouds, I saw Maurice's pale sleepy face. We reached the farmhouse, stopping at the back door.

Maurice drummed his fingers on the window. A minute later the door opened.

'Come in,' an old man said in German.

I ducked and stepped down to the uneven red-bricked passage and walked through to the kitchen, a newly white-washed rectangular room with a low sagging beamed ceiling.

It was here I met Captain Rumbold, the proud, tall, thick-set, bullet-headed Prussian, with whom I was destined to share some very tense and exciting moments. As we came in he was in the act of pushing a plate away on the well-scrubbed bare table near the low latticed window—doing this and picking his teeth with a broken match. He didn't look up immediately, probably due to preoccupation with his thoughts.

When, however, he saw me he jumped up, clicked his heels and greeted me in perfect English.

I liked him on sight. He exuded strength of character and something which made me happy to have him as a guide.

He and Maurice ignored each other. While Rumbold was talking to me, Maurice took off his leather jacket and cap and slung them on an old couch.

Out of the window, I saw dawn breaking over the fields. 'Frederick is getting you some grub,' Rumbold said. 'I'll see you later—when you wake up. We'll have a chat then, huh.' Stooping, he picked up a huge ginger cat which he carried through a low doorway on the right.

'Those damned Germans,' Maurice said, a minute later, shaking his head in disgust. 'Dull, stupid morons. No imagination. No compassion — nothing except a brutish understanding of life.' He glanced cautiously over his shoulder at the door. 'That Rumbold. As fearless as a buffalo. But no imagination. Paris was full of them during the war. They were like ducks out of water. . . . Do you like Germans?'

'I don't know any,' I said, which was true. Anyway, I wasn't getting involved in racial arguments. Enough bitterness already existed in the world.

Frederick, the man who let us in, gave me bacon and eggs. It was the first food I'd had since leaving London. After coffee, he took me to a large room at the back. Rumbold was sleeping in a bunk near the window. I chose one near the door. With all the excitement and anxiety I'd been through, I wasn't hopeful of getting any sleep. But as soon as my head hit the pillow, I was away. . . .

When I woke up it was already dusk. An old woman shook me. Then she asked me whether I would like a bath.

'Thank you,' I said.

'It's next door to here. Shall I run it?'

'Please,' I said.

While I waited for this, Rumbold came in.

'Sleep well?' he asked.

I nodded.

'Good.' As I got out of bed, he stared at me. 'You're a big fellow,' he added smiling. 'Used to walking?'

'In a way, yes.'

'Good. You're going to get plenty of it. We start at ten. When you've had your bath, I'll see you again.'

'O.K.' I said.

The bathroom was small—the tub just big enough to sit up in. I studied the clothes on the chair—the thick blouse, the flannel shirt, long underwear, breeches, boots which laced up

56

to the knee and the armpit holster. . . . I'd left my passport and money with Lamond in Paris. After the bath, I dressed in these strange clothes. Then Rumbold came in, grinning.

'Everything fit?' he said, scrutinising the outfit.

'What do you think?' I said, turning round.

'They look all right. . . . What about the boots?'

I glanced down at them.

'They seem all right.'

'Then everything is what you call fine and dandy. Now we go to the kitchen.' He opened the door and I followed him. 'Hungry?'

'Yes,' I said.

'Good. How about a meal? There's roast sucking-pig, sauerkraut, potatoes. This, by the way, will be your last hot meal until we reach Big Francis' place.'

'O.K.' I said. We sat at the long table. 'Where's Maurice?' I added.

Rumbold pulled a face.

'Gone. . . . And jolly good riddance. I can't stick those Latins, those decadent morons with their belly-aching.'

I asked him where he'd learnt his English.

'Cambridge,' he said proudly. 'Took a post-graduate course there in 1930. Wonderful town Cambridge.' He took the top off a silver dish and cut me a large chunk of pig. 'Help yourself to spuds.' I did that. 'You like the French?'

'I don't know them very well,' I said.

'They're a nation of egotists,' he said. 'I like the French women. They're more feminine than any other women. They know how to make love. They are exquisite cooks. Good mothers. But the men—pah! They're like the Italians. All would-be Casanovas. What conceit! No gallantry. No humility. Very little intelligence. They see a pretty girl and they think she must of necessity be crazy about them.'

He wagged his head and munched his food. I asked him what his politics were.

'I'm sentimentally an anarchist,' he said with his mouth full. 'I'm violently opposed to groups, political dogmas and everything else which conspires against the individual. I loathe civil servants, football clubs and old comrades associations.'

It was soon apparent that Rumbold was excessively fond of Rumbold. But his was a pleasing egotism, possibly because what he said was for the most part free of slogans and cliches. After the meal he showed me a big automatic.

'Ever use one of these?' he smiled. 'I hope not. You were too young for the war?'

'Yes,' I said.

He gave me a demonstration on the weapon's use. I had fired a revolver before. I remembered how on our last vacation with Uncle Henry at Flackwell Heath in Bucks, the old man had taken Rick and I down to his private shooting range in the lower field. We used old tin cans as targets and Rick beat both Uncle Henry and me.

I took the automatic to pieces and then reassembled it. After this I was instructed how to load and unload it.

'This gadget,' Rumbold said, pointing to an additional piece of mechanism, 'is a silencer.'

I glanced out of the window. A dusky sombre silence lay on the fields. The day was drawing in its frazzled ends. We would soon be on our way. An old frau, with a face brown and wrinkled as a walnut, cleared the table. A cat on the sill was blinking supinely and enigmatically at the dying light. Putting the automatic in the holster, I wondered if I'd ever have to use it.

Rumbold briefed me. He said we had over a thirty kilometre walk before we were on the other side of the Curtain. Once there, I was to act the part of a deaf mute.

'You can't speak and you can't hear anything,' he said.

'I understand.'

'You quite sure?'

I nodded.

'All you do is this.' His face went vacant and he kept touching his lips and wagging his head. 'Get it?' he grinned. 'Do that and leave all the talking to me.'

After this he fell silent—just sat there staring morosely at the floor and looking as though he were living in the backwater of some half-forgotten tragedy. Night crawled rapidly up the sky. It was surprising how quickly it got dark over there. Shadows were almost running out from the buildings and the stone walls in the fields.

Suddenly it was time to move. Rumbold got up and put on a knapsack and stared at his rugged face in the blurred mirror over the sink.

'Between the frontier and our destination,' he explained later, 'is a string of bases—barns, belonging to people in sympathy with the West. We shack up in them during daylight and walk only by night. I take you to Big Francis near Slany. Then I'm finished.'

Rumbold was about my height—6 ft. 2 ins., but of slightly slimmer build.

We left the farm by the back door and cut across the fields, keeping near the hedges until we reached the wood. Walking directly behind him, I wondered why he carried those trenching tools fixed to his broad brass-studded belt.

Inside the wood he turned and beckoned me to join him. Then the loud flutter from startled birds broke the eerie stillness. Suddenly we left the narrow path we'd been following and walked through the silent battalions of fir trees. Now the wood's dark bulk was rapidly intensifying. Soon it was necessary for Rumbold to use his torch. The wood's surface, matted with dead pine needles and cones, was soft as a carpet, and the only sounds we made were when we stepped on dead wood and one of us sniffed or coughed. I wondered why Rumbold was so silent. He moved like a huge panther, his big head swivelling all the time as though he constantly expected to meet trouble.

After two hours' solid walking the calves of my legs were beginning to protest against the strain imposed on them. At the end of the wood we entered a field and Rumbold glanced at his phosphorescent watch.

'We're a little ahead of time,' he whispered, pausing at the brow of a hill. 'These hikes are planned like military operations.' He fell down in the grass and added, 'We'll rest here a while.'

Lying on his back, he rolled a cigarette. Then as he cupped a match, I saw his eyes squint and wrinkle at the ends. Down there in the valley a road was lined with skinny poplars like giant umbrellas.

'That Maurice,' Rumbold said. 'He doesn't like me. I feel it. It's curious—I mean, how you sense things like that. We've known each other for—oh, it must be two years. Yet we've never had a cross word. I think we have a chemical antagonism.' Sighing, he dragged at his cigarette. 'Funny fellow,' he added. 'I think he's nagged by his spouse. He looks the type, don't you think?'

I made no comment.

Ten minutes later we moved on. Sometimes when we passed farmhouses, I'd see faces float up to lighted windows, and in the roads long fingers of light from speeding cars raked dark hedges and stone walls.

All the time we'd been walking, I felt an ever increasing fear creeping into my being. It was something new to me. I'd been scared before of course but not in the way I was now. I think it was imagination more than anything else. Every sound I heard in the woods and the fields we passed through had me reaching for my gun.

Rumbold, however, was a tower of strength. Nothing apparently perturbed him. He reminded me of a tank. We walked mostly in the dark, making very little use of our torches. He knew every single path, every dip in a road; what fences, gates and stiles to climb.

The farther we went, however, the more warily Rumbold walked. Although he said nothing to me, I felt that he knew exactly where the dangers were. Sometimes he'd suddenly stop dead in his tracks, grab his automatic, hold his breath and listen. Then without a word, he'd snort like a petulant animal and plod on through the darkness.

Later on, tension seemed to leave him. Then he began to quiz me about my antecedents.

'What part of England do you live in?' he whispered, after we'd climbed a fence and dropped down into a field which rose suddenly to another wood.

'London,' I said.

'You worked there?'

'Yes.'

'In Whitehall?'

The moon was rising but clouds obscured its progress up the western sky.

'Not likely,' I smiled. 'That's where the civil servants work.'

'Yes, I know. Aren't you a Government man?'

'No. . . . I'm a boxer—a professional boxer.'

'That so? It just shows you. You never know who's who. I thought you were an agent.'

'Not me.'

He sighed, blew his nose and added, 'We get all sorts on this long walk in the dark. Mostly people coming out from that communistic slave-kennel—women as well as men. You should see them! Mostly people in late middle-age who've waited too long for the communistic paradise to appear— people who in their youth slaved for those 5-year plans the materialistic morons were always instituting at the outset of the régime. They buy diamonds and then try to get away to spend their old age in one of the decadent democracies where they can do what they did as kids—say boo to a goose and without fear of being denounced by their sons and daughters.'

'You hate the Commies?'

'No. I hate their attitudes towards life—the way millions and millions of human beings are enslaved and worked to death to create a state—a super state visualised by those half-baked Oriental pipe-dreamers. In time people become conditioned like ants. They're never happy unless they're slogging their guts out. They lose their egos and become part of a big ego— the Slavonic Termite Ego. People who yearn to escape to our side are the incorrigible individualists. The stories they tell! One fellow told me they were asked to give a whole month's pay for the cause of peace. They still fall for that peace line the Commies are always shouting. . . . It makes me want to vomit.'

We reached another wood and Rumbold rolled a cigarette I asked him if he liked his life, guiding people through the Iron Curtain.

'No, I hate it,' he said. 'I long to breathe and to think without having to worry about people being blown into Kingdom Come any moment. I ought to be sitting in clover really. My trouble is and has always been gambling. You would think a fellow with my consistent bad luck would pack it up. Had I done so a few years ago, I wouldn't be doing this now. But I've got a hunch that it's due to change any day now.'

I asked him about his family.

'They were all killed by a bomb in 1943,' he said. 'That illustrates the Rumbold luck. This is what happened: We'd moved from Prussia in 1938 to a house outside Cologne—in a little town called Sindorf. The old man's idea of paradise. He'd saved all his life to achieve it. He'd never known such happiness. Then war came. I was sent to the Russian Front. That same year the family was wiped out—bang! Just one stray bomb. It just shows you how useless life is. It took nature millions of years to evolve us Rumbolds and one of your airmen a couple of minutes to make us virtually extinct.'

'You hate the British?'

'No. Why should I? I hate nobody—just people's attitudes towards existence. That's all. I take the view that ordinary existence is fraught with danger from germs, earthquakes, floods and all the rest. But not content with that, some people must add to the terror and misery of existence by inventing H-bombs and all the other diabolical devices for annihilating our poor benighted species.'

Five hours after setting out from the barn near Plauen, we came to our first base—a little farmhouse nestling in a valley between the hills.

'Here's where we kip,' Rumbold said, pointing to a long barn on the right. 'Here's where we can shut ourselves out from all the darkness.'

'How far are we behind the Iron Curtain?'

'Not as far as you think,' he replied. 'To get here we had to make many detours. If we'd travelled as the crow flies we'd have got here in less than half the time.'

We ran to the barn, keeping to the shadowed part of the hill. Clouds had vanished and the moon was climbing vigorously up the western sky. It was almost as light as day—a strange awe-inspiring moonlight which exposed a scene vaguely familiar, like some place I'd known a long time ago and had forgotten.

After creeping through a ragged hole in the barn, we passed threshing machines and other farming implements. Rumbold shone his torch on a vertical ladder nailed to a loft about fifteen feet above. 'Follow me,' he whispered.

Later, when we were lying in the hay, we munched the pork sandwiches we'd brought with us. Rumbold unscrewed a thermos flask, filled the cup of it with coffee and said, 'Have a swig.'

It was warm in the hay—warm and cosy. For the first time since I'd known about Rick I felt relaxed.

I wondered about Rick—what he was doing now, whether he realised what he was up against. It seemed incredible that we should both be on this side of the Iron Curtain.

We took off our boots. Outside I heard bats squeaking.

'Feeling tired, huh?' Rumbold said.

'Yes, are you?'

'Not very. I never get very tired these days.'

'We must have walked forty kilometres,' I said. 'I was nearly all in.'

'How are your feet?'

'Not too bad.'

'Know where we are?'

'No.'

'Only a few kilometres inside the Iron Curtain,' he said. 'We had to take the route north. But now we're inside the Curtain, we've got to watch out. I don't want to scare you. There's no need to. If we use our wits, we'll be O.K. Anyway, I'm a professional. My organisation has existed for six years. We've got the whole thing more or less taped now. We've made mistakes, of course. Several of our guides have been killed. But not lately. We've conquered the art of bribing officials and obliterating all traces of those poor misguided wretches who tried to arrest us.'

While he was talking, I wondered how old Motty and the boys at the gym would have reacted to what he said. What would those English crowds at the Oval and Lord's have thought of all this.

I yawned. I was becoming overwhelmed with a wonderful weariness. For the first time since I'd known of Rick's predicament, nothing mattered.

'You ever killed a man?' Rumbold said.

'No.'

'Would you be scared to?'

'I wouldn't like it very much,' I yawned. 'But I suppose it would all depend on what the circumstances were. I don't think anybody kills just for the sake of killing. Wild animals kill to eat or to win a mate or for their own existence.'

'You're probably right. . . . Here. Swallow these.' He gave me two pink pills. Then he took two himself. After this he wriggled down into the hole he'd made in the hay. A moment later, he was fast asleep.

10

I NOTICED things on this long walk I'd never troubled about before—insignificant things that helped to make up this strange new world of mine. Sitting in the hay, I watched dustycobwebs shimmering in odd corners of the barn, with husks of bluebottles welded to them. Needles of sunlight full of dancing dust motes pierced small holes in the corrugated roof. Rumbold lay with his hands behind his fat red neck, staring at the roof, his eyes blind with some intriguing speculation. Sometimes his tongue wandered between his thick lips like a thing enjoying a separate existence.

The thump of horses' hooves on hard ground and the sound of squeaking cart wheels outside told us the day was nearing its end. Shadows were already marching up the hills. When the noise outside died away, Rumbold consulted his watch. It was quite dark in the barn. 'We'll eat and then push on,' he said.

Reaching for my sandwiches, I wondered what this second lap of my walk in the dark would have in store for us. After drinking what remained of the coffee, we descended the ladder. At the bottom, Rumbold stopped and whispered that he was picking up food the farmer had hidden for us. Two haversacks packed with sandwiches and a thermos flask full of coffee for each of us, hung on a nail behind a threshing machine.

'It's part of the organisation,' Rumbold said, giving me one of the haversacks, which I slung over my shoulder. 'It took a long time to get all this laid on.'

I followed him out of the barn into the dark field. A cool breeze was blowing in from the east. Rumbold led the way up the hill. All the light we had was a handful of stars flung across the sky. As we neared the top of the hill, I was startled by a huge hare which jumped up immediately in front of me and ran a frantic zig-zag course with its long ears up.

'What a beauty!' Rumbold exclaimed.

'It scared me stiff,' I said.

'Me too,' he chuckled.

We plodded on across fields, through woods and occasionally entered a lane. Then sprawling before us like a black apron carelessly splashed with phosphorescent paint was a wide valley.

At this time I was wallowing in a sweet sorry-for-myself sadness.

'We've got to take a long detour,' Rumbold said. 'These are what take the time. It wouldn't have been necessary had not a reckless amateur killed a cop here a couple of years ago—stabbed him and left him for the whole bloody world to see. So to be on the safe side we make a long detour and avoid trouble. . . . Is that all right with you?'

'I'm in your hands.'

He moved on, still talking.

'You've got to realise that if we're stopped the odds are they'll lumber us inside. You never know. But you don't go inside if you can help it. Tell you why. There's no return ticket. So it frequently happens that you have to kill the conscientious types. It's not pleasant. But it's imperative. So don't be surprised what turns up.'

'I'm with you all the way.'

'Good.'

We followed a faint footpath curling through the fields, now kicking stones, now staggering over ruts. It was early morning. The wind had dropped and an uncanny silence had settled on the countryside.

'From now on,' Rumbold said, 'keep your ears skinned. This is the number one danger spot. So keep your hand on your gun and don't be afraid to use it. The snag about this part is the prowling dogs. The type the cops use in this country are nearly human in their understanding. The blasted things will stalk you for miles without barking, without even disclosing where they are. Unless your ears are trained, you can't hear the damn things either. Then when you get to a point where a patrol is, they suddenly bark. The only way to deal with them is to kill them. But that's not easy. They're like will-o'-the-wisps. First here. Then there. Then they'll be some other place. But never far away from you.'

'How do you tackle them?'

He stopped and shone his torch on a cardboard box containing diced meat.

'With these,' he said. 'There's enough cyanide in each piece to kill a dozen dogs. They can train the wretched things to do anything except control their appetites.'

I never said anything.

'You don't approve,' he said.

'I like dogs.'

'So do I. But I like my life better. Perhaps you're not yet aware how important your existence is to you. It takes time. I'd been flirting with death for years before I got wise to her intentions. Now I avoid her like the plague.'

We climbed a gate and entered the dark field. The moon was up now. It discovered a narrow path for us—a zig-zagging path running through dense undergrowth on the outskirts of a wood.

'Keep your eyes and ears skinned,' Rumbold whispered, as he took the lead. We had to slacken pace. Unseen branches and straying bramble leads kept holding us up. I grew more and more aware of the tension that was tying my tummy in knots. It was what Rumbold had said about those dogs. I could feel the wretched things watching us. When we came to an open space, sparsely populated by old oaks, Rumbold suddenly stopped dead in his tracks, taut, alert. 'There's a dog behind us,' he whispered. 'Hear it?'

I listened. Did I hear it! No, sir. All I heard was something ticking in my ears. 'No,' I said.

Ducking behind a portly tree, he took out his box and carefully laid two pieces of meat on the ground.

'I hate doing this,' he said, 'I'd rather feed it to the brutes' masters.'

He beckoned to me to follow him to another tree. Standing in a shadow, we watched an alsatian creeping into a patch of moonlight, its nose to the ground. Suddenly it stopped, raised its head and looked quickly each way. It was a beautiful specimen, with a huge noble head and exquisitely shaped pricked ears. It ran to the meat, sniffed it, then wolfed it. It made no fuss about dying—just rolled over and sighed. It was uncanny. While we stood there I fancied that the sigh from the poor dog was running around in the trees above us. . . .

Leaving me, Rumbold went to the dog. I saw him grab its hind legs and drag it into a thicket. 'Shan't be long,' he whispered.

Then I heard his trenching tools hitting stones as he dug the dog's grave.

'Sorry about that,' he said, as we moved on through the mottled shadows and silver moonlight.

In the valley a car's headlights were spraying the hedges of a lane.

'That looks like the cops,' Rumbold said. 'They seem to be very restless tonight. I don't like it.'

We ran down the hill to the lane. Crawling through a hole in the hedge, we slid down to the road which led to a town.

'This is perhaps the diciest part of the whole journey,' Rumbold whispered. 'Tell you for why. We've got to pass through this small town. It's the only way we can cross the river. Anyway, if we're stopped you just play dumb like I showed you. Leave all the talking to me.'

'O.K.'

We rounded a bend and there fifty yards ahead was a red light in the middle of the striped barrier-pole which barricaded a level-crossing. We stopped. The man in the signal box on the left stood over a row of levers. Slipping his automatic in his right jacket pocket, Rumbold indicated to me to do like-wise. I didn't like it. Something warned me we were in trouble. A train was thundering through the night. Hoo-hoo, it shrieked. We moved on quickly. Just as we reached the level-crossing, the train raced past like a black duck, with a white plume of smoke waving behind its chimney.

While we waited for it to pass Rumbold told me to put on

the plastic mac I carried. He slipped his on too. Then the barrier-poles rose. As we crossed over, the signalman pulled the levers and glanced down at us suspiciously. Then just as I thought we were safe, we came face to face with two cops.

They'd stepped out of a shadow bulging from a wall and said something to Rumbold who stopped just in front of them. The shorter of the two gave me a critical once-over. Then he came up and said something. Shaking my head, I pointed to my mouth. In the pale light from a street lamp, I saw the other cop's eyes glowering at us under thick arched black brows. He carried his rifle at the ready. I didn't like the look of these characters. They were so palpably trigger-happy. This, I thought, is where we get our chips. They kept gabbling and gesticulating to Rumbold. Finally, he gave them papers. One of them shone a torch on them while the other read them aloud.

When they'd finished reading, they walked close to me. They wore sort of bluish uniforms and caps with shiny peaks. They started gabbling. All I did was to point to my mouth and wag my head.

What's the score? I thought, when Rumbold started to argue with them. Were they going to take us in or not? I was surprised that they hadn't frisked us for arms.

It was when Rumbold grinned that I stopped sweating. Then the cops laughed. Rumbold gave them each a cigar. They looked at me, sadly wagging their heads. Rumbold pointed to his mouth and then indicated that I'd been a deaf mute since I was a kid. He took my arm and we moved on, waving to the cops as we went.

'They wanted to take us in,' Rumbold said later. 'They would have done too had it not been for those faked papers. I explained that our car had broken down way back. He asked where it was. I told him. Incidentally, we have a contact to cover this alibi if our bluff's ever called.'

We hurried across the cobbled bridge. Peeping over, I saw boats of every description moored to the banks and black water tumbling and gurgling on its way to the valley.

'Are we O.K. now?' I asked, after we'd climbed a gate and entered a field.

'No. You're never O.K.' Rumbold said. 'There's always

snags in this business. You go on thinking you're as safe as houses and then you're suddenly lumbered.'

We spoke in English. Rumbold told me how he hated cops —'those legal gangsters who would swear your life away for a rouble.' He was talking loudly and gesticulating. On the other side of the hedge was a narrow road.

'Hark!' I said, hearing something. 'What's that?'

He stopped and cupped his ear.

'All right, throw up your hands,' a voice said in English. Swinging round I saw them covering us with their rifles. There were two of them—two shortish people. They came out of the hedge, slowly and with a torch shining on Rumbold and me. One of them looked like a woman.

We put our hands up and stopped.

'What's the idea?' Rumbold said.

My neck was sweating.

'You'll see,' the woman said.

Rumbold spoke to them in Czech.

'You don't have to speak that language,' the woman said. 'We understand English perfectly.'

As the man came forward shining his torch on us, the woman looked through the sights of her rifle trained on us.

'Get in the lane,' she said. 'Along there and through the gate. Keep your hands behind your necks.'

Rumbold went ahead of me, almost creeping along, yet as taut as a bow-string. How remarkably calm he was! What was on his mind? I'd have given the world to have known. But it was just as well I didn't. Had I done so I might have cooked our goose.

As we walked through the gateway, I moved ahead of Rumbold.

'Get back,' he snarled, moving ahead of me. The next second he swung round and started blasting at the cops with his automatic. I didn't even see him reach for his gun—just saw those two vivid flashes. When I turned round the cops were falling down. What an experience! The woman came down head first, her rifle rolling in front of her. Then the man who'd rolled past her had stopped near to where I was standing in the lane.

'Quick!' Rumbold whispered, bending down and grabbing the woman's feet. 'Take her arms.' As we picked her up, I saw a jeep without lights on the other side of a road. It was parked on a grass verge—standing there precariously and slightly on one side.

'God, that was a near thing!' Rumbold sighed, as we crossed to the jeep.

'You're telling me,' I said.

'We'll dump them in the rear,' he returned, as we lowered the woman to the ground. I was panting and sweating. Rumbold left me and pushed the jeep into the lane. After we'd loaded the bodies in the back of it, one on top of the other, I got the reaction. It hit me for six. Never had I been so scared—never quite so bewildered and confused. But Rumbold was like an iceberg. He amazed me. He took it all in his stride.

'You drive these things?' he said, staring at the jeep.

'Not too well.'

'O.K.' he said. 'Get in.'

I sat next to him. He had no trouble in starting the jeep—just pressed the starter and off she went.

'That's the nearest shave I've had for years,' he sighed as the jeep roared through the lane. 'Know something? We outwitted them. The poor stupid bastards. . . . Being shot was the last thing they expected. What amateurs! You'd have thought they'd have frisked us for guns.' He sounded tough and he looked fierce—an animal almost. 'They thought they'd got some easy pickings,' he went on. 'They're typical of the modern generation. They don't think quickly enough.'

He was driving furiously, swinging round bends at such a high speed it was a wonder I wasn't thrown into a hedge. We rode some way in silence.

'These people are conditioned by slogans,' he said. 'They're fed with them every day. We have slogans in the West too, especially in advertising. Somebody spends a fortune extolling the virtues of a soap-powder. It's just a good powder. But we fall for the name. Then somebody spends twice as much on advertising another good powder and most of us switch over. There's none of that over here. You either buy the one thing they tell you about or go filthy.'

I wasn't interested. The shooting back there had overawed me. I hated death—hated the very thought of it. And those bodies kept rolling about in the jeep and giving me the creeps. I kept thinking how only a little while ago they were thinking people. Now they were so much dead meat.

When the hedges fell away, I caught glimpses of cattle in the moonlit fields. Once, I saw a horse throw up its head and gallop hell for leather across a field. All the time I was scared that Rumbold would crash into another vehicle for there was no room in that lane for two vehicles to pass each other.

We ran up a hill and along a plateau for several kilometres. Then we roared between a double row of skinny poplars. The fields on the other side of them were painted with silver moonlight.

'Know what I think?' Rumbold said, breaking the long silence, 'the couple in the back were probably tipped off about us. Did you know they had women cops in this country? Of course you did. I believe you have them in England now, don't you?'

'Yes,' I said.

'It was their own fault,' he went on. 'The trouble was, I didn't expect them so soon after the others had stopped us. But I should have done. When you see the dogs you can bet your life the country's lousy with cops. It never fails. Whenever I've seen dogs, I've always seen bags of cops.'

11

ABOUT a half an hour later we turned into a rough track and bumped our way through a forest. Now clear of the road, Rumbold decided it was safe to switch on the lights. He had to. He couldn't have driven without them. Talk about the Black Hole of Calcutta! It had nothing on the darkness in this forest. . . . What a sinister journey it was!

The track suddenly narrowed and was badly scarred with ruts, many of which were hidden by giant ferns which grew lavishly and promiscuously on either side. Birds, startled by the jeep's engine, were constantly falling out of trees and flying screaming into the blackness of the forest. Progress was of necessity slow; so bad were the ruts in places, we could barely crawl along. Here and there old tree stumps all but blocked our way. At the end of the track we came to an old gravel pit.

To by-pass this, Rumbold drove the jeep up a steep bank and zig-zagged through the trees and bushes. The ground was soft and littered with dead cones and pine needles. The strong smell of pine reminded me of the wood in Flackwell Heath in which Rick and I played as kids.

'Know where you're going?' I asked Rumbold.

'Sure. To a graveyard.'

He wasn't serious. We were smack in the heart of the forest now. What an outlandish place! By the look of the tangled undergrowth nobody had ever been here before. It was like a jungle.

'We'll bury them along here,' Rumbold said, stopping the jeep in front of a mass of young saplings. We jumped down. I followed him through the crowded trees, impressed by that air of casual belligerence he'd had since the killing. It reminded me of that mortuary keeper in Paris—that fellow with the leather apron.

Handing me one of the trenching tools, Rumbold said, 'We'll dig them a grave. . . . That's the least we can do for them. But don't think I'm doing it out of altruism. It's expediency. Nobody finds them and nobody's worried.'

He shone the light and we both started to dig. It was a long grave, about three feet deep. After we'd stripped the bodies of all clothing, we dragged them into the grave and buried them feet to feet. It was a wretched, tiring job. And I was glad when it was all over. When we'd filled the grave Rumbold mumbled something in German. Then we picked up the clothes and threw them in the back of the jeep.

'You see how it is,' Rumbold said. 'You meet trouble, you dispose of it and then you bury it.'

'As long as they're not found,' I said.

'Found! Don't be silly. Who's going to come here? If

anybody does, it's unlikely they'll find the bodies for months. By then the grave will be buried with dead leaves and you'll probably be Prime Minister of Britain.'

He was relaxed now, relaxed and happy. You could tell that by the way he drove. There was no hurry, no tension manifest in his manner. What pleased me most was his awareness of the ruts and the holes in the track we followed.

I wanted to tell him why I was here—how I was taking Rick's place in the hospital. I felt at one with Rumbold now. He could probably give me facts of the Q-plan, the odds of my getting back to the West alive. But Maurice had taught me a lesson—that you said nothing about your particular racket when in transit. . . .

A red fox crouching in front of us, blinked furiously and defiantly at the headlights. Seeing it, Rumbold stepped on the gas and for a moment I thought we'd run over it. But it was too quick for him. Leaping to the right, it plunged into the hissing undergrowth.

'You never quite get those devils,' Rumbold murmured.

Suddenly I thought, what's the harm in quizzing him? He can only shut me up.

'Ever heard of the Q-plan?' I asked.

He took his foot off the gas.

'Who told you about that?'

I told him.

'What happens?' I added.

'You mean from our point of view?'

'Yes.'

'I don't know. We never function when it's operating. We know about it. We know of the helicopters; the squads of searchers equipped with walkie-talkie outfits. We know of the specially trained dogs and all that. But just what it's like to be the quarry I don't know. Must be pretty tough.'

He slowed down. The trees were pretty dense just here. Pulling out his compass, he asked me to shine the torch on it.

He glanced at it quickly and then stopped. 'We're going the wrong way,' he said.

He dodged round trees and then changed course.

'Did they tell you why I'm here?' I said.

'No. I don't want to know, either. It's none of my business. My job is to pick you up and deliver you to Big Francis. I'm not interested in the details. If I knew all that went on, I might be too scared to do my job.'

We jogged on. Rumbold sat there, hunched and featureless in the dark.

'Never seen people killed before, huh?' he said, breaking the long tedious silence.

'No,' I said.

'Lucky boy. Once you've tasted war, smelt the stench of dead bodies and seen the agonies of the wounded, you're never quite the same again. War accelerates experience and learning. It makes you old and cynical when you're still young in years.'

What I'd experienced tonight wasn't war. But it affected me the same. I felt much older and wiser than I had yesterday; that I'd never be quite the same again. I'd lost something. Hitherto I'd always been a bit of a stick-in-the-mud; a stuffy sort of bloke—typically English. A dart-thrower and a cricket fan. Although a non-drinker, I liked the matey atmosphere of the English pub. But don't get me wrong, we had murders and crimes of violence in England. But somehow we kept them separate from our way of life. They were with us but not of us. They always shocked us. They always hit the headlines. But we relegated them to an un-English world—the underworld of spivs and spies; stick-up men and homicidal maniacs. They were 'bad shows.'

'What's on your mind?' Rumbold said.

'Nothing much,' I said.

We hit a gravel track, rocking and swaying like rodeo-riders.

'You don't want to think too much,' Rumbold said. 'It seldom helps. Events have their own spacetime, their own logic and geometry. What's more they seldom conform to wishful thinking. The politicians see to that.'

We left the forest at last, bumping and wobbling down a steep bank to a lane. Suddenly we were in the open, free of darkness and morbid speculations.

'What now?' I asked, as we ran up an incline through a gateway and into a field.

'We dump the jeep,' Rumbold said, jumping down. 'Then we burn the cops' clothes.' He pointed to a fence. 'Give us a hand.'

I got down and we walked over to the fence—a temporary affair erected to prevent cattle falling into the old sand pit beyond it.

'Down there,' Rumbold said, 'is a tangle of bushes. We push the jeep over. Once it hits the bottom it will, I hope, sink to where it can't be seen. I've often wondered whether I'd ever have to use it.'

We lifted a pole resting on two X-shaped posts and laid it on the grass to the left. Then Rumbold collected the cops' clothes and laid them under the petrol tank.

'Get me a hammer and chisel from the toolbag,' he said.

While I was doing this, he cut the buttons from the uniforms and put them in his pocket. Then he hammered a hole in the tank. We stood there waiting for the tank to empty. Then we dragged the petrol-soaked clothes away from the jeep.

'Give us a hand,' Rumbold said, pushing the jeep up a mound. I put my shoulder to the tailboard and pushed. At the top, we gave it a final shove and then stopped.

It started slowly, wobbling over the bumpy ground. Then as it gathered momentum, it suddenly leapt over the side like a giant black frog and disappeared.

One . . . two seconds passed. Then—crash! It hit the bushes and sank, we hoped, to its last resting place.

'What a stink of petrol!' Rumbold said.

We replaced the pole. Rumbold picked up some of the petrol-soaked clothing and I the remainder. We carried it to a valley. Here Rumbold set light to the boots. When these had been blazing for several minutes, he dropped the clothing on them.

'Won't this be seen?' I said, as a huge feathery red flame leapt into the air.

'Maybe. Who can tell? If you stop to worry about possibilities like that you're finished.'

'What about the buttons?'

'I'll show you.'

He searched for a rabbit's hole. There was an old one near

75

some bushes. Rumbold dropped the buttons into it. Then he kicked the soil and buried them.

'See. It's so simple,' he said. 'The bodies, the jeep, the buttons are buried and the clothes are burnt. Now we're free from all encumbrances. Know what? When those cops don't show up at their station, a search will be made for them. When they don't find them some cynic will probably suggest that being man and woman, they've gone off to live together in another world. But who cares? I don't. You finish one story and start another. That's life. A long process of next to next.'

As we moved off across the rolling fields, I thought of those tracks the jeep must have made in the tall grass near the gravel pit—how anybody seeing them would guess what had happened. . . . So what? It was as Rumbold said—futile to worry about situations over which you have no control.

The sky was marbled with clouds and moonlight. We were behind schedule, a fact which worried the German. Fortunately, the way was down hill. We ran and then dropped back to a walk.

'What made you take up this business?' I asked.

'The dough. That's all I'm in it for. It pays three times as much as an ordinary job.'

'How did you get mixed up in it?'

'I met Big Francis. I was a prisoner of war in Russia. A pal of Francis' was in my outfit. He told me that if ever I reached Prague I was to look up Big Francis—a racketeer and a half. I escaped from a P.O.W. camp just outside Moscow with a character named Lou, a Bavarian. He got caught. Silly devil went into a café and was twigged. I went on. Luckily, I knew the language. I speak seven languages almost fluently. I finally reached this country. I was practically all in, I knocked at a cottage and spun a hard luck story to a girl who gave me her husband's suit. What for?' He laughed. 'She liked me.'

'Did she know who you were?'

'Sure she did. I told her I was a prisoner on the run. That didn't bother her. She just wanted a man—crazy for one. Her husband was fighting in Leningrad and she hadn't had a man for a long time. I learnt a lot about love and devotion from that baby. A lot about life too. I'd been a P.O.W. for a long time.

I'd done a lot of thinking. I used to wonder what about that wonderful world I believed in as a kid—that kindly world; that world of brotherhood, of love, respect and sincerity. What a pipe-dream! It was that young wife who taught me the biggest lesson of all. Yes, sir. She taught me that everything except the perpetuation of the species is incidental and ultimately unimportant.'

'What about love?' I said.

'Love. . . . Pah! What is it? A fever produced by hormones— a fever which makes us see an ordinary girl as a goddess. It snares us into marriage. Not until after five years of nagging and nattering do we see the girl as she really is. Then we say— whatever I could see in her, I don't know.'

That was Rumbold at his best. He loved to air his cynicism; to shock conventional blokes like me with his denunciation of all life.

'So you met Big Francis,' I said, trying to change the subject. He nodded.

'Quite a character.'

'Intelligent?'

'Oh, yes. Very much so. A man of vision, too. That's why he is where he is today. He knew what would happen after the war—that the Commies weren't going to settle down like turtledoves with the Western Powers. War had regenerated the Soviet. It left them strong. They were well organised. Armed to the teeth. Had it not been for the A-bomb the Yanks dropped in Japan, we'd all be digesting in the Russian bear's stomach.' He paused and sighed.

'As you know,' he went on, 'it went the way Big Francis said it would. This country—well, you know the treachery that followed the end of the war here. It was a sorry story. Big Francis was in on the ground floor. He cultivated the Red leaders. He surveyed the land between Prague and the border. He worked out safe routes for his human traffic. He bribed his way into the very heart of the police force. He had no politics. No feeling. No compassion. He's therefore as invulnerable to treachery as is possible for a human to be.

'Things have changed of course. We've had to alter our technique. Radar has bitched the use of planes in this business.

Then there's short-wave radio, helicopters. We've had to return to the primitive methods of working.'

'How long are you going to stick this life?'

He shrugged.

'God knows. Depends on the sort of cards I'm dealt. But when my luck changes, I'll go as far away from civilisation as possible. A desert island maybe. That'll be it. I'll get myself a beautiful popsie and we'll settle down on a desert island— as far away from Homo-sapiens as possible. It's an old man's dream, of course. A symptom of senile decay.' He threw up his head and laughed at the stars. 'But that's me, boy. That's me.'

When we reached our next base, dawn was breaking over the world, a warm, yellow friendly dawn.

I was happy to bury myself in the hay again; to shut out the world. . . .

12

RUMBOLD woke me up. Opening my eyes, I saw him pouring himself out some coffee.

Sitting up, I fingered hay-dust from my ears, yawned and then looked about me.

'Listen to those rats squealing down there in the barn,' he said.

They made almost as much noise as pigs. I drank some coffee. Things looked pretty glum this evening. We were too near to the end of this long walk in the dark for my liking. I wanted to go on and on forever. . . .

I thought of Rick then—how this time tomorrow Rumbold would be talking to him instead of me. Then it struck me for the first time that maybe nobody had told Rumbold that Rick and I were identical twins. What would happen if they hadn't? He'd probably think Rick was me. But they were bound to tell him.

'By the way,' I said. 'Who you bringing back with you?'

He smiled.

'I never know till the last minute. Probably just as well. If I knew earlier I might be too scared to do the job.'

Our last stage was the roughest. I'd never seen such weather. But it didn't bother Rumbold. Indeed, he seemed to enjoy it. The wind sounded like a horde of screaming devils charging through the woods.

'I like this weather,' Rumbold said, as we entered a wood. 'It sabotages police efficiency.'

Our destination was a mile or so south of Slany—a small village at the foot of a hill. We reached it as dawn was breaking. Just before we got there, I saw the mental hospital in which Rick was incarcerated, standing solitary and foreboding on high ground above the village.

As Rumbold guided me to a sand pit about a hundred yards from the old mansion which Big Francis had made his H.Q. I had an awful feeling that something terrible was going to happen.

'This way,' Rumbold said, running down a path. 'We go through a tunnel. This leads to a cellar in the house. It was used by the Free Czechs during the war.'

The entrance was hidden in a tangle of bushes in the pit. You'd never dream it existed unless you saw it. We crawled along a dark tunnel. At the end of this, Rumbold led the way up a ladder at the top of which he pushed a trap door open. I followed him into a barely furnished room in which two old Jews were fast asleep in two bunks. Feeble gaslight flickered in a dirty globe. Rumbold closed the trap door gently.

'We can't get into the other part of the building until later,' he explained.

Two empty bunks on the far side of the room attracted his attention.

'We'll sleep there,' he said, pointing to them. 'But what about food. . . . Hungry?'

'No, thanks.'

'Me? I'm having vodka,' he returned, going to a cupboard. 'Like one?' He glanced back at me over his shoulder.

'No, I'll turn in,' I said, looking sideways at the shuttered windows.

I'd just about had it. What with the weather and the realisation that I was at last at the end of the road, created a feeling in me akin to death. Never have I been so tired, so wretched, so anxious to escape from reality.

Rumbold swigged vodka. I undressed. What a treat to be naked between clean sheets! As I lay down, I heard one of the Jews roll over on his side, and groan in his sleep. The other snorted. The wind was still hissing furiously out there in the bushes.

I climbed into the top bunk.

'What is it you say in salutation?' Rumbold said, turning to me and grinning.

'Cheerio,' I said.

'Ah, cheerio,' Rumbold repeated, holding his glass to his lips. 'By the way, this is the best thing they have on this side of the Curtain.' Then throwing back his head, he swallowed the vodka in one long gulp. After licking his lips, he grinned obscenely and added, 'All I want to complete this bliss is a beautiful girl.'

13

WHEN I woke up Big Francis was staring at me from a chair. I thought I was dreaming. The broad forehead, the scanty grey hair, the impish blue-grey eyes slightly upturned at the ends and that wicked glint in his eye reminded me vividly of the younger Voltaire I'd seen sketched in a book we had at home. Francis was, of course, much bigger, much more robust than the master cynic of France, but he had the same rascally look about him as the Frenchman had.

Sitting up, I rubbed my eyes with my fists, yawned and wondered who he was.

'So you're Harry Hammond,' he said in English.

'That's right,' I said, looking around for Rumbold.

'Glad to know you.' He stood up and came to me, his arm outstretched. 'I'm Big Francis.' We shook hands. 'They tell me you're a boxer.'

'That's right.'

He stepped back and surveyed me.

'What's your weight?'

'Fourteen stone.'

'Stripped?'

I nodded.

'How old?'

'Twenty-four.'

'You don't say . . . . What a wonderful age—twenty-four! Tell me. What sort of a trip did you have?'

'Not too bad.'

'Good. . . . And Lamond? How's he keeping?'

'O.K. I guess.'

'So you're a scrapper, eh? Well, I wish you luck.'

'I guess I'll need it.'

'You'll need it all right. . . . Hungry?'

I looked at my trousers folded over the back of a chair.

'Mind chucking them?' I said, pointing to them.

'Not at all.'

He went over and collected them.

'Catch.'

He threw them and I caught them. While I was pulling them on I noticed that the Jews and Rumbold had gone.

'Know something?' Big Francis said, going to the window and opening the shutters. 'You fascinate me.' Golden light suddenly flooded his harsh red face. 'Know why? You're a contradiction to everything I believe in. I've seen heroes. Fellows who did the craziest things when they were scared. But I've never met your type before. Did Lamond tell you what you're in for?'

'Yes,' I said, slipping on my clothes.

'And you came here of your own free will?'

'That's right.'

I washed in the enamel basin to the right of the window.

'Well, you're either barmy or a very brave man,' he went on. 'I wouldn't do what you're going to do for all the diamonds in Africa.'

I shrugged and soaped my face.

'No, sir, not for all the loot in the Kremlin. Anyway, let's have a cup of coffee.'

I put on my blouse and then followed him along a passage. We entered a low-ceilinged kitchen where a long table was laid for a meal. 'Sit down.' He pulled out a chair and I sat down, wondering where Rumbold was.

'I've lived for nearly sixty years,' he went on. 'I've seen the lot—bravery, cowards, suicides, murderers—the lot. But you're the only person I know who'd willingly walk into that madhouse and submit himself to all the tortures those twisted lunatics can think up. And all for what? To save your brother. . . . Tell me, kid. Why is it? Why do you think his life is more important than your own? It doesn't make sense.'

'I'm not dead yet,' I said.

He looked at my shoulders and chest.

'No. That's true. If I can help it you won't be either. But I've got to warn you.'

'I know all about it—the Q-plan, your love of your own skin.'

'Good for Lamond. He's a crook but he's sincere. I'm glad he told you, kid. As bad as I am, I wouldn't wish my worst enemy in that place. Those doctors! They're not human. They're fiends. Why they think up more diabolical ways of destroying a man's soul than the devil himself. Believe me, I know. I've seen men in courts—seen them with my own eyes get up and denounce themselves as traitors—as creatures unfit to live. Men—men who before had honour, pride, self-respect. What's the world coming to when men will do that to their fellow-creatures? I'm a crook. I'm a bully. I'm even a killer. But I couldn't do that. What's at work in the world? I'll tell you, kid. The devil our forebears dreamt up has become a fact —flesh and blood. A man in a white coat and a beard. Instead of a fork, he has a hypodermic syringe. Instead of fire, fantastic drugs. What's more he'll bargain for your soul. If you don't agree to his terms, he'll pinch it anyway.' He threw up his hands.

'I'm glad I'm able to help people. I do it for gain. No virtue in that. But I could hate my work, couldn't I? When I snatch somebody away from those monsters in white jackets, I'm happy.' He sighed. Then clapped his hands. A fat woman came in through a doorway. 'Coffee please, Lotty.' She didn't even notice me, just grunted something and then returned to the kitchen.

Big Francis was steamed up. He got up and started to walk about the room wagging his head and hunching his shoulders like a prima donna. It was a fine day. The wind had dropped. Birds were singing. The smell of roses pervaded the room.

'When I spoke to Lamond over the short-wave, he said you knew what you were in for,' Big Francis said. 'And I said, "Who's leg you trying to pull?" Then I said, "Well, obviously the kid can't know all that goes on in that loony bin."' "He does, you know," Lamond said.'

'Look, all I'm really interested in is this: Is it true that once Rick's over the border, you'll get me out of the hospital?'

'Sure—sure. But don't jump ahead, laddie. Don't forget that you'll be due for the first treatment tomorrow—so Jan tells me. Jan, by the way, is our inside man. He's the nurse in charge of your brother. He's the man we're relying on to get your brother out.' He looked at his watch. 'He'll be here very soon. Your brother was to have a sample of the treatment today but he was too full of dope. So they postponed it until tomorrow morning. You'll be there instead.'

'I don't want to know. All I ask is one thing. When my brother is across the border, just get me out of there. It shouldn't take any longer than forty-eight hours. I can take all they can give me in the meantime.'

Big Francis shook his head.

'O.K.,' he said, coming over and patting my shoulder. 'It's a deal. But don't forget. Once the balloon goes up even I'm not safe. Even the officials in my pay get panicky. Know what they're liable to do—turn this place over. We're tipped off just as soon as the Q-plan goes into operation. And what do we do? I'll tell you, kid, we go underground. And we stay there till it's all over.'

The frau came in with a pot of coffee, she put a cup in front of me.

'You'll need some grub,' Big Francis said.

'I don't feel hungry.'

The woman poured me out a cup of coffee.

'Does Rick know I'm going to take his place?' I asked when she'd gone.

'He hasn't a clue. What do you think we are—mugs? No,

sir. He doesn't even know that he's getting out today. It won't be explained to him until the last moment.' He looked at his watch. 'The switch will take place between 1.30 p.m. and 2 p.m. That is the time when the wing is deserted. The doctors are eating—yes, those monsters eat too.'

'How is it proposed to switch us?'

'Now you mustn't ask questions. But I can tell you it's all laid on.'

I sipped my coffee.

'And once my brother is across the border, you can get me out of the hospital?'

He nodded.

'But that's all. I'll be perfectly frank with you. That's all.'

'And you can rely on this nurse—this Jan?'

'There you go again. What do you say—oh, yes. With all other things being equal, yes. But you can't judge what men will do in a crisis. Not all, anyway. This Jan—he's like so many people here—dissatisfied. He wants to get to Paris where his mother is. He's helping us for no other reason.'

I finished my coffee. He poured another. Then he told me what I had to do. First I'd have to have a short haircut. A man was standing by to do that now. After this they'd give me a hospital dressing gown, pyjamas, slippers—everything Rick was wearing.

One of the Jews I'd seen asleep came in and spoke to Big Francis in rapid German. He said Rumbold was losing heavily at poker.

'So what?' Big Francis said, gesturing. 'What's the matter with you guys? He's always losing. So leave him be. I'll see him when he's broke.'

'I don't like to see a man lose like that,' the Jew said. 'It's unnatural.'

'He gets a kick out of it,' Big Francis grinned. 'He's what you'd call a financial masochist. He dreams of winning. He has big plans for that day. But I'll bet you anything you like that once he did win, once his dream came true, he'd be lost. He wouldn't know how to cope.'

Sad-eyed and slightly bewildered by what Big Francis had

84

said, the Jew bowed, shrugged and then returned to the poker game in the basement.

'Poor Rumbold,' Big Francis sighed. 'If he wanted to he could make a fortune. I've taught him how to stack the cards. He knows all the answers. But do you think he'd cash in? No. I've begged of him to take a little—just a wee bit from each of my clients. It would be so easy. But does that thick-headed Prussian take my advice? No. And why? He believes in Providence—he believes that one day he's going to hit the jackpot. He doesn't believe in forcing fate to put a move on. He seems to have the idea that his lot has already been mapped out for him.' He stopped and wagged his head in fake bewilderment.

When somebody knocked on the door, Big Francis yelled out, 'Come in.' It was Jan, the nurse from the hospital—a fat quiet man with straw-coloured hair, fierce dead staring blue eyes and big red lips. The sight of me apparently startled him for his mouth suddenly dropped open and he blinked as if unable to believe what he was seeing.

Big Francis introduced us. Jan's hand felt like a dead mole.

'I'll see you after we've cut the hair and dressed him,' Big Francis said. 'Meanwhile, go to the basement and pick yourself up some change, Jan. The Prussian's down there playing with a couple of naïve Jews. It should be good pickings, boy.'

Jan nodded apathetically and then went out, staring at me.

'Notice anything queer about him?' Big Francis said.

'Not particularly.'

'Poor devil,' he sighed. 'He's got it bad. No wonder. You'd have it bad too if you'd seen what he's seen. That's why he's a hop-head. He finds reality a nightmare. Look what he's seen! After a few days' treatment normal intelligent men are suddenly reduced to gibbering idiots; when sentenced to death slap-happy lunatics whoop with joy. . . .' He glanced at my cup. 'More coffee?'

'No thanks.'

That was Big Francis. Always talking. He never let up. I had to give him full marks. By the time he'd finished, I had no illusions about the future. He saw to that. He saw that I had the broadest view of the shape of things to come. All my instincts urged me to turn back. But I wouldn't listen. For the first time in my life, I was doing something for somebody else.

Draining my coffee, I noticed Big Francis staring at me, that his eyes were mere slits of light.

Pushing the cup away from me, I said, 'What do I do now?'

'Get your hair cut,' he said.

He took me to another room where a stunted, stockily built man awaited me. As I sat in a chair opposite a mirror, Francis told him what to do.

The man put a sheet around me.

'I'll be back when you're through,' Big Francis said, leaving me alone with the barber.

'All right,' I said. The barber said his name was Oscar. He spoke French with a Parisian accent. Picking up the electric clippers, he said, 'What a pity to cut all this curly hair off.' But he seemed to relish the job. He pushed those clippers like an enthusiastic lawn-mower, whistling while he worked. And I sat there, staring pop-eyed at this horrible mutilation. As the last of my crowning glory fell about my shoulders, my heart sank. Never have I seen anything more abject; more sorry than I looked without my hair.

'I've cut to allow for two days' growth,' the barber grinned. 'That's what I call real crafty. Get the idea? When they cut your hair in the hospital, they leave nothing; you're as bald as an egg. Your brother's head is prickly with hair just like yours is now. It's little details like these which can mean all the difference between life and death . . . . Now if you will come this way, I'll give you the pyjamas, dressing gown and slippers.'

He whipped the sheet off me. I looked like somebody from Dartmoor. In a cubicle later, he threw me the clothes I had to wear in hospital. When I was dressed, Big Francis brought Jan to see me.

'Here he is, Jan,' Big Francis said with gusto.

Jan stared at me sceptically.

'You think they're alike?' Big Francis said.

'Alike!' He clasped his hands and rolled his blue eyes.

'What about the scars?' He gave Jan a magnifying glass. 'So?' he said, after Jan had scrutinised my face.

'They're unimportant,' he said. Then he explained. Nobody

86

had seen Rick except the reception doctor and the other two nurses who shared the watch with Jan.

'They wouldn't notice scars,' Jan added. 'They notice nothing except the clock.' He looked at me. 'It is a good thing Dr. Klaus didn't see your brother. He has eyes like a hawk. He sees everything. He was expected to arrive from Moscow yesterday. But something detained him. He sees you tomorrow.' His face went suddenly sad.

'How is my brother?'

'All right. . . . Most of the time he's been asleep.'

'But he's all right?'

'Yes. He's fine.' He gave Big Francis a searching sidelong glance. 'Does Monsieur know about Dr. Klaus?'

'Don't tell me,' I said. 'I'm more interested in my brother. Did they hurt him?'

'There was no need for that. He was asleep. His only discomfort would be a hangover.'

Big Francis looked at his watch.

'The basket is all ready I presume?' he said to Oscar.

'Yes, sir.'

'I'll be popping along,' Jan said. He smiled at me. 'You'll see me in the hospital. Big Francis will explain everything.'

He left us. When he was gone Big Francis showed me a laundry basket about five feet four inches tall and wide enough for me to squat in. It was fitted with wheels so that it could be pushed. I got in and tested it. It was a tight fit.

'Sheets will be packed on top of you,' Big Francis said. 'And you'll be taken to the linen room. As soon as you get there you get out. On the opposite side of the corridor you'll see a door over which will be burning a blue light. That is the bathroom. You go there and wait for Jan. When you close the door it will automatically lock itself. You wait for Jan to collect you. He will take you to the room your brother occupies. Your brother will get in the basket. Jan will put sheets on top—the dirty linen. All this has only been possible because I have the local laundryman fixed. He doesn't know exactly what goes on. He's not interested. All that interests that boy is the cash I pay him.' He paused and winked at me. 'It talks all languages. . . . Have you any questions?'

87

'How long shall I be in the basket?'

'Fifteen minutes. But don't worry. The canes are loosely woven so you'll have no trouble breathing. You'll be a bit stiff maybe. But what's that? Nothing.' He glanced at his watch again. He told Oscar to make a 'phone call. 'You like the way I do the switch with your brother?' he said, when the barber had left the room.

'Yes,' I sighed. I was thinking of the man from Moscow—Dr. Klaus. How he was coming here specially to see Rick. 'This Dr. Klaus. Who is he?'

'A neurologist,' Big Francis said. 'Need I say any more? I don't know what he'll do. Jan tells me his treatment varies. Apparently nervous systems differ in human beings. So you get the treatment which your nervous system responds to best.'

The door opened. Turning I saw Rumbold, pale, excited. 'Ah,' he said coming over to me. 'I am so glad you're not gone. I wanted to say good-bye and wish you all the luck in the world.'

'Talking about luck,' Big Francis said, while Rumbold was pumping my hand. 'How's yours?'

'It was shocking. But during the last twenty minutes it's changed. I can't do anything wrong. It was so good, I got scared. I said to myself, it can't last. What shall I do? Then I thought of the Englishman. How meeting him had probably changed my luck. So I ran up and here I am.'

'I hope it continues,' I said. 'And thanks again for getting me here.'

His face went solemn. He pouted petulantly at his thoughts, wagged his head and looked at me.

'Well,' he sighed, 'it is to be hoped that you won't end up by cursing me for getting you here. . . . Anyway, until better times.' He clicked his heels and held out his hand again. 'Au revoir.'

'Au revoir,' I said.

Rumbold bowed first to me and then to Big Francis. 'Now I return to my luck.'

Big Francis was shaking his head all the time and staring at Rumbold as he might at some pitiable child.

'He'll lose,' he said. The sound of a lorry stopping outside excited Big Francis. 'They're here,' he said. 'This is where we depart. I hate to see you go in there. But there's nothing I can do about it. It's either you or your brother. You still have time to change your mind if you want to.'

'I'll be O.K. All I ask is—just get me out of that hospital when Rick's safely over the border.'

'I'll do that.' We shook hands. Then Big Francis called Oscar. The little barber came in and wheeled the basket in front of me.

'I'm ready when you are,' he said, grinning at me.

I got in the basket. Oscar laid the sheets on top of me. The canes pressed into my shoulders. When I moved my head, they stroked my nose. Through the tiny apertures I could see bits of the room. There was no difficulty in breathing—no feeling of being cooped up except when I moved my shoulders or my head.

'Take him away,' Big Francis said.

I could feel Oscar pushing the basket and heard him mumbling something to himself. He stopped at the front door, I presumed it was. Then I had glimpses of men's shoes, parts of their legs and the floor. The basket was tilted. As the men moved me, I heard them grunting. They spoke in their native tongue. I smelt the fresh air heavy with the perfume of roses. Slashes of yellow light lay sourceless in the road. Suddenly I felt them raising the basket apparently to the tailboard of a van. It wobbled. One of the men jumped up and pulled the basket inside the van. Alone, I heard somebody revving the engine. . . .

14

WE were on our way to the hospital. No turning back now. No more wishful thinking. The world in which miracles happened had vanished. I was on my way to get the big kidney punch. How would I take it? That's what scared me. I didn't want to turn yellow in front of those Commies. I'd have rather died first. Don't get me wrong. I wasn't all that scared of being hurt. I was no hero. But so far I'd no reason to think I was a yellow-belly either. I'd taken some punishment in my time. After all I was a professional fighter. Pain had been part and parcel of my game. You had to be able to take it. If not, you'd had it. It was the same in this adventure. It reminded me of a big fight. But where I was at a disadvantage was that I never knew what I was up against. Anyway, the bell hadn't gone yet. There was perhaps yet time to assess the opposition's strength and conceive a way of beating it.

The ride to the hospital was rough. What a slap-happy driver! He took all the corners at full speed. Perhaps it was the squeals and whines of tyres and road that urged him on. Most of the time I was moving like a rocking horse and my nose seemed intent on pushing its way through those loosely woven canes of the basket.

Presently the engine groaned up a hill and speed was reduced almost to a walking pace.

Soon after we'd stopped, I heard the tailboard clatter as it fell. Then somebody jumped in the van and pulled the basket to the edge. A bloke wearing what looked like a nurse's uniform dragged it out. He and another man lowered it to the ground. They wheeled it to a freight lift. I heard the men shout to each other. A minute later, the gates crashed and the lift whined as it climbed the shaft.

On the way up all that had transpired since I'd said good-bye to Motty flashed through my mind. It seemed an eternity ago— that I'd lived a whole life since then.

The lift shuddered to a standstill. As the gates crashed open the smell of ether hit my nostrils. The wheels of the basket squeaked as somebody pushed it out of the lift.

I guessed where I was—in the hospital and on my way to the linen room. The basket was getting me down. My kneecaps were bursting through the skin, my calves ached. Would the journey never end! How long was this blasted corridor anyway! Just how long can they be! I felt like screaming. I couldn't stick it much longer.

When at last I stopped, I waited eagerly for the person with me to beat it. Peeping through the apertures of the canes, I saw his white trousers and white canvas shoes. Then I heard him blow his nose. After this he left. The door slammed to. One—two minutes passed before I got up. Never had I been so glad to stand up. It was heaven. I heard the sheets I pushed out fall to the floor. Then I shot up to my full height. This was the linen room all right. Shelves all round the walls were packed with it. I picked up the sheets I'd pushed out and put them back in the basket. Then I tiptoed to the door. Opening it, I poked my head out and there directly opposite was the door over which burned a blue light. The corridor looked endless in one direction. It was lined with windows on one side and white doors on the other. I slipped out, closing the door behind me and ran to the bathroom, still feeling wretchedly stiff. The door was ajar. I went in, stared at the tub, the enamel washbasin and the chromium fittings and then closed the door. After this I made a check. Big Francis was right—the door was locked. Bars in the rectangular window which looked down between this and another building to an area, jolted me. I was a prisoner. A yellow patch of light on the top part of the building opposite mocked at me. Everything was so still, so bright and so still out there. I looked at my slippers and the cheap red flannelette dressing gown I wore. Then I got to thinking about Rick. He was so near and yet so far. Closing my eyes I tried to concentrate on him to see if I could get any reaction. But I was constantly distracted by the tick-tick-tick of a nerve in my ear. A few minutes later I heard somebody walking outside. I ran to the door, pressed my ear to it. Somebody coughed. A door squeaked open. There was a few minutes' silence. All I heard was that almost insufferable tick-tick-tick in my ear. I was excited. Once I wanted to yell, 'Rick—Rick.' He and I together could beat the whole world! That's how crazy I was. But something wiser than I hit that idea on the head. At last I heard them—those wheels of the linen basket. I fell on my knees, closed one eye and pressed the other to the keyhole. But all I could see was a bit of wall and floor. A door banged, the squealing wheels ran away. My heart sank. Sitting on the edge of the tub, I muttered a silent prayer, 'God,' I said, 'get that boy safely over to the other side.'

15

How long was it? Time had no meaning now. But I guess it must have been nearly half an hour before Jan opened the door.

'O.K.,' he said in a gruff voice. 'Let's go.'

He went first and waited in the corridor.

'This way.' We turned left and walked about fifty yards along the corridor and went into a room on the right.

This was it. This was where Rick had been. This was the end of the walk in the dark.

It was just an ordinary hospital room, small, spotlessly clean, with a cot on the right. By the look of the dishevelled covers it was obvious Rick had got straight out of bed. The thought of his having been here only a few minutes before gave me a strange feeling of propinquity. Then irrational thoughts began to swirl in my mind. Why was I bowing so meekly to their orders? Why the hell didn't I knock Jan for six and escape? Then Rick and I could team up and flee together to England and sanity.

'He's clear,' Jan said. 'Everything went off exactly as we had planned it. At dusk Rumbold will escort him west. If they take the short cut they should be in Paris in a couple of days.'

Moving to the barred window, I saw the sunny silence down there in the hospital grounds. There were green lawns sloping to a wood, red buildings, tennis courts, red paths. Everything looked so normal, so serene. . . .

'What's the matter?' Jan said.

I swung round.

'Nothing—nothing at all. Why? Do I look——'

'Oh, no,' he cut in, anxious to pacify me.

'About getting out of here?' I began.

He wagged his head, compressed his lips.

'We're fixing that,' he said.

'Think I'll make it O.K?'

We looked at each other.

'Why not? Your brother did.'

'Yes, but this—this Q-plan?'

'We can't avoid that, can we? We can't keep the powers-that-be away from this room till you're safe across the border.'

'This Klaus?'

Jan squinted and nodded. The name obviously distressed him.

'Yes?' He stared wide-eyed.

'What's he like?'

'You mean physically—well, he's short, but his head is enormous. It makes him look top-heavy. His face, despite the beard is like a rat's. I want to give you a tip about him. He's a madman. He has a one-track mind. Struts around like a god. If things don't go his way, he screams and raves like a child.'

'What do they do when they give you the treatment?'

'It varies. Some get the needle. Others are put into the cells naked. It all depends what sort of a fellow you are. We don't all behave the same, so they say.'

'What's the idea of putting you in a cell naked?'

'To outrage and subdue your ego. It's insulted and humiliated so much that it soon becomes a sniffling, toadying creature that has no shame, no pride, something that readily denounces itself as a liar, as a coward, a cheat, as anything they want it to be.'

'How long does that take?'

'It's like I said. It depends on the person. Some egos react quicker than others. Some even act as though they're not responding to the treatment. It's all so strange—so horrible. It's getting me down.'

'Can you tell me how long it takes for them to kill your soul?'

'A week . . . ten days maybe.'

'How do they begin?'

'Look. I don't want to discuss it. Tomorrow you will see for yourself. He will be here with the others at about 9 a.m.'

'But can't you tell me what he will do?'

'No. He'll test you.'

'How?'

'It will depend on his diagnosis of your nervous system. His tactics vary. It's uncanny. I don't know what does it. Sometimes he coos and kids a patient; sometimes he explodes,

93

at other times he just spits right in a patient's face without warning.'

'What a bastard!'

'It all started with the scientist named Pavlov—this conversion cult did. He experimented on animals. Conditioning reflexes, they call it. Pavlov found that certain shocks changed animals normal behaviour—made them neurotic. Well, what they did to the animals, they now do to human beings.'

Fear—a strange awful fear began to creep into my being. It was the thought of losing my soul, losing my identity—the thing I'd known all my life—ME. I grew agitated. I couldn't keep still. There was a feeling in the pit of my stomach—a feeling that I was going to blow up. I must have started to mutter, for I saw Jan watching me, his eyes narrowed, that small vertical line between his almost non-existent brows deepen.

'You'd better get into bed,' he cooed, coming over to me.

'No, thanks,' I said. 'No, thanks, old boy. Not me.'

'But you must. Somebody might come. They'll see you like this and blame me. I'll be transferred then. And all your chance of escape will go.'

'I'm—I'm so——'

'Yes, I know,' he cooed, taking my arm. 'I was a fool to tell you. They're all like that. All scared of losing their power to identify themselves.'

'It's not that I'm a coward. I'd gladly die fighting. But—but to, to be——'

'Please, come on,' he broke in, tugging me gently. 'I'll give you something. It will calm you—banish all fear.'

I stared at him. Who was he? Jan. Who was Jan? Couldn't he be a phoney? Couldn't he have made a bargain with Big Francis? O.K. I was here in place of my brother. Only Jan knew that. So—so he didn't have to do anything. He could leave me to take the rap.

'Let go, you bastard!' I snarled.

He dropped my arm as he might a red hot cinder and stared at me in horror.

'You're—you're not going to do anything foolish, are you?' he said tremulously.

'I know you,' I said. 'You want to dope me—prepare me for them.'

'You're becoming hysterical,' he sighed. 'Don't yield to it. Do that and you're finished. You've got to trust me. Really you have. I'm your only hope. You're mine. Only when I get you out of here, will I be able to join my poor mother in Paris. I've been waiting years for it. There were times when I was nearly there. Then something happened. Something always happened.'

I calmed down. He smiled.

'This drug won't hurt you.'

'How do I know?'

'You can't possibly know, can you?'

'What about you taking one?'

'With pleasure.' He went to a cupboard, took a key from his pocket, unlocked it and took out a box of capsules, shaped like skittles. He swallowed one. 'What about it?

I took one from the box and swallowed it. Then I asked if I could have just one more look out of the window. I was irrational. I know that now. But it was very real to me then— this feeling I had that after this the world out there would never look quite the same again.

'Just one look,' I said.

I walked to the bars and there they were—green grass, the trees, the brown soil, the birds, the sun and the sky. My world. I looked round at Jan. 'And your world,' I said. 'Will it—will it ever be the same again?'

'It's just your nerves,' he cooed. 'You're getting the reaction. Your nervous system can stand just so much. Then it breaks down. You don't want that to happen. You'll need all your nervous energy for tomorrow. It's a big day for you. Get over tomorrow and half the battle is won. So be a good fellow and go to bed. If there's anything you want I'll get it for you.'

'It was the same when we were children,' I said. 'We had our own world. Then nature did something to us. Our voices broke. We grew beards. We had strange feelings. And that— that world of childhood was no more.'

It was so unlike me to talk like this. Even in my state, I realised it—I seemed to be two people—or it may have been

95

that what I had gone through had changed me, but something of that old stick-in-the-mud remained.

The drug had a rapid action. I was already feeling relaxed. That horrible tension which resulted from what Jan had told me about Klaus, had gone. I got into bed—into Rick's bed. Fancy, I thought, the old so-and-so was here less than an hour ago—his face on this same pillow, his feet in these sheets—lying here, looking at the same things as I am and now—now he's in Big Francis' place, where poor Rumbold is losing his cash at poker and tonight—tonight he'll embark on that walk in the dark. . . .

'There's one thing I must have clear,' I said.

'Yes.' Jan came to the bed.

'As soon as my brother is across the border, you'll get me out of here.'

'Yes. But why are you so——'

'Why!' I cut in. 'Out there it's me against anybody. I've got a chance. I'm not shackled. But in here I am. I haven't a hope in hell. Understand?'

That day was endless—the longest I'd ever lived. You can see how it was. It wouldn't have been so bad had I seen Klaus —seen him and got it over with. I'd have had no time to think, no time to brood. I'd have got it. And that would have been that. Minutes dragged like hours. It seemed an eternity before a clock somewhere out there struck the hour.

Jan came to me.

'I'm giving you something to put you to sleep,' he whispered. 'I'm going off duty. A new man comes on. I'll see you at two tomorrow. You'll have seen Klaus by then. . . . Will you promise me something?'

'What?' I stared at him.

'Don't lose your head. Try to remember when you see him that you're only here for forty-eight hours—you'll be out of here at two in the afternoon, day after to-morrow.'

He held out his hand. There were two pink tablets in the palm.

'Take these.' He gave me a glass of water. 'And don't forget. Whatever you do, don't lose your head.'

I swallowed the tablets.

'I'll do my best not to and thanks—thanks a million.'

I closed my eyes. He was moving almost noiselessly about the room. That was the last I remember until I woke up and found myself face to face with Klaus.

16

IT was like waking up in a nightmare world. I remember how scared I was when I first saw him—saw that rat face, the eyes like black buttons behind the thick ridged lenses, the twin vertical lines above that long pointed nose, the fidgety muscles of the lean black-bearded jaws and the chin which was conspicuous for its absence. The other faces were dimmed by this monster's. . . .

I blinked a couple of times in an effort to convince myself I was awake. Suddenly he yelled, 'Sit up, thief!'

Thief! I was still befuddled by sleep.

'I said—up!' The double back-hander across my mouth, cut the membrane inside the lips. The salty taste of blood incensed me. I sprang up. Two musclemen seized my arms and held me. So you're Klaus, I thought, glaring at the monster. The infamous Dr. Klaus. Remembering Jan's advice, I suddenly relaxed. Then I noticed a snub-nosed blonde with cropped hair, no lipstick or powder, peering at me as she might at a strange germ. Next to her stood another chinless tartar.

'Look,' Klaus said, between clenched teeth, 'we don't waste time here. It's too precious. Our approach to criminals like you is determined by long experience.' He had an Oxford accent. 'This is the position: Either you tell us where you've hidden the film stolen from the Soviet Union of your own volition or we'll create conditions whereby you'll be happy to tell us anyway. The advantage of the first alternative is that it saves us a lot of time and trouble. And you a lot of pain.' He bent down, his face quite near mine.

'But——' That was as far as I got.

'Don't you dare speak until you're told to,' he screamed, giving me another back-hander.

Something came alive in me—something alien and vicious. Pins and needles danced over my scalp. My muscles swelled. I was quickly imbued with amazing energy. Klaus' hideous face—the rodent teeth, the loathesome eyes snapped something in my brain. It all happened in a second. I must have broken away from the musclemen and grabbed Klaus' gown. I remember coming to and finding myself punching his face with everything I had. . . . Three, maybe four, seconds passed. Then I got it. It felt as if a bomb had exploded in my head. A blinding flash dazzled me. Then I went out. . . .

I woke up in a cell. What an awakening! My lips were a million times thicker than normally. My eyes struggled to see through swollen flesh. The bump at the back of my head was as big as a turkey-egg. Pain! Every square inch of me throbbed and ached almost unbearably. I could just see the feeble light filtering through a grating high up in the wall. I was stark naked and lying on a cold stone floor.

As I tried to rise, pain stabbed me like a stiletto—in my back, chest, stomach. I blinked, confused and stupefied at the padded walls that rippled and wobbled, bulged and stretched like things seen in distorted mirrors.

Panting, I stared about me like some newborn thing striving to co-ordinate what I saw, to remember what happened and who I was. Only the pain was real. God knows how long I'd been there. I kept passing out. Time had no meaning. Nothing had for what—oh, it must have been hours. I got to a point where I knew I was hurt—that breathing through my nose was difficult. It was curious. I had a feeling that I was fighting Hanslip, that he'd knocked me down and that I had to get up. I kept trying to, getting on my knees and then passing out.

I'd somehow managed to crawl into the light from the grating and was now staring at the raw and swollen knuckles of my right fist, seeing the black congealed blood, the skin broken at the knuckles.

Suddenly, I remembered hitting Klaus and clenched my teeth. Something was wrong with them! My tongue explored the empty cavities belonging to those that had been kicked out.

98

Pain in the jaw muscles scared me. Had they broken my jaws? I champed a couple of times. Then I licked the lacerated membrane inside my mouth. What a beating! I'd never had anything like it. I checked my limbs for fractures. They were O.K. I took a deep breath. Apart from general soreness, my ribs were apparently O.K. too.

The sun came out and dust motes sparkled and danced in the yellow needles of light.

So I'd had the treatment! Or had I? Perhaps it was yet to come. What they'd given me was probably only preventative medicine.

I noticed I was panting like a nervous animal. Sweat was pouring from my naked body.

What now? I remembered Jan's warning. I realised that I'd killed my chances of getting out of there. What would happen? They'd keep me here indefinitely. Nakedness was probably a phase of the treatment. Next would come the spitting, the jeering. I'd tell them who I was—that I'd taken my brother's place. Then they'd bump me off. That was O.K. by me. There was nothing left to live for anyway.

I suddenly relaxed. Hope raced away from me like a dog from a trap. My spirit wilted and withered. I'd had it. . . . This was the end of me. It didn't matter. Nothing did except pain. . . .

O.K. I thought, let them come and spit at me and see what I care. Let them do what the hell they like. Let the bastards crucify me. . . . Apathy and supineness followed. I grew weary—so tired that I was unaware of the cold and the hardness of the floor. All I craved was oblivion. . . . At least that was how it was at first. Gradually, however, I grew aware of something running beneath the abject and demoralised me—something whispering incoherently and with an urgency that demanded attention. The hell with it, I kept thinking. I'm tired. Want to go to sleep. Soon I was straining my ears to catch what was being said. At last I heard, 'Box clever, boy. Box clever.' It was Motty's voice. Suddenly there he was staring at me through the ropes. The walls had vanished—there was just the ring and that spotlight shining on me.

'It's no good,' I said, and then passed out.

When I came to they were there—three musclemen with rubber truncheons and a tall, lank doctor in one of those long white gowns—staring at me.

Blinking at them, I thought, this is where I get my chips.

'Get up,' the doctor said in English.

I tried to, but failed. He yelled something to the others. I was grabbed and yanked to my feet. They let go of me. I staggered. My knees wobbled. Never have I felt so weak— never quite so wretched. The doctor checked my pulse. One of the musclemen helped me on with my dressing gown. Later, they took me to a lift at the end of a long corridor—a freight lift it looked like.

Where were we going? I could just totter. Two musclemen supported me. To my surprise, they took me back to my room on the top floor. Here the doctor examined me—testing my reflexes, my heart and breathing. Then he quizzed me.

'Are you giddy?' he asked.

'Not now.'

He wrote something on a chart. While he was doing so Jan came in, looking at me in a squinty alarmed manner. He said something to the doctor who nodded. I was put on the bed. The doctor came over.

'Are you prepared to behave yourself?' he asked in English.

'Yes,' I said.

He whispered something to the others. Then he faced me again.

'Any more trouble and back you go to the cells.'

'There won't be,' I said, catching Jan's eye.

He asked Jan if he required an extra attendant.

'No, sir. I'll manage. He's hardly fit to start any more trouble. If he does, I know what to do.'

We were left alone. As soon as the others had gone Jan gave me a drink—something that made me feel on top of the world.

'Thanks a million,' I whispered hoarsely.

'You'll never learn, will you?' he said.

'The hell with me. What about Rick? Did he make it?'

'Yes.'

He sat on the foot of the bed.

'Why didn't you play it the smart way?'

100

I sighed.

'It was Klaus——'

'You know what you've done to him—broken his jaw and nose. It's a wonder they didn't kill you.'

'I'm glad—I'm glad I did that—so jolly glad.'

'It's an ill wind that doesn't blow some good. He won't be fit to see you for at least a week.'

'So what?'

'Don't you see? The treatment's postponed. The question now is—are you fit enough to leave on schedule?'

'How long have I got?'

'Until tomorrow afternoon.'

'I'll be O.K. by then.'

'How do you feel?'

'Terrible.'

'You took one hell of a beating I'm told. They said——'

'I don't want to know.'

'You were crazy.'

'What else could I do? He hit me twice. I'd done nothing.'

'Thank your lucky stars you're not staying. I hate to think what Klaus has in store for you.'

He helped me to lie down.

'I'm due to go underground at 2.30 tomorrow,' he said. 'If you're not well enough——'

'Don't worry. I shall be,' I cut in.

I fell to thinking of Big Francis—how he'd had such an apparent admiration for me. I knew why now. He must have known the drill—what a bloke like me would get.

'About tomorrow?' I said. 'What's the drill?'

'It's going to be tougher than we thought,' Jan said. 'You'll have to do some fighting. That's what scares me. You're not fit for that.'

'I'll decide whether or not I am. What's the drill?'

He thought about it.

'At 1.30 tomorrow, I'll take you to the bathroom,' he said. 'At 1.40 the door will be unlocked. You then nip across to the linen room and hide behind the door. Directly ahead of you you'll see the laundry basket you came in. It will be overflowing with dirty linen. You're supposed to be in it. A few minutes

101

later a guard—a fellow your size—will come in. He'll think you're hiding in the basket. When he gets to it, you overwhelm him. I'll give you cord to tie him up with. Before you do this, you strip off his uniform. Then you'll gag and tie him. After this you put on the uniform. It should fit. The fellow you'll tackle is about your size. I told his boss I'd like him on duty in the wing—just in case. He knows what you did to Klaus. . . .'

'I do all this and then what?'

'You get out of here. Leaving the linen room, you'll turn left. At the end of the passage running at right angles to the corridor, you'll see the lift. When you get in it, you press the basement button.'

'I get out by myself?' I said in surprise.

'Yes.' He took a paper from his pocket. 'This is a rough sketch of the way out.'

'Then what?'

'Halfway down the hill, you'll find a grey getaway car. You'll have an hour before the scream goes up.'

'What do you do?'

'I told you—I go underground.'

'Can't I go with you?'

'It's not possible. Your only hope is by travelling at night. I'll give you a map and compass. It should only take you two nights at the most to reach the other side.'

I thought over what he'd told me. It was nothing like what I'd visualised.

'Why can't you get me out the same way as you got me in here?' I asked.

'It can't be done that way. Guards have orders to search anything going in or out.'

'Why?'

'That's the new drill. It started today.'

'A bit of a coincidence—'

'It's not that. Klaus tightened up on security. Maybe stool pigeons have been talking to him.'

I studied the map he gave me.

'How do I get past the guard at the main gate?' I said.

'That's up to you.'

'Isn't there another way out—a back way?'

'Sure. But it's more dicey still. The man at the gate sits in an office. It should be simple to sneak up and hurry through with your face turned the other way. If you're quick, he won't see who you are. Being in uniform, he'll probably think you're a colleague.'

I didn't like it. It stank to High Heaven.

'Tell me the truth,' I said. 'Why are you leaving me to my own resources?'

'Because Big Francis has packed up and gone to Paris,' Jan said. 'He's been tipped off that if anybody escapes from here, he can't expect protection. There's a new chief of police in Slany—a Moscow-trained hoodlum—who's unbribable.'

'I see. . . . What it amounts to is that you'll be leaving before me.'

'I've got to. I'll be number one suspect. I'm taking no chances.' He looked sheepish. 'You can't blame me for thinking of myself first.'

'That's fair enough. But it's not like Lamond said it would be. But never mind. I'll get out. Tell me, do the guards carry guns?'

'Yes.'

'How do you know I'll have an hour's lead on them?'

'The doctor's won't know you've gone till they visit your room. That will be about an hour after you've left.'

'Where you going?'

'I've made my own plans.'

'What about those barns we stayed at on the way here? Can't I shack up in them?'

'I know nothing about them. They're in Big Francis' set-up. I only work for him. He's told me nothing about his set-up.'

'But isn't there some place I can hide—till the scream has died down?'

'There's not enough money that would tempt anybody to hide you. Big Francis obviously had to tip off his contacts that he was leaving. They'd guess why. They'd know the balloon was about to go up. . . . Sorry and all that.'

17

WELL, there it was. That was the set-up. Jan kept his word. He produced the cord, map and compass, which I put in my dressing gown pockets. Then he escorted me to the bathroom. I was still in pain—still aching all over. But much of my strength had returned.

'You're sure you're strong enough to tackle this guard?'

'You wait and see.'

He looked at his watch.

'Wait ten minutes and then nip over to the linen room. I'll pop along and see the other nurse on duty—send him downstairs for something. When he's gone I'll unlock the door. Then I'll go to the check point and tell the guard I believe you're hiding in the linen closet. I may even come back with him.'

'Before you go. Which road leads west?'

'The left fork at the bottom of the hill,' he said. 'But don't keep on it too long. It could be a death-trap.'

'I wish you all the best,' I said, shaking his hand.

'Same to you. Let's hope we meet in happier circumstances.'

He left. I waited ten minutes and then nipped across to the linen room. Standing by the door, I saw that Jan could easily have double-crossed me; that this could be a trap to cover his own escape. If not this, it could be a ruse to get me moved elsewhere. Having done this, Jan could quit his job in the ordinary way and go to Paris at his leisure.

Suddenly the whole thing seemed to be full of snags. Would a guard tackle me alone? It seemed inconceivable that he would. The only reason he might would be because his colleagues were at lunch. These speculations started me sweating. Was it wise to risk being killed? Wouldn't it be better to wait in the hope that a better chance of escape popped up later on?

Then I heard them outside—the clamping feet, the whispers. 'In there in the basket.' It was Jan.

The door was kicked open. The man hesitated. Then moved

in warily—gun in hand, head swivelling. I didn't hesitate. It was now or never. I'd never felt so strong! Leaping like a gazelle, I landed on his back, my right arm round his throat. Reeling back, he tried to shake me off, but I was too strong for him. I squeezed his throat for less than a second, then down he went.

I worked fast—undressing him wasn't easy. As I yanked off his tunic he came to and I had to sock him on the back of the neck. He went out. I left him lying in his underwear and shirt. After tying him up, I gagged him. Then I slipped into his things. The tunic was tight across the shoulders, but the breeches and boots fitted me to a T. I laced the knee-boots and then tried on the cap. It was a size too big. But that didn't matter. It was all the better for it. I could pull the peak over my swollen eyes. . . .

So far so good. There was nobody in the long corridor outside. Only the yellow splashes of light that streamed through the windows and those dead-pan white doors. Jan had been correct. The lift was halfway along a narrow corridor. . . .

Seeing somebody, I suddenly stopped. It was a sister wheeling a patient to the lift. What should I do? It was no good turning back now. But what if she saw my black eyes and swollen lips! I had to chance it. Pressing on, I walked with my head bowed, my hand on the gun which was loose in my tunic pocket. The sister had already wheeled the patient in the lift when I got there. I only saw his white face. Luckily, she was staring at him when I came in. I stood facing the indicator, my back to the sister.

'Floor?' I said in German.

'First,' she replied in the same language.

I waited anxiously for her to say something more. The lift descended. She didn't speak again. The lift stopped. The gates crashed open. As she passed me, she turned round to look at me but I was too quick for her. Before she could see my face, I turned away. When the gates closed, I stared at my puffed eyes, the black half-moons beneath them, the swollen nose and the swollen lips. What a sight! I stabbed the last button on the indicator. The lift shuddered and then began to whine. The gates opened on to a long stone-floored corridor. Glancing at Jan's plan I started to sprint. When I was halfway to the door at the far end, a little man in a chef's outfit left a huge kitchen, his head bowed, a cigarette slanting across his long white chin.

I slowed down, walking with bowed head. I was happy to see him turn left and enter another corridor.

Wanton yellow light of the afternoon played with the shadows of nodding flowers in the beds surrounding the lawn outside.

Reaching the four steps leading up to a red path, I saw a mist of fine water from the half dozen whirling sprays on the spacious lawn. Sucking in air and cursing my trembling limbs, I took a quick look at Jan's sketch. I stared ahead. This is it, I thought, hurrying along the path in front of me. At the end of this I turned right and there directly ahead were the main gates—red wired gates, with an office on the left.

As I reached the path two nurses left the building beyond it—walking quickly towards me, arms folded and eyes downcast. They didn't see me.

Just before I reached the gates, I saw two patients wheeling themselves out of a ward on the second floor of a building and on to a verandah. A nurse was following them. As they stopped, she bent down, said something to one of them, then they all stared at me. This is where you start running, boy, I thought. Then they started! What a noise! It was as if hell itself had broken loose. There were what—at least six sirens and that hooter which went off in a series of jerky blasts.

I reached the gate and there he stood—this fat man with a blue moon face and popping blue eyes. Standing in the office doorway at the main gates, he scowled at the grin I gave him. It was an impudent, stupid grin. But it was the only thing I could think of doing at the time. It was his face—the look on it—the look of outraged incredulity. I drew near him, saw him clench his fat hands, square his jaws. That's all the poor devil had time to do. He didn't know what hit him. Never even saw it coming. I'd never socked anybody quite so swiftly or so accurately. He just fell back against a table and then slid down to the floor. I yanked the telephone flex from its socket. The sirens were still wailing. All the verandahs were now crowded with doctors, nurses, patients. What did I care? I was outside that torture-chamber and halfway down the hill was the car Jan had told me about.

I ran to it. Nothing could stop me now. Of that much I was sure. Turning the ignition key, I wondered how the gears worked. It was a universal change. After a shaky start, I stepped on the gas. . . . The relief of being out of that torture-chamber was infinite. It gave me delusions of grandeur. What I didn't realise was that there was now no hour's grace—that the first stage of the dreaded Q-plan was already in operation. As my foot left the clutch the car shot forward down the hill. What a beauty she was! It was as easy to steer as a Rolls. I'd forgotten all about those wailing sirens now. Nothing mattered—nothing at all. . . .

Reaching the village, I was surprised to see how beautiful it was, the quaint cottages, the lovely flower gardens. The only person I saw was an old lady in black weeding her garden, apparently undisturbed by the sirens still wailing up there at the hospital.

After swinging the car into the left fork, I saw a dead straight road ahead. It wasn't until I'd gone nearly a dozen kilometres that I suddenly realised I was on the wrong side of the road— driving on the left instead of the right.

I'd passed nothing so far. The road was still straight, still empty. I didn't like the look of it. It seemed as if somebody had warned off all the other traffic. Suddenly I decided to get the hell off that road. Turning into a lane, I glanced at the instrument board and I wondered about oil and gas. How much was there? Then glancing in my driving mirror, I saw a motor-cyclist creeping up on me.

This won't do, I thought, pressing the gas pedal flush with the floor. The car shimmied; the engine hummed like a power station. Chummy on the motor-bike fell rapidly away from me. Very soon we parted company for good. I started whistling, 'Let's all sing like the birdies sing.' I thought of Rick. How he was living with Rumbold. He'd now be shacked up in one of those barns. Had Rumbold told him about the cops he'd killed? Had he discussed me with Rick? It was most unlikely. Big Francis had obviously briefed him what to say and what not to say. It stood to reason. If Rick knew I'd taken his place he'd never leave this side of the Curtain without me.

18

I FELT better on this road—safer and less tense than before. The countryside was at its best. It wasn't unlike Sussex in places—rolling country and very green. Some of the fields were crowded with cattle which grazed blissfully in the sun, oblivious to such things as Q-plans, H-bombs, bacteriological warfare and all the other diabolical devices which in the last decade had turned the once sane world into a madhouse.

I'd been driving hard for about an hour. It was now time I dumped the car. Very soon the air would be full of buzzing helicopters, the roads blocked with police cars. Hunters with dogs would be working the fields and the woods. Oh, yes, I had no illusions. This little flip in the car, undisturbed and as cosy as it could be, hadn't blinded me to all the dangers that should now be prodding the highways and by-ways like sensitive fingers.

But for all my awareness, I was by no means downhearted. Indeed, a new optimism had flowered—one that gave me confidence that, come what may, I should finally get through safely to the West. Looking about me, I saw lots of acres—plenty of space for a fellow to move around in.

Driving through the mottled shadows of the lanes which went to God knows where, I looked around for a place in which to dump the car.

It was dynamite now. Somebody was bound to have seen me in it—that motor-cyclist I'd seen soon after I'd left the village, for example.

Nobody could have asked for a better marked man than I was. Apart from my swollen black eyes, my thick bruised lips, there was my uniform and cropped hair. I'd be standing out a mile even to the most witless person.

I followed a narrow lane winding through the hills and wondered where I was going. My compass said I'd been travelling south-west for over an hour. There'd been no roads leading directly west—at least I hadn't seen any.

Most of the time I was looking for helicopters and road blocks. Why hadn't I seen any? Was this Q-plan as hot as they'd made out? Perhaps I'd been over-rating its efficiency?

Reaching a small hamlet at the bottom of a hill, I saw a signpost pointing directly west. 'To Womback,' it said. The place wasn't on the map. What did that matter? It went west. So off I buzzed. Cow-droppings in the narrow lane or track suggested it hadn't seen a car. I drove carefully through hedgeless fields, passing numerous poplars infested with hundreds of cawing crows. It was way beyond these—when I was in the remote country that I heard the first helicopter. I was still following the track and hugging a tall hawthorn hedge when I saw it hovering over a wood like some fabulous spider waiting to pounce on its prey. My heart started to work overtime. The insides of my hands were weeping copiously. My mouth had gone as dry as the cracked soil in the road. So far so good, I thought. They haven't seen me. I descended a hill. Here the track got tougher. Old ruts scarred the path and huge brown stones blistered it so badly I was forced to slow down to a crawl. The car wobbled. It wasn't liking this ride any more than I. . . .

Suddenly I saw it—the first house I'd seen for over an hour, a dirty grey stone farmhouse. It squatted in a hollow under a hill its outhouses looking very black in the sun. I took my foot off the gas and looked back over my shoulder. The helicopter was out of sight. But something else worried me. Did this crude track end at the farm? If it did, then I'd have to ditch the car. But I thought, it must go to the place on the signpost.

I left the hawthorn hedges behind and followed the track through a field. Way over to the left near a broken fence, I saw a farmer wheeling a bicycle with one hand and wielding a stick with the other. He and his dog were driving a herd of black and white cattle towards the farmhouse. I sailed past them. As I did so, the man shielded his eyes from the sun and stared at me.

Standing on the other side of a stone wall at the farm a stout woman watched me approach with all the interest of a scientist.

'Where does this road lead to?' I asked her in German.

'Womback,' she said.

'Are there any main roads there?'

She nodded.

'Going west?'

She frowned and pouted.

'I don't know where they go to. You get to Prague from there. That I know.'

I thanked her and as I drove on I wondered how she'd reacted to my bruised face. Would she tell her man about me when he returned? What was the use of worrying? This was all very well. She'd say nothing. . . . O.K. The man I'd seen with the cows would say nothing. . . .

'But there's always the radio,' I muttered.

I slowed down and thought of Rumbold—the way he'd dumped that jeep. He'd know the right things to do, I thought. Me? I'd had no experience, except that walk in the dark to this side of the Curtain. But you soon learn. Be up against it for any length of time and you can always pull something unexpected out of the bag. I knew I was due to resume my journey on shank's pony. It wasn't a pleasant thought. I was very much in love with this car. I hated parting with it. Without it, I'd be exposed to view—so conspicuous in my uniform. But I couldn't chance riding much farther. A description of it must have been broadcast by now.

Pulling up at a gate on the right, I jumped out of the car and stared at a field which sloped to a tangle of bushes—blackberry or hawthorn, I think they were. It's just the job, I thought. What a God forsaken place! I drove into the field and down to the bushes. What a lucky boy, I said, as I entered a tunnel of foliage. It was a tight squeeze. Nobody could see us in here. It couldn't have been better. Once I was tempted to burn the car. But what was the point? It would probably take days before they found it and with luck I'd be on the other side by then.

After taking cigarettes, matches and a wallet containing money and snaps of a buxom blonde woman with frizzy yellow hair from the tunic, I stripped off. It was senseless to keep it on. I'd have to go ahead in the pyjama jacket and hope for the best. You never knew what your luck was going to be. It was this

110

thought that kept me going. Who knows, I thought, I might chance upon a civvy jacket just my size.

Such was my optimism. I emerged from the bushes and looked around for a place to sit down. It was still warm. But what would it be like when the sun went down? I chose a grassy spot between some lofty bushes. A few minutes passed. Then a buzz in the sky had me looking up again. But I needn't have bothered. It was only a passenger plane. I lay down for a while, closing my eyes and feeling the sun warm on my face. Then I got to thinking about the gun—how I hadn't seriously thought of using it. I sat up and pulled it out of the holster on the belt I'd buckled round my waist.

It was easy to work. I loaded and unloaded it three or four times. Then I realised just how lucky I had been. For example, where would I have been without a compass? It was all right during the day. I knew the sun rose in the east and set in the west. But since the moon was late rising and I had no idea of star geography, I'd have been hopelessly lost at night.

It was funny how possessed I was with these things—how indifferent to such vital factors as food, drink and a place to sleep. It wasn't until later—much later that I began to contemplate them.

It was while watching bees working the blackberry blossom that I likened myself to these tenacious and industrious insects. Like them nothing would daunt me. If it was the last thing I did, I'd prove to myself that this Q-plan could be beaten.

The sun was already sinking and night had begun its slow march up the sky. It wouldn't be long now before I could start moving. Sometimes when I heard a distant car buzz past, I wondered what old Motty and Jo were doing back home; just how far old Rick and Rumbold were from that farm on the other side of the Curtain. Suddenly it was dusk.

I felt so safe in the dark, so remote from the lunatics who hunted me. Indeed, I might have been sitting in a field at Flackwell Heath, waiting for Rick before returning to Uncle Henry's farm.

I didn't feel like moving. To pass away the time, I recapitulated all I'd experienced since I'd got that cable from Nina. What an incredible journey it had been! It was like being suddenly catapulted into a strange new world which had different values, a faster tempo, a geometry all of its own. My adventures were reminiscent of Alice's in Wonderland. It seemed to me that there must be hundreds of different worlds on this planet—the peasant's world. The world of the big-time gamblers. The underworld of crooks. The cloak and dagger world in which characters like Rumbold and Big Francis lived. The world of narrow confines belonging to air crews and that of fanatics fighting in jungles. . . .

19

It was still dark when I woke up—dark and chilly. For a second or so I couldn't make out where I was. I'd fallen asleep on the grass beneath a bush. As I stood up and my hand wandered automatically over my cropped head, a chill ran down my spine. Where was my crowning glory? My tummy was rumbling. Suddenly, it all returned—all the terror, the hunted experience in the night. By now the whole country would have been told about me and from now on I should have to move only under cover of night and as warily as one lost in a land abounding with quicksands.

Leaving the bushes, I climbed to the high ground wondering what time it was. It was too early for the moon. Down there in the valley lights of a farmhouse gleamed invitingly.

I felt lost without Rumbold and too tired to walk tonight. Perhaps it would be as well if I laid low for a few days. By that time the scream would have died down.

Dropping the automatic in my hip pocket, I set off through the bushes to a fence which separated them from the field on the other side of which was the farmhouse. This stood back from the lane I'd been following before I dumped the car.

What could I do at the farm? Steal eggs and appease my hunger? That was an idea. The logical thing to do however, was first to eat, then get a jacket and cap from somewhere and afterwards press on to the west.

The faint mutter of a radio at the farm reminded me again that I was immersed in a sea of trouble. How many descriptions of me had they broadcast so far? I wondered. Dozens probably. Nearing a barn, I stopped and listened to somebody talking in Czech—somebody all beefed up about something. Reaching the door, I was happy to find it unlocked. A piece of rope kept it from blowing open. Inside, I found a pen of thick straw. Just the job, I thought, lying down.

A crowing cock awakened me. Sitting up, I shivered. Gosh, was it cold! Dawn had just broken. What should I do? If I stayed here a search party might find me. If I moved on, I was bound to attract attention. So there I sat feeling for about the first time in my life between the devil and the deep blue sea.

I had to do something. The longer I stayed on this side of the Iron Curtain, the more the chances of being recaptured increased. It was better to take risks—to push on at every opportunity.

Peeping through a hole later, I saw a girl dressed in a jersey, breeches and wellingtons, leaving a shed on the far side of the yard. She looked about eighteen—short, blonde, with dishevelled hair and no make-up. Passing a car—a pre-war Ford it looked like—she picked up a bucket and then disappeared in the house.

A few minutes later two sturdy peasants left the house with buckets, crossed the yard and entered a long black milking shed on a mound beyond the manure heap in which some white leghorns were scratching. When they disappeared, I looked for telephone wires. The idea of somebody 'phoning the cops and telling them where I was scared me. The only wires I saw were those belonging to a radio aerial on the farmhouse. So in the event of my being seen I had a chance of getting away before anybody could raise the alarm, for what I remembered of what I'd seen yesterday, the nearest house to here was the farm where I'd spoken to the woman.

When the girl joined the men in the milking shed. I decided to take a chance. The only person in the house would probably be the house frau. With a bit of luck, I thought, I might talk her into selling me food and a jacket, which I could pay for with the currency I found in the guard's wallet.

Nipping out of the barn, I ran across to a side window and peeped into what was apparently the living room. While I was

113

doing this somebody cleared his throat of phlegm. I stood there petrified for nearly a minute before he spoke. Turning I saw an old man, stunted, deep-chested, with a wild white beard, pink face and twinkling blue eyes.

I asked him if he spoke German.

'Ja,' he replied, frowning suspiciously.

'Could you sell me some food?' I asked, suddenly remembering my cropped hair, battered face and pyjama top. I thought by the way he suddenly smiled, he was going to say yes. Instead, he whistled to the family in the shed. As he did so, my hand flew instinctively to the gun. Turning, I saw the girl framed in the shed doorway—standing there taut and manifestly belligerent. What now? The old man shouted something in his native tongue, gesticulating wildly as he did so.

'Who are you?' she called in English.

'I've lost my way,' I explained. 'My car broke down. Could I buy food and drink?'

Glancing over her shoulder apparently at the men in the shed, she moved towards me, slowly, her head slightly bowed, her eyes fierce and shifty.

'Where do you want to go to?' she said, just before she reached me.

'Prague.'

'You're English, yes?'

I hesitated.

'You are, aren't you?'

'Yes,' I said, slipping the gun from the hip to the right pocket.

'Prague's fifty kilometres from here,' she said.

The men left the shed, carrying pitch-forks and looking as if they expected a rough house.

'They're not going to get tough, are they?' I said to the girl. The old man had moved to the other side of her. I backed to the wall.

'He's the Englishman,' she called to the men.

'Him they describe on the radio?' said the taller of the two in German.

'That's right,' I said, pulling out the automatic and pointing it at him. 'I'm the bloke all right as you can see from my face and my head.'

They looked at each other, pale, terror-stricken.

'Put your hands behind your heads,' I added in German. 'And don't try anything funny. Do that and you'll get it.'

Up went their hands.

'You're being foolish,' the girl said.

'That's your opinion. But nobody gets hurt unless they try something. All I want is food, a jacket, a hat. Tell you what. Let's go inside. I'll open the door.'

I did that. The girl went first. Passing me, the men swivelled their heads as if to get a better look at me.

'We're milking the cows,' the girl said, as we went into the long, low-ceilinged kitchen.

'It won't take long,' I said.

Just then a woman as round as a top came out of the scullery, wiping her red hands on her apron.

'What goes on?' she bellowed in German, staring at the others.

The girl told her who I was and what I wanted. The woman squinted at me.

'I'm not a bad man,' I said. 'Do as I say and everybody's going to be O.K. . . . Will you please get me some food?' She looked at the old man who nodded vigorously. One of the other men said something in Czech, I guess it was. She smiled wistfully, nodded and then returned to the scullery. A few minutes later she came out with a half leg of pork and a white towel. She laid the meat in it and tied the ends.

'A little bread,' I said.

'Ja, ja,' she said, returning to the scullery.

'Now all I want is a hat and jacket,' I said to the others.

'I'll get them,' the girl said.

'No. You stay where you are,' I said. 'Pop can get them for me.' I looked at the old man. 'You understand?'

He nodded sombrely. When he left us the old lady gave me a glass of milk. She seemed less scared than the others. I liked her frank and friendly grey eyes, her bold stare.

'It's nice of you,' I said, when she put the bundle on the table beside me.

'We've got the milking to do,' grumbled the taller of the two younger men.

'I'll be away from here in a few minutes,' I said.

The old man returned with the jacket and a cap with a shiny peak. The jacket was a tight fit but it had to suffice. I got the old man to help me on with it, while I covered the others with the gun. The cap was O.K. I told them all to go to the milking shed and reassured them again that provided they didn't start something nobody would get hurt.

The girl went first. As they trooped across the yard, I decided to steal the Ford we passed and get as far away as possible before they raised the alarm.

'The car works, doesn't it?' I whispered in German to the dimmest-looking of the two young men.

'Ja, ja,' he said.

The cows were all ready for milking, chained in their respective stalls with the suction gadgets of the electrical milking equipment attached to their teats.

The men put their hands down and by their apparent docility none of them had any intention of tackling me. I surveyed the shed. There were only two small dusty windows, hardly big enough for the smallest to get through.

'The door locks from the outside,' the girl said.

'Thanks.'

'You'd better hurry. This is a collective farm. The other partners are due any minute.'

'Where did you learn to speak such good English?'

'I shouldn't bother about that if I were you. The padlock locks automatically. All you do is to close it.'

'Just one thing—the ignition key to the Ford?'

She spoke to the smaller of the two young men and he felt in his pocket. Then gave me the key.

'Petrol and oil O.K?' I asked the girl.

She spoke to the same man, who nodded.

'How much?'

'The tank's full,' he said.

I looked at them each in turn. They were all smiling in that dumb embarrassed manner of people whose routine has suddenly been upset by a situation with which they cannot cope—a sort of oafish nervousness which would seem more natural behind the bars of a zoo cage than in human company.

116

'I'm sorry to have to do this,' I said, speaking to them in German. 'It is my life that is in danger.'

They all nodded as if they understood and sympathised with me. I figured they were Sudeten Germans whom Hitler had tried to immortalise in 1938.

'Good-bye and thanks a lot,' I said.

They nodded and smiled.

I backed out, feeling a bit of a fool with that gun in my hand. After I'd locked the door, I suddenly remembered that I needed a knife.

I ran to the kitchen and took a sharp pointed one with a wooden handle from a drawer in the kitchen table.

The car—a V-8 in excellent condition—was easy to start. Turning round, I drove through the front gateway, turned left and followed the track along which I'd travelled the day before. This was in very bad condition. Just here it wound its way up a long hill to the south west.

How far had I driven? It must have been about five hundred yards when the men appeared. I'd just reached the brow of the hill when I saw them ambling down the track. There were three of them—three peasants. Seeing me, they stopped in the track and I thought, they probably recognise this jalopy. But I'm not wasting time with them. They must have realised this too, for when I stepped on the gas, they got off the track, moving thickly like carthorses that had been suddenly hit. The car roared and quickly developed a wobble. Thinking one of the wheels was loose, I took my foot off the gas-pedal. The car slowed down. Over my shoulder I saw the peasants staring at me. One of them—a raw-boned red-head with a face splashed with freckles, shook his huge fist at me and yelled, 'Swinehund,' or something like that.

I didn't like it. I was unlucky meeting these hayseeds. Now what? I had to face facts. This is when the fun begins, brother, I thought. Not a million years from now, you'll hear the call of the hunters. Those old helicopters will start abuzzing. Oddly enough, I was no longer scared. That's what freedom does to you, imbues you with terrific optimism. It was just what the doctor had ordered for my morale.

The jalopy roared on, churning up the dust. The track

abounded with ruts and holes obscured by bouquets of grass. When hitting these I'd leave the seat and nearly be thrown out. The track ended in a lane about five miles from the farm—a lane going direct west. What luck! My spirits rose. But not for long. At the bottom of the hill the engine conked out opposite a pond in which two white ducks were swimming. A village was less than a hundred yards away.

A woman, wearing a sun-bonnet and wheeling a barrow, came towards me. She was the last person I wanted to see. Jumping down I went to the back of the car, and waited until she drew level, then I slid under the chassis and lay there till she'd gone past.

There was no time to check up on the car. Those young men I'd passed had probably already sounded the alarm. My best plan was to beat it west as fast as my legs would carry me.

Grabbing my food, I looked either way to see if anybody had spotted me. Then I ran up a bank, ducked under a wire fence, and walked back up the hill, keeping close to the hedge. On the right, a man driving a tractor, suddenly stopped and shaded his eyes with his hands and looked at me. Ignoring him, I ran up the hill, alarmed at my unfitness. Perhaps it was due to the bashing I'd got in that hospital, or possibly to the lack of food.

I walked for hours, crossing numerous fields. Then I came to a wood of mixed beech and elm trees, with fairly thick undergrowth. It covered the whole side of a hill as far as I could see. Seeing nothing of the hunters all day, I began to think I'd got away with it. It was a nice smug feeling. Well, if things continued like this, I'd soon be back with Rick, Motty and the boys in London.

All day I'd been in the hot sun and now I was in a wood I could feel the sunburn stinging my forehead and face.

Coming to an open space in the trees, I heard a plane roaring. 'Hell!' I exclaimed aloud. 'It's a bloody helicopter.'

It was so low—almost touching the tree-tops. It was hovering and I could see somebody in the opaque observation carriage, with glasses to his eyes.

This is it! I thought. This is where I really get my chips. Panic grabbed me by the throat. Next I knew I was running hell for leather into thick bushes, oblivious to the brambles which cut my breeches and hands. The ceiling of foliage above me was, thank God, very thick. But I could still see the dark outline of the helicopter moving my way. I squatted in a bush, staring up. It stopped too. No, I thought they can't see you, Harry. It moved on like a giant spider. Hearing the trickle of water, I looked left and saw a tiny spring bubbling above a crack in the wet clay surface. Getting down on all fours, I drank greedily of the sweet spring water.

Standing, I wondered how far I was from the German border. Since I'd been travelling west practically all day, I couldn't be a million miles away from it. What infuriated me was thinking that I'd beaten the Q-plan. This complacency was typical of my mentality at that time. Being on the run creates special attitudes and dwarfs your imagination. Although this psychology enables you to take big risks it can result in utter disaster.

The helicopter had changed all that. It set me thinking of hunters equipped with short-wave radios, and helped by dogs. It created a picture of men studying a map on which was a red ring. I could hear the bloke in charge say, 'Our quarry is inside the ring. We surround him and then close in. It's as easy as that.'

I pressed on, keeping to the thickest part of the wood. While wading through the undergrowth, I realised that my only hope was to break out of this wood and infiltrate through the enemy lines.

To move more freely, I cut the pork into chunks and tossed the bone away. Then I stuffed the chunks in my pocket with what remained of the bread.

About this time I heard them in the distance—those blood-hounds baying way over in the eastern section of the wood. Their enthusiasm suggested they were hot on my trail. This was real trouble. As long as I kept running I felt I could keep ahead of them. For they were bound to miss my scent occasionally and would take time to pick it up again. But I was unfit for a marathon run. What I wanted was a nice river abounding with reeds in which to wade. They'd never get me then. But what a hope! There were no rivers on this hill. My only hope of finding one was to make for the valley.

Only one thing was in my favour—the ascending darkness.

Shadows in the wood were already assembling. What I've got to do now, I thought, pressing on, is to get the hell out of here quickly. Darting along a track to the right, I ran two hundred yards and came to a field. Stopping to get my wind, I listened to the buzzing helicopter and that mournful baying of hounds way over in the east.

This was no time to dally. Night would soon fall. Already the last of the light in the sky was closing like an eye and the valley was glittering with lights. I ran on through the rough frustrating grass, leaping like a gazelle. Below the buzz of the helicopter, I heard the laboured breathing of a train. Then way down below me the railway swung into view. It snaked its way up through the hills and vanished from sight behind the hedge in front of me.

With a bit of luck, I thought, I might be able to jump that train. Suddenly, the air was full of noise—that excited urgent baying of the hounds which had broken away from the wood and were now dashing through the tall grass after me.

I almost fell through the hedge separating the field from the railway. God knows how I did it. A steep grassy bank was on the other side. I half ran and half slid down it, thinking, if I get caught now, I'll die. It seemed so damned unfair after all I'd been through, after all the lucky breaks I'd had, that I should get captured almost within sight of freedom.

Just as I reached the metals, the engine was rounding a bend, the light on its breast spraying the banks and the track way ahead.

After running across the metals, I stood by a bush, listening anxiously to the engine labouring up the gradient. Above me an ominous finger of light from the helicopter was sweeping toward the railway.

It was now or never. The train thundered past me, hissing and puffing like some disgruntled and exhausted monster slinking away from some lost battle.

A dozen box-cars rumbled past. Then I started to run. Seeing an iron ladder running to the roof of the next car, I grabbed it, pulled myself up, got a toe-hold on something and then finally started the slow precarious climb to the roof. But I was in no hurry. That white finger from the helicopter's searchlight was still probing the vicinity. At the top of the car I looked towards the plume of smoke waving behind the engine. Just then a piece of grit flew into my eye.

'Damn it!' I growled. My eye wept. The stinging grew almost unbearable. I had no handkerchief—just the cloth I'd wrapped the pork in. I pulled this out of my pocket, segregated it from the bread and meat and then wiped my eye with it.

It was funny how this slight discomfiture suddenly divorced me from my fears. When the grit was out, I stared at the long skinny caterpillar of swaying trucks behind me and counted my blessings. The passing of the train just at the time when I reached the track couldn't have been better.

It was the second break I'd had since Jan had got me out of that hospital. But I wasn't free yet. My compass told me the train was travelling north. Moreover, my pursuers would have seen the train. By now they were probably talking to colleagues in the north that I was on it. So this was hardly the time to count unhatched chickens. Any moment now somebody might stop the train which was still climbing the gradient. I got back on the ladder. But it was too soon to jump down on the track. The thing to do was to get as far away from those dogs as possible.

Looking up, I was horrified to see that damned helicopter belting along behind the train. Someone in it was flashing a light, probably in the hope of attracting the guard's attention. It was way down almost level with the dark bushes which loomed on either side. Where was the guard? I hoped he was enjoying a pipe in his van at the tail of the train and dreaming of Marilyn Monroe. But he was bound to hear the noise of the helicopter sooner or later. What then? Would he have the sense to know the pilot wanted him to stop the train? Would that frantically winking light up there enlighten him?

The helicopter was creeping up on me, car by car. When the winking stopped, I climbed down to the last rung. The search-light came on then, sweeping slowly over the tops of the cars and creeping nearer and nearer to me.

'This is where we part company,' I said to the train, as I slid off and hit the cinder track which ran alongside the metals. Rolling into a ditch, I lay face down while the train thundered past. A few minutes later, I sat up and saw the helicopter halfway along the train, hovering above it like some fabulous flying spider, its searchlight stabbing the darkness between it and the roofs of those swaying box-cars.

Ten minutes later, I crawled up a bank and went in search of a place to sleep, confident in the thought that I had for the time being eluded my pursuers.

20

A REDDISH squirrel with eyes like black beads was looking at me from the trunk of a tree beyond the bushes in which I'd slept—its bushy tail fanned, the lobes of its nose throbbing like a heart. I don't think it approved of me. Or perhaps it was the lousy day. Grey clouds smeared the sky. The light was bad. Standing up, I felt my beard. I don't know which was the longest—that or my hair. The squirrel suddenly decided it wanted nothing more to do with me. Swinging round it flew up the tree and had disappeared in a jiffy.

After scoffing two slices of pork and the last of the black bread, I left the bushes, feeling that I must almost be at the German border. This was wild, almost hillbilly country—nothing but wild grass, brambles and old tree stumps. Most of the timber on this part of the hill had been felled years before. Only the stumps remained. Linden and birch saplings lined the track I followed in the hope of getting a wider view. Down there in the valley a black hut crouched in some foliage. Beyond it a silvery stream snaked its way past a rash of caravans and cottages.

Just as I was thinking that its population was asleep in bed, I heard the patter of feet emanating from a bend in the track. Stepping neatly behind a bush, I removed the automatic's safety-catch and slipped a finger through the trigger-guard. The footsteps stopped. A red bandanna wound round a girl's head appeared between the branches of the bush in which I was hiding. Then I saw the dusky smiling face, the exquisite teeth flashing white.

'Stand where you are,' I cooed in German.

'Oh, now, please Mister,' she said in English, as she contemplated the automatic, 'is this a nice way to receive a little girl like me?'

I guessed she was a gypsy, about seventeen. Curly black hair was alive and leaping over her shoulders. The deep-set brown eyes spaced wide apart in the oval high cheek-boned face had the latent explosive qualities of an A-bomb. The small lobes of the slightly curved nose flared and might have been fashioned by a great artist.

'He say you speak English,' she gabbled on, fingering her enormous yellow earrings.

What was the score? I didn't get it. 'He say that, huh. . . . So what?'

'I speak very good English. My mother she was English. But I don't understand this—this "so what?" you say.' She frowned. 'What that mean—"so what?" '

'Who are you talking about?'

'Mister Joe. He English too. He see you come down the hill. He say, Anna go and tell the man I want to see him. He say, I go myself. But maybe he shoot first and say he sorry afterwards.'

'How does he know I've got a gun?'

'They say on the radio you armed.'

'Who is this Joe?'

'Just drop the gun, Mister, and I'll tell you.' The husky Cockney voice was right behind me. I dropped the gun, raised my arms and tried to cope with the goosepimples emigrating down my limbs. 'Step out in the open,' he added. 'And don't try nothing. Tell you why. Me trigger-finger's awful nervous.'

What a contemptuous voice! Who is the sonofabitch? I thought, stepping on the path.

'Pick up his gun, Anna,' he added to the girl. 'Then join the party.'

He was shorter than I imagined—no more than five feet one, I should say—a sharp-featured, unshaven, Cockney type, with bushy eyebrows like white wire and a short beakish nose.

He came round in front of me, pointing the old rifle at my chest.

'Tell me—are you the geyser what did a bunk from that hospital near Slany?' he said. 'But of course you are. Look at

123

your mince pies. Your garden hose. . . . Well, I must say, they've certainly made a mess of you, chum. By the way, name's Higgins. Joe Higgins. Means nothing to you, does it?'

The girl came out of the bushes holding my automatic and staring at me with feline curiosity.

'Where's the party?' I asked, wondering how I was going to get myself out of this one.

'Where I am taking you, chum!'

'No,' said the girl.

Higgins stared at her.

'What do you mean, no?'

'You no take him anywhere.'

I'll never forget the look that came into that Cockney's eyes when he saw that she had him covered with my automatic.

'Blimey,' he managed to gasp, 'blowed if you don't mean it, too.'

'Drop rifle.' He did that. She glanced at me. 'You pick him up.'

'Rifle?'

''Course rifle. What you think—pick him up?'

I stooped, still looking at her, and snatched up the rifle, thinking, Where's the catch? The way that baby held my automatic! I didn't like it. She had all the confidence of a gangster's moll.

'They'll hang you for this,' Higgins said.

'If you have your way—yes.'

Higgins looked at me. He had put his hands round his neck and seemed resigned to the situation.

'Don't worry,' Higgins said.

'You told my father not to worry when they send him to salt mines too. Anna no forget. She has what you call a wide memory.'

'Who is he?' I asked

'Him. . . . Police informer. Me take him to Uncle Leo's hut. Then I tell you everything.'

I carried the rifle at the ready. I was more at home with it than the automatic.

'We go now to Uncle Leo's,' this Anna said.

The path wound through the bushes to the valley where the

stream was. I couldn't make head nor tail of this set-up. I didn't know whether I was walking to freedom or into the jaws of death.

Higgins, wearing old blue jeans, a check shirt and a floppy straw hat, walked with his buttocks wobbling above his bandy legs. At the end of the path at the foot of the hill, the black hut I'd seen earlier, appeared. Higgins knew his way. We followed him along a stony path to the back door which was wide open. He climbed the three steps and went inside like a disobedient dog into a kennel.

'My uncle out hunting,' the girl explained. 'No be back till dark.'

'You don't know what you're doing, you silly cow,' Higgins said, facing us. 'They'll hang you for this.'

'Sit down.' She pointed to the unmade bunk under the window behind him. Looking round, he slouched over to it.

'They'll hang you the same way as they did that Borocoff woman.'

'Shut up.'

'But be sensible, Anna,' Higgins said. 'You know who he is. The one they spoke on the radio about—the criminal from——'

'How far am I from the border?' I asked.

'Do not worry,' she smiled. 'Anna look after you.' She pointed to a chest of drawers. 'You find cord in the bottom drawer.'

I got it out.

'Tie him.'

Higgins seemed only too pleased to be tied up.

'Jolly good,' Anna said, when I'd finished. 'What me call you?'

'Harry,' I said.

'All right, Mister Harry. You do good job. Where you learn to tie man like that?'

'I was a Boy Scout.'

'I see.'

'Who's he?'

'Me told you. Police spy. He come and pretend to be trapper. He mix with my people. Then he tell the police what they do. My father, he go to salt mines because he told police.'

Higgins snorted and shouted, 'Don't take any notice of her,

125

mate. Know what she'll do? Hand you over and collect the reward.'

She looked at me.

'You no believe that?'

'Me?' I smiled. 'I should say not. You wouldn't do a thing like that to me.'

She shook her head. I wasn't so sure. . . . She looked capable of doing anything to any fellow.

'Look,' I said. 'I've got to be on my way.'

'Watch out for her, mate,' Higgins said.

'I say you no go,' the girl said.

'O.K What do I do?'

'Wait.'

'How far are we from the German border?'

'You'll never make it,' Higgins cut in. "Every inch between here and the border is black with coppers. Why don't you tell him, Anna, what you're after?'

'Twenty kilometres,' Anna said.

I raised my gun and covered the girl.

'Look,' I said conversationally, 'I like you. I appreciate all you've done for me. But I've got to be going. Will you please give me back my automatic?'

Staring contemptuously at my rifle, she sneered, 'Oh, so, that's you, huh. Big bad Englishman.'

'Just put it on the dresser.'

'If I don't?' she said defiantly.

'I shall have to kill you,' I said facetiously.

Higgins laughed.

'You do that to young girl—young girl who save you from this vomit. You tie me up. Know what they do? They untie Higgins. He tells what I do. They get big rope, take me to tree and—string me up. Not very nice, huh? I mean for Anna—Anna who save you. You do what my mother used to say—bite the hand that saved you. A nice thing. And I—oh, never mind. Do what you like. Tie me.' She held up her wrists. 'Go on.' There were tears of outrage in her eyes. 'Do that, pig! Then you see. But I can get you cross border. Me know southern route. Go by self and you soon die.'

'What can I do with you if I don't tie you?' I said.

126

'Me come with you. Anna show you way cross border.'

Higgins was laughing.

'What's on your mind?' I asked him

'Listen to her and you're due for the big sleep,' he said.

I turned to Anna. She looked so sincere.

'What will you do across the border?' I said. 'What about our people?'

'People,' she scoffed. 'There's only Uncle Leo. Him! No ood. Him try to make marriage with me. My father he'll kill im—so—so me want to go to the other side so I can marry a ich American and have lots of children like Charlie Chaplin's ife.'

I looked at Higgins' bulging shadow and decided to gag him. Anna was O.K. At least I thought she was. My intentions in ringing her along were strictly selfish. All that really concerned ne was getting across that border.

'You're a mug,' Higgins said. 'She'll two-time you. You don't now these gypsies—thieves, liars, cheats.'

She frowned at Higgins.

'Put something in his mouth.'

She asked what for. I said, 'To stop him shouting.'

'Ah, yes, yes, of course.' Anna went over to the foot of the ed, picked up a dirty sock and stuffed it in Higgins' mouth. I hope you like the taste of Uncle Leo's feet,' she laughed riumphantly. 'He no wash them in six years.'

She joined me at the door. 'Quick.' She caught hold of my and and we ran together along a path of cracked soil webbed vith exposed roots of trees. A hundred yards farther on we ame to a towing path by the river I'd seen earlier.

'We go north,' she said, swinging to the left.

'But you said the only escape route was to the south.'

'Yes, but only for Higgins' ears. When he get free he tell olice we go south. So they won't look north.'

We stopped to get our wind and stared at the tall rushes that vere swaying drunkenly in the breeze. Then we ran on, keeping o the towing path.

'How far do we run?'

'Not far. We stop just up here round the bend. Then we borrov ld Philip's boat. He is the poacher. It is a very good boat.'

127

It was tied to a stump of sawn-off sapling in the thick rushe We got in it. Anna grabbed one of the paddles and I the othe

'We go up as far as we can,' Anna said, over her shoulde 'It is a good way. Dog no smell.' She knelt down at the ster and started paddling like an expert.

'Who are you really?' I asked, when we were clear of th reeds.

'I'm a gypsy girl. All alone. They take my father. He go t the salt mines. All he do is to borrow a cow. They say he sto it. Not my father. He think I should have fresh milk. He sa when I grow up and am big girl he take cow back to farmer. Tha Higgins, I think he was the one who told the police. So m father, he now in salt mines. . . . My mother she died last yea I lived with my relations. I was to work in the mill next week But I no like it—shut up all day—noise of the machines.' Sh stopped paddling. 'And doing the same thing a million times day. It's no good for Anna. So when I see you—big and wha you call handsome Englishman, I say I go with him. . . . Kno what I was going to do? I was going to run over the border. M father say many Americans over there—rich Americans. He say Anna, you marry an American. Then send for your old dad. H crave to sleep between sheets, my father. Silk sheets.' She wagge her head. 'Him not a very very good gypsy. He once broke int a mansion and went to bed. Nobody find him. He stay in be two days. This was near Prague before the war. Before he marr my English mother. Why they no catch him? Because they wer in Berlin. So my father strip naked and lay between the sil sheets. He never forget that. When he get old, he say he slee all the time between silk sheets. It was his idea of—of Paradise.

For nearly a mile the river curved and narrowed. The curren was stronger and progress twice as slow as when we set out To the west a steep grassy bank rose to a fir wood. Farther o we saw smooth brown boulders over which clear water bubble and sparkled in the sun now clear of the fast scattering clouds

Anna suddenly steered the boat to a stretch of tall rushes o the west bank. I watched my image wobbling in the shimmerin water, the waves running away from us. A piece of dead woo grew excited when the waves from our boat reached it. We were going straight for the rushes. As the stern hit them, Ann ducked and put her paddle in the boat. As she did so a flock of moorhens soared above us.

I jumped ashore first. Anna handed me Higgins' rifle which I put on the grassy bank. Then she held out her arms, smiling light-heartedly as she did so.

'You're—you're very big man—strong man,' she said as I caught her. 'I like them big and strong.'

She stooped and picked up the rifle. Then linked my arm with hers. We walked rapidly to the hill.

'Do you think anybody saw us on the river?'

She shook her head confidently.

'No. . . . No, I'm Anna. I know these cops. Fools. They always work the same. Like the silly insects. Everything go all right and they are all right. But somebody like me—we do things they no expect and what happens? When Higgins tell them we go off together, they act just the same as they always do. They think we go south and then west. Every fugitive go that way. Why? It is the quickest and the easiest. Soldiers go that way in war. So the police think because everybody go that way, we go that way. But not Anna. Instead we go north. Nobody go this way. Why? It is too difficult. You easy get lost in this forest.'

We jumped over a small bush and Anna looked up the hill.

'Here the wood slant all the way. You understand? North, I mean. So we have cover all the way. Nobody see us from the valley. My father show me this way. I was little girl. This was when Germans come. My father, he go this way during war. He act as guide for underground. Sometimes I go with him. Clever, yes? Father he dress soldiers as gypsies and we all wander up this way. I think one day I go out this way too. I do this when I am eighteen and marry American soldier and have big car.'

21

FROM where we stood near the top of the hill we could see the stream winding like a silver snake through lush meadowland, yellow with buttercups. To the south were the caravans and the cottages I had seen earlier. A road pointing like a black finger to the west was choked with slow-moving traffic. I could see why. A mile or so ahead there was a police check-point.

Anna started to climb again. I went up behind her wondering what is going to happen if we succeeded in escaping from this side of the Iron Curtain.

The morning was gathering speed. Gusts of birds squealing like mice passed over us. I caught up with Anna who appeared to be lost in the pathos and beauty of her youth. What enchantment! What mystery! this young girl had. When we reached the forest she grew aware of the squirrels and other animals.

'You like the forest?' she asked.

'Yes,' I replied.

Her route to the border was about three times longer than the one to the south.

'But it is very much safer. What is it you say—More haste less speed?'

I was enchanted by the long lances of misty light which stabbed the mantled tree-tops. It was warm. When the breeze dropped the incessant hum of insect life in the forest was accentuated.

Anna was staring at me in wonderment.

'So you like the forest, yes?'

'Don't you?'

'Me ask you first.'

'I told you,' I said. 'And you?'

She gestured. 'Trees, bushes—more trees, more bushes,' she said in that bracing urgent voice of hers. 'Cawing birds. Beastly insects.' Wagging her head vigorously, she added, 'No. I long for the smoke and for the sight of people. When I was a little girl we went to Prague, selling baskets and telling fortunes. Good days. Hot streets swarming with people. Girls in silk stockings and funny hats. The smell of scent. Wonderful shops. People staring at us. My mother she love things. She say, Anna, that hairbrush. Look at it. So beautiful. Please get it for me. I look. I love it too. I say, God meant poor Mama's hair to be brushed by you. And the hairbrush seemed to smile and nod at me. So I go in the shop and when nobody look, I pick this hairbrush up and pop it under my dress. Mama say I'm clever. When I grow up, I no hawk baskets. I have a big house. I dress in silks. And I tell the rich their fortunes. . . .'

'But that's stealing,' I said.

She wagged her head.

'No. . . . I think that. I say to Mama, is it stealing?' She sighed and wagged her head. 'Poor Mama. You should have seen her face. "Stealing, baby," she say to me. "Oh, no. Nothing you ever get for your Mama is stealing. . . . For your father—yes, that is stealing. They put you in prison for that. But not your Mama." '

I laughed.

'Why you—you laugh?'

'Oh, nothing,' I said.

'Now tell me about you—your Mama.'

I told her my life story as we went along—about Mother and Dad, Rick and me as kids. About Joan and how I was a boxer. She asked no questions. When I was finished, I quizzed her about her education. She could read and write—that was about all. But it didn't bother her. A girl didn't need to be educated, she said. Especially a girl like her who had made up her mind to marry an American.

She hated work, she said, because it left little time for the things she really enjoyed in life.

I said, 'How hard do they work on this side?'

'Like the bees—all work. No time for dreaming. My people are very unhappy. They no longer go where they want to. They are forced to work like the fools who live in houses. No more lying in the sun and watching the clouds race over the sky. These Communists! Pah! Toil, toil, toil. All their lives they work. For what? To get old. Then you die—worn out by work and life has passed you by. Those people are always saying— One day we shall have everything we want. But it never happens. My father tell me. When he was a boy people enjoy themselves. They danced round the fires. They sing songs. They look happy. But today—do you see many people smiling? Do you hear people sing? No. They yawn and look miserable. They sit and listen to other people sing on the radio. They grow scared of each other. Everywhere there are people like that Higgins. They tell tales and there's trouble. All they want to do is to get you in gaol. Mother told me in England when she was a girl everybody could say and think what they like. Is it still so?'

'More or less,' I said.

The farther we went the thicker the trees became. Here and there we stopped to sip water from springs. I offered Anna some pork. She turned up her nose. Then she began looking about her. Sometimes she wandered off the path and I'd lose sight of her. Once she was away for fifteen minutes. When she appeared she was carrying a hedgehog.

'This is good,' she said, holding it up.

'How the devil do you eat it?'

'I show you.'

She found some wet red clay and covered the hedgehog with it.

'Now we get wood and build fire,' she said.

We gathered an armful each, then she stacked the dead branches like a pyramid. The blaze lasted nearly half an hour. She waited until the embers had turned black, then she scraped them away. The clay was hard and almost black now.

'You see,' Anna said, cracking the clay shell. 'This is the gypsy's oven. See the quills, they all come away with the crust. Like this.' She pulled it apart. 'And the meat is cooked in its own juices.'

Quite frankly, I didn't like the look of it. But I'd been so long without a hot meal that I took a chance and nibbled the piece of meat Anna gave me in a big leaf. It was delicious—like sucking-pig.

While we were eating, she sat crossed-legged staring at me, her big brown eyes soft and quizzical.

'Those black marks under your eyes—they always there?' she said.

'No. I had a fight.'

She nodded and smiled quietly to herself.

'And your hair? What is that like when you've got it?'

'Curly and black like yours,' I said.

'And this brother—this Rick you tell me about—he has the same hair?'

'Exactly.'

' I see,' she said, nodding speculatively.

After we'd eaten, I lay back on a mossy bank, my face to the sun. What a long time ago it seemed since I was working in

Motty's gym. Yet it was—what? Just a matter of days. But look what had happened to me! All I hoped was that Rick was safe—that what I'd suffered hadn't been in vain.

Feeling Anna's fingers tickling my lips, I opened my eyes. She looked no more than ten years old. The glint of mischief in her eyes challenged me. But when I reached out to pull her to me, she wriggled away.

'What they call you?' she said, biting a stem of dried grass.

'Harry.'

'Mister Harry?'

'No. Just Harry.'

'Harry,' she repeated it to herself. 'Me think Mister Harry's better. You let me call you Mister Harry, yes?'

I was amorous. It was the first time I'd felt this way since Joan's death. I looked at Anna long and warmly. When she accepted the challenge, I thought I was getting away with murder. I reached out for her hand. Withdrawing it, she shook her head slowly and said, 'Please Mister Harry—please none of that what you call the sex.' A squirrel running up a tree suddenly distracted her. 'Look!' she cried, 'isn't it a silly thing.'

Our eyes met. There was no warmth in her gaze now, just the glitter of an excited child. . . . That was all it needed to cool me down. . . .

22

AT dusk we came to an old ruin, standing in a hollow at the bottom of a field which rose to about 400 feet to the west. We'd just left the forest and Anna remembered the ruin when she'd been here with her father during the war.

'What was it?' I said.

'They say it was where—where the—ah, yes, where the monks lived many years ago.'

We stepped over the remnants of a wall. One part of the monastery was still intact. But undergrowth had closed in and almost hid it from view. Pointing to a path, Anna said, 'Somebody been here.'

Stooping, I examined recent bruising on branches and rambling leads from blackberry bushes. The path led to an opening. I went first, crouching under an archway of foliage, stepping over rusted cans, now pulling a branch aside so that Anna could pass.

The opening to the building had once formed part of a doorway. Peeping inside we saw a stone floor, littered with dead leaves and broken twigs.

'Look,' Anna said, pointing to a heap of hay on the far side near the turret-window through which the last of the dying light was filtering. 'Somebody make a bed, yes?'

It looked that way. The room smelt of dead leaves and hay. There was nothing except this litter. Walking to the hay, I said, 'It looks as if somebody has used this place recently.'

She nodded agreement. Kicking the hay, I discovered there was more than I imagined. Spread out it made a big bed. Anna fell down and tested it.

'It is better than the hard ground,' she said.

'It is indeed.'

She jumped up, glancing at me sideways.

'Don't worry,' I said. 'I shan't eat you.'

'You—you, be good, Mister Harry.'

'What if I'm not?'

'I shall have to kill you,' she pouted.

'Would you?'

She nodded—nodded and stared at me in that solemn sad way young girls have.

'You sleep near wall.'

'Why?'

'Because I'm no hemmed in.'

'What you mean is that you want a way out in case I make a pass at you.'

'Make pass?' she frowned. 'What is that—make pass?'

I reached out and grabbed her.

'This,' I said, trying to pull her to me, but she was too wily to fall for that.

'Me no like pass,' she said, pouting.

'Very well, me no make pass,' I said, aping her accent. 'Me go to bye-bye.'

I walked over to the hay and lay down near the wall. Looking

134

up I saw her surveying me sceptically. 'Maybe I make my own bed over there.' Swinging round, she pointed to the other side of the room. Stooping, she gathered an armful of hay. After laying this down, she returned for more. Having made the bed to her satisfaction, she came over, pecked my cheek and said, 'Be a good Englishman, Mister Harry.'

'Good-night,' I said.

It was a long time before I went to sleep. It was the myriad of nocturnal noises—the squeaks and the scratchings; the howl of the wind; the hay hissing as Anna twisted and turned in her sleep. I started to count sheep. Suddenly I was fighting for the World's Heavyweight title. . . . I was doing this, when my opponent socked me on the jaw. . . .

I woke in horrible pain, bewildered. What had happened? I'd been coshed. Blood, warm and sticky, was trickling down my neck. Pains shot up on both sides of my temples.

I suddenly remembered my automatic. It had been in my breeches pocket. I felt for it. It was gone! So was the knife. . . . My head was spinning like a catherine wheel. Thinking of Anna, I jumped up and stared at her bed. It was empty!

Where had she gone. . . .? Wasn't it obvious? She'd given me the old one-two and hopped it. Where was my cash? Just as I was feeling for the wallet, I heard a noise outside. . . . Running through the archway of foliage, I came out the other side just in time to see the huge ape-like figure ascending the hill, with what looked like Anna over his shoulder.

I nearly went crazy. Who was it? Pain no longer bothered me. I was haring after that gorilla like streaked lightning. He'd reached the steepest part of the hill on the west of the ruin, moving slowly, sturdily, and looking very black and sinister against the starlit sky.

Had he killed her? It looked like it. Anna wasn't moving. What should I do? One thing was obvious—I had to out-manoeuvre him—steal up ahead, wait for him to pass. . . . And then. . . .? I daren't think about it. The mere thought of attacking him made me want to roar like an infuriated beast. I went after him, teeth and fists clenched—doing this and thinking, He's got a gun, boy. . . . Don't forget that. . . . One squeeze of the trigger and you're so much dead meat.

I started after him ape-like. Who was the sonofabitch? A tramp? Possibly. He'd returned to the ruins to sleep and had found us there. First he'd knocked me out, probably with my own gun and then poor Anna. Where was he taking her?

I was sweating. It kept dribbling off my forehead and running down my face. I was creeping up on the sonofabitch. Suddenly he stopped and put Anna down. What's he going to do—rape her? The mere thought of this froze me. I started to charge him. But he had a gun. I stopped and fell down in the grass. He mustn't see me. Not yet, anyway. But he was bending. What was he doing? I couldn't stand it any longer. I started barking like a dog—barking as I did as a kid. They used to say 'You can't tell the difference between Harry's bark and that of a dog. . . .' That did it. He jumped up, gun in hand. It had fooled him. He really thought it was a dog. I kept it up, barking savagely now. It did what I wanted—had him walking towards me. I ceased barking; scrambled away to the left and waited. He came on, automatic at the ready, his head swivelling, his huge shoulders hunched as if in readiness to meet a sudden attack.

I waited a few seconds. Then I crawled away to the left in the tall grass, my heart thumping nineteen to the dozen. Suddenly, I saw Anna, dark and inert in a grave of grass. Then I heard the tramp. There was no time to see any more. He was returning. I could hear his sturdy legs thrashing through the grass. Rising, I saw him coming towards me, walking slowly, cautiously, his head still swivelling constantly. I had to tackle him before he reached Anna. I had to remember he had a gun. . . .

One . . . two seconds passed. He was panting and muttering gibberish. Suddenly his dark bulk loomed just above me. I didn't think—didn't have to think. It seemed as if I was sitting on a spring. When he was almost on top of me, I shot up from the grass like a ferocious man-eating tiger. He never had a chance to shout. My right arm wrapped itself round his thick neck and all I heard was a strange whinnying noise. I was squeezing with all I had. Suddenly he collapsed. We fell down— me on top of him. But my arm didn't budge. It was wrapped round his neck like a piece of lead piping.

It was strange—how I kept holding the sonofabitch—doing

this long after he was dead. When I realised this, I let go and as the head hit the hard ground it rang like a bell. I was wet through, almost exhausted. Suddenly the moon swam clear of a cloudbank—a full awfully clear moon it was. Then I saw that horrible face, the red tongue forced out of the big mouth; the eyes squeezed clear of their sockets stared at the universe with horror—with all the horror he'd ever known. It had wanted to escape but death had trapped it at the last second—trapped it and made it everlasting.

'Anna!' I heard myself shouting. 'Anna!' I was on my feet running to where I'd seen her in the grass. I saw then how the monster had just untied the cord which had secured her feet when he heard me bark.

I untied her wrists and then picked her up, whispering, 'You're all right now. . . . It's, it's Mister Harry, Anna. You hear? It's Mister Harry.'

I could feel her heart thumping against my chest, feel the warmth of her body soaking into mine. She was still out. I stroked her forehead and waited.

A few minutes later her head wagged like somebody coming out of a nightmare—she was doing this and whimpering something incoherent.

'You're all right,' I said, as she started to struggle with me. 'It's Mister Harry.'

Her face was contorting, as if with pain and she kept fighting me.

'It's me—Harry,' I said.

Suddenly her arms closed around my neck and she whimpered, 'Oh, Mister Harry. Mister Harry. . . .'

How she trembled! Poor kid! There was nothing I could do for her except let all that pent-up fear go free. . . . I'll never forget it—the way it swept through her like a tornado. . . . I guess it was the first time this child had ever seen the human animal at its worst.

When the storm had run its course, she walked back with me to where the tramp was lying on the grass. Stooping, I searched for my automatic. As I picked it up, I saw Anna quietly contemplating the throttled corpse, her beautiful face devoid of all horror, of all fear and hate. It was like that of a Madonna.

'You kill him, Mister Harry?' she said, breaking the tense silence.

'It was either him or me,' I said, leading her away. She was looking at me with intense, almost child-like admiration and in the moonlight she looked so beautiful, so young and beautiful.

When I'd told her how I'd woken up to find blood on my neck, I asked her if she'd heard the brute enter the monastery.

'No. Me asleep,' she said. 'Me wake up to find something stuffed in my mouth; my legs and hands tied. I tried to struggle. He pick me up and throw me over shoulder like a sack. I nearly go mad. He put me down in grass and kiss my throat. Then I hear dog bark. Me faint then, I think.'

A bump on my head as big as a golf ball felt like an erupting Vesuvius.

'He came there to sleep, me think,' Anna said. 'He see us. What he do to you?'

I bent down and asked her to feel the bump.

'How terrible. It hurt very bad, yes?'

'And how!'

We searched the ruin for Higgins' rifle, but the tramp had evidently thrown it away.

We left the ruins and climbed the moon-splashed hill on the west side, walking slowly. Fear was apparently still with Anna, for she kept glancing over her shoulder, as if expecting to see that brute following us. And I would say, 'It's all right. He can't hurt you any more. Can't hurt anybody any more.'

At the top of the hill, we stopped and checked the compass.

'How far are we from the border?'

Anna couldn't remember.

'Me no think properly,' she whispered.

'He—he didn't assault you, did he?'

I turned her round to the moon, seeing her tear-stained face, pale, twitching. Suddenly shaking her head, she said, 'No, no. The dog, he save me.'

'That was me. I bark.'

A tiny smile played around her mouth.

'Me bark too,' she said. 'Me bark like dog, grunt like pig and crow like the cockerel.'

Then she was her old self again, volatile, garrulous, argumentative.

'You marry?' she asked.

'I was. I told you in the forest. Don't you remember?'

'Ah, yes, your wife die. . . . But you have sweetheart?'

'No.'

'What you—fibber?'

'But it's true. My wife's only been dead about three months.'

'Why—big man like you! Why no sweetheart?'

'Don't you understand? Wife only been dead three months,' I said.

'You still love her, Mister Harry?' she asked. 'Yes?'

'Very much,' I said.

She compressed her lips and shook her head disconsolately.

'That is bad. It like wishing for something you can never have. She no come back. You only have memories of her, Mister Harry. They not very—very what you call it—satisfying.'

'Nothing is,' I said. 'Life consists of countless efforts to achieve something which always eludes you.'

'My mother say "piffle." You and me. We together, yes?'

'Well?'

'That is real.' She pointed to the moon. 'That real. But memories—why they have no, no what you say—substance.'

We came to a barn and found a squat calf's shed full of clean straw.

'See if it's empty,' Anna said.

I crawled in and she followed me. We sat in the dark for a long time without speaking. Then she came near to me and put her head on my chest. 'Your heart is real too, Mister Harry,' she whispered. 'I hear him thump-thump.'

I lay down and she cuddled up close to me, a little scared and a little unsure of herself, like a child. I could feel the warmth of her body mingling with my own. It was strange. There was no fire in my blood—just serenity. I don't remember ever feeling quite so much at peace in this world; quite so spiritually and chemically attuned to anybody, as I was to Anna.

She must have felt the same, for she lay there in my arms breathing evenly and when she fell asleep, she turned to me like a child to its mother and put her arm round my neck. . . .

And there we were as complete as any two people could be in the world. . . . But for how long? That's what I thought, as I lay there thinking about everything. How long was anything complete and at rest—only the dead enjoyed that state permanently.

23

THE squeaking wheels of a cart woke me up. Anna, whose arm was still around my neck was fast asleep. Light streaming through the entrance splashed on her rumpled face and played in her wild, black hair. How beautiful she looked asleep, how young, how innocent and how much softer and whiter was her skin than when she was awake. . . . It had a tanned silky quality. I didn't move—just lay there listening to the thumping hooves of a heavy horse and the squeaking wheels of a cart. I had no idea of time. It was another fine day. I could smell the sun and the manure out there in the farmyard. A faint rumble in my tummy reminded me of food.

'Hans, where are you?' a voice called in good German. My spirits rose. We'd made it—at last! We were on the West side of the Curtain.

Anna suddenly tore herself away from me like some scared horrified thing.

'It's only me,' I whispered. 'Only Mister Harry. Remember? Mister Harry.'

She blinked furiously and then recognising me, she relaxed and yawned.

'I'm—I'm sorry,' she said, sitting up. 'Please forgive me. I have the bad nightmare. I dream terrible things, Mister Harry.' Straw was entangled in her dishevelled black hair, her eyes puffed with sleep.

'You know something,' I said. 'I think we're in the Western world.'

'Really?' We stared at each other gently. Then she came and snuggled up to me like an affectionate daughter. What to do?

Should we chance it and see if the voices I'd heard earlier were German?

'No,' Anna said. 'It's not worth it.'

We left the shed about ten that night and cut across hills to the west. It was cool and a fresh wind blew in from the north-east. The moon rose just after midnight. By this time we'd reached the wood which was to play such a big part in our future. I led the way along a narrow path, pausing now to duck under low branches, now to pull a bramble lead away from Anna's skirt. The going was tough. Anna, who was stockingless, was apparently used to the thorns and stinging nettles. Reaching an open space where trees had been felled, I stopped and surveyed the scrappy moonlight lying ghostlike on the bushes. It must have been nearly three a.m. We passed through the long shadows slanting from trees and eventually came to another thicket.

'Can't you carry me?' Anna said.

'It's too deep for that. I should probably fall on my face if I attempted it,' I grinned.

How right I was! It was the thickest undergrowth we'd met so far. I hadn't a clue how wide it was. My idea was to try and make a path for Anna to get through.

While I was doing this, I suddenly lost contact with the earth. One minute I was stamping down bushes; the next falling through air. Bang! My buttocks suddenly contacted the ground. What a painful reunion! It felt as if my head had been jolted off my neck. Down I went head over heels for ten—maybe twenty feet. Then I fell again. This time I landed on a clump of thick blackberry bushes.

Shaking my head, I removed some tenacious thorns from my posterior. Then I tried to sit upright. A sharp pain shooting through my shoulder made me holler, 'Ouch!' It was my right clavicle. Was it broken?

'Where are you, Mister Harry?' Anna shouted. 'Where are you?'

'Here,' I yelled.

'What happened?'

'I fell.'

'Me come down.'

'Be careful how you go.'

'You hurt bad, Mister Harry?'

'Haven't checked up yet.'

'Don't move till Anna come,' she said.

'You'll break your neck,' I said, as I heard a scouting party of stones running ahead of her down the steep bank.

'Not me, Mister Harry,' she said. 'Me gypsy girl. Me know all about these things.'

She arrived on top of a heap of sand which she'd pushed down.

'Catch hold of my hand.'

Looking up, I saw her standing in front of me. But only for a second or so. Her body suddenly bulged and wobbled like something in a distorted mirror. Then it blew up like a huge balloon and burst in a blinding yellow flash. . . .

24

SKINNY blue lupins were swaying drunkenly all around and up there—way up near the sky green leafy branches were waving their condolences to me. How nice, I thought. How positively charming. Everything was in fact obviously sorry for me except the birds that squealed and fussed around in the trees. The selfish brutes couldn't have cared less how I felt. They were too domesticated—too absorbed with feeding their young to bother about me.

I smelt Anna. Then I felt my head in her lap, those long tapering fingers of hers stroking my scalp. It was so—so soothing.

Day was breaking at last. White wisps of mist crawling surreptitiously round the bushes, looked like part of a spook world.

'Am I in heaven?' I whispered facetiously, as Anna's fingers touched my lips.

'Yes, you are, Mister Harry,' she smiled bending over me.

'Have I been out long?'

'No—no, half-hour maybe. Feeling better?'

142

I considered it.

'I think so.'

'Can you sit up?'

'If you help me.'

She did that.

'Let me help you off with your jacket.'

'What for?'

'Because I want to take off shirt.'

'But what for?'

She shook her head impatiently.

'You're—what you call him? Ah, yes. You are a big inquisitive little boy, Mister Harry.'

After she'd helped me off with my jacket and shirt, she asked me to stand up. I did this, feeling the air cold on my bare skin.

'Stand like a soldier like this.'

She jumped to attention and stood like a woman Redcap waiting to be inspected by Viscount Montgomery. She stared at my shoulders fearsomely.

'Me no like,' she said, pulling a face.

'What?'

'Your shoulder. It fall down one side. It no good. It mean the bone is broken.'

'I could have told you that.'

'I go for bandage. It is important. My father had one once. Mother, she show me how to put bandage. So I get one. You wait here and watch the birds, yes?'

She helped me on with my shirt and jacket.

'Before you go,' I said. 'What have you done with my gun?'

'I put him in your pocket.'

She touched my lips with her fingers again and then left me. I tried to persuade her to let me go with her. She wouldn't hear of it. The bank was much too steep for me to climb, she said. I must stay there like a good boy.

'Where you going?' I asked.

'Find cottage.'

'Be careful.'

'When I'm awake, I'm always careful, Mister Harry. Somebody stop me, I kill him.' Her eyes flashed like brown glass in

143

the sun. Her hair was so tangled it looked as if it had never been brushed.

'I want to come with you,' I said.

She stopped and swung round, staring at me like an irate mother.

'You stay put as Mr. Higgins say. No move. If you do, Anna she be very cross with Mister Harry.' Her lips broke open, a lovely smile spread over her face. It was rapidly getting lighter. I saw her run to the bank on the far side of this disused gravel pit.

'Anna, I love you,' I called, as she climbed the bank.

'Piffle,' she called back.

'But I do.'

'Me—me a gypsy. Piffle, Mister Harry. Piffle. That's what my mother say. Men love, she say, piffle.' She stopped and gripped the branch of a sapling. For a moment, I thought she would have to slide back.

'Don't be too long,' I said. 'I'm in awful pain.'

'No—no. Be back in no time.' She started to hum a tune then and up she went to the top climbing like a cat.

'Don't forget—I love you.'

'Piffle!' she called, as she swung round and waved at me. 'Piffle, Mama used to say.'

I could just see her up there, now standing with arms akimbo, here eyes full of mischief, her lips parted in a glorious smile.

'Don't be long.'

'Bye, bye blackbirds,' she called.

'Hurry,' I said.

'As quick as I can.' She waved and then disappeared into some bushes.

What was it? I tried to figure it out—why I was suddenly so sad now. A premonition? Maybe. I stood up and listened. All I heard was the singing birds; the incessant hum of insect life. I wanted to kick myself for letting her go. But it was too late now to call her back. The pain in my shoulder was worse than the one at the back of my head. I guessed it *was* a fractured collarbone. I felt weak. My legs were rubbery. I was anxious right from the start. So much so I couldn't keep still. I looked about me. Bloom was everywhere—white, pink, blue. Up there where Anna had disappeared, grey squirrels scampered up the silver bark of ash trees, their bushy tails spread like grey wings. The new sun was clambering up the sky.

An hour—maybe two hours later, I began to panic. What had happened to Anna? If I asked that once, I asked it a million times. It was my fault. I should never have let her go, I thought. It was obvious what had happened. A patrol had picked her up. She was now probably being grilled by the cops.

What to do? If I left the pit, she'd probably return. Then she'd go looking for me. In that event we might never meet again.

I spent some time watching bees vacillating between the pale pink blossom of the blackberry bushes. When she didn't show up, I decided I could wait no longer.

Slouching through the truant bramble leads, I looked for the easiest place to climb. There wasn't much choice. Anna had chosen the easiest bank.

I hadn't climbed anything as steep as this since I was a kid. It wasn't going to be easy. I needed at least a six-foot run to get to the top of the bank. Then as I went up I'd have to concentrate on my shoulder. Walking back, I braced myself and then made my run. Halfway up the bank, I suddenly stopped and afterwards slid down.

I had a longer run next time. To do this, I had to stamp down half a dozen lupins. A new species of pain invaded my shoulder and was giving me hell. But there was no time for self-pity.

I walked back over the lupins and stared at the bank. Then I made my run. It was more successful than the first. It took me within a yard of the top. To keep there, I grabbed the branch of the sapling—the one that saved Anna making a second attempt—and pulled myself to the top.

White flowers powdered the open space before me. Here trees had been felled and the undergrowth allowed to grow unchecked. Looking about me, I wondered which way Anna had gone. Moving forward, I watched a half grown rabbit jump out of a bush in front of me. It pranced like a ballet dancer, its ears and white tail up. A blackbird with a vivid yellow beak flew squawking after it.

Moving through the tall grass towards the clearing, I saw no

145

sign of Anna. But just before I reached that carpet of white flowers, the sound of cracking twigs halted me. It must be her, I thought, listening. More twig-cracking excited me. Where was the noise coming from? It got worse—so loud in fact I expected to see a whole Army corps. Suppose it was a Czech patrol? It could have been. Although I thought we'd crossed the border, I had no proof that we had succeeded. Moving into a blade of yellow light stabbing the tree-tops, I walked with my hand on the automatic.

I crept past a clump of bushes and then out into the open space. There were only a few old trees in there. When the twig-cracking continued, I took cover behind a sturdy oak, I think it was. In the event of shooting, I had adequate cover.

Listening, I heard somebody walking. Then just as I got the automatic out of my pocket, a voice said, 'Drop that gat, Bub.'

A plague of butterflies played around inside my tummy.

'I said drop it, Bub—drop it before I drop you.' I let go of it; heard it thump the ground. 'Now feel your neck with both hands.'

'Can't be done,' I said. 'I've fractured a collarbone.'

I saw them then. There was about a dozen of them—G.I's with Tommy-guns—all camouflaged like bushes. I couldn't see the speaker.

'O.K. Stand where you are,' he added, coming up behind me. 'No smart moves.'

'Don't worry,' I said. 'I'm in no mood to be smart—just talkative.'

He came round in front—a big top-sergeant with red hair and pink-rimmed blue eyes. He carried a Tommy-gun at the ready.

'You with the dame?' he said, pushing back his helmet with his forearm. His buddies had me surrounded, all of them staring and gaping at me.

'Where is she?' I said excitedly.

'With the captain. We got word to find you. Think you can walk to the jeep over there?'

'Yes,' I said. We moved off through the glade. 'How far we from the Czech border?'

'About ten miles.'

'Did you find the girl?'

'No. She found us. She was after a bandage.' He smiled to himself. 'Quite a dish. What is she—gypsy?'

'Yes,' I said. 'What did she say?'

'Told us about you.' We followed a narrow path to the track where the jeep was. A lank Southerner with a long neck and a gaunt chinless face, was driving the jeep. He and the sergeant helped me into it.

'What else did she say?' I asked the sergeant as we set off along the crude track running between the trees.

'Nothing—but what a dish!' The sergeant stared at my face then, squinting at and disapproving of my black eyes. 'Say—they're beauties. Where did you get them?'

'I got beaten up.'

He sat up and folded his arms, apparently absorbed in the subject.

'What for?' he asked, as we wobbled over ruts.

'Talking,' I said.

'No kidding?' He glanced at me sideways.

'No kidding,' I said.

'Mean—just for talking?' he said incredulously. 'Hear what he says, Hank?' he added to the driver.

'What's that, Red?' Hank said.

'This guy—know what he got—know what he got just for talking? A beating up.'

'You don't say.' Hank took a sudden interest in me.

'He says so. Ain't that right, Bub?'

'It sure is,' I said.

'What did you say, Mac?' Hank said. 'What did you say that made them beat you up?'

'Just a few words,' I said.

'No kidding?' Hank cut in. 'Well, what do you know. . . . Just a few words and he gets beat up.'

'It doesn't sound right,' Red said. 'Go on, feller. What else?'

'That's all. I say a few words——'

'And they let you have it?' Red broke in.

'That's right,' I said. Who'd beaten me up? They didn't want to know. The *dramatis personae* of the act was unimportant. All that concerned those boys was the actual beating up—where I'd been hit, how many times, did I bleed much—stuff like that.

147

'You don't say,' Red drawled, when I'd finished. 'Well, what d'you know. . . .'

Leaving the wood, we turned into a narrow lane and drove for a mile or so on the switchback road between the trees. Then we reached H.Q.—an old mansion standing in its own grounds away from the road and beneath a parasol of branches of a giant fir tree. We turned left and drove through a white gateway and along a gravel path snaking its way through a neglected lawn.

'The captain said for you to wash up before you saw him, Mac,' Red said, when the jeep came to a standstill.

They both jumped down and reached up to help me.

'That moss on your pan,' Red added, after I joined them on the gravel path. 'You'll want to scrape it off, won't you?'

'Where's the——' I began, stroking my bearded chin.

'The doll, Mac?' Red cut in. 'One of our girls is looking after her. She's cleaning up too, I guess.'

I stopped, so that he could lead the way.

'No, you go first, Mac,' Red said. Just beyond the porch we passed a sentry and then entered the spacious foyer, the walls of which were panelled. At the end of this we turned left by the stairs.

'Bathroom's on the next floor,' Red said.

I went up first. The stairs were bare but lino had been laid in the corridors.

The bathroom was spacious and full of mirrors which reflected me wherever I looked. What a sight! I couldn't believe it was me I saw. What with my cropped head, my battered sun-scorched grimy face, I looked like somebody out of the Stone Age.

'Well, who would believe it!' I exclaimed, looking at Red in the mirror.

'Don't like the look of yourself, huh, Bub?'

'Look at me! Just look at me! No wonder you had me covered in the wood.'

He laughed. 'Yeah. You looked like a cross between Boris Karloff and Humphrey Bogart.'

Black and white tiles on the floor cried out for a scrub. The bath was black and sunk into the floor. Red turned on the water. Then he left to get me soap and towels. When he returned he said the mansion had belonged to a baron. I started to undress. Outside the window, a fir tree nodded a hello to me. The grounds were crowded with these trees. Looking out the window I was surprised to see two German cops in earnest conversation on the neglected lawn.

'Who are those blokes?' I asked Red.

He came over and looked at them.

'The German law.'

'What do they want?'

'I wouldn't know.'

Steam billowed up from the bath, condensing on the walls, which were streaming with rivulets. As Red pulled off my boots, he laughed.

'What's funny?' I asked.

'That gypsy girl.' He cocked a brow, as he glanced up at me. 'Guess what she wanted to know—how to get an American husband.'

The socks were stuck to my sore, red feet.

'What a dish!'

'She's O.K.,' I said.

'Sure—sure, she's O.K.,' he added quickly. 'Swell kid. Kind of cute too. Boy, was she worried about you. Wouldn't budge till she'd exacted a promise from the captain that we brought you here.'

I slipped off the pyjama jacket and Red frowned gravely at my fallen shoulder.

'Say,' he drawled. 'This—it don't look so good. You fell you said?'

'That's right.'

'We gotta nurse—a good kid. She'll fix it. Doc's gone over to another sector.'

I tested the water and added some cold to it. Then I got in and slid down.

'Is it O.K?' Red asked.

'Fine.' It was too. Never had I enjoyed a bath so much. It was so good that it was some minutes before I noticed the huge black bruises on my body and limbs. Red saw them too. He stood staring at them, his eyes straining from their sockets in surprise.

149

'Well, blow me down,' he drawled. 'What decorations . . . ! Boy, you certainly got a beating all right. What did they do—kick you?'

'I don't know. Never felt a thing. I bet that annoyed them. There's not much fun for a sadist, if his victim feels none of the pain he's dishing out.'

'But gee! Just look at those medals! Boy, you sure been in the wars. Who were they?'

'Don't know,' I said. 'They could have been gorillas or apes. It's certain they weren't human.'

I lay in the water, wallowing in the warmth that soaked into and soothed my weary body.

'I seen a guy beaten up one night in The Loop,' Red said, after he'd lit a cigarette. 'That's in Chicago. Boy, did they lam into that poor guy!'

'Is that so?' I soaped my body. What an age this was! How people loved violence. Why is that? I wondered. Is it a guilt symptom . . . ? Is it something we all wanted to dish out so as to make us feel a little better about this cockeyed era in which we found ourselves alive in this world—this era of fear, of monstrous machines and diabolical destructive devices. We were all suffering horribly with frustration and inferiority and did we secretly yearn to be cruel because being cruel made us feel a little better . . . ?

25

RED dried and shaved me. What a nice fellow! With this done, I surveyed my new self. Despite my cropped hair and bruises, I looked almost my old self. . . .

'I should say,' Red said, 'that with time you'll probably look more or less like Mrs. Hammond's boy.'

He gave me a complete new outfit—B.D.V's, a khaki shirt, drill pants and a leather jacket.

'Now we'll go and see the captain,' he said, when I was dressed. 'Know something? He's the swellest guy in this man's army.' Opening the door, he stood to one side and bowed me out. 'Jones,' he said. 'That's his name. Captain Kelloway Jones.'

'What will he want to know?'

'Search me. He just sent me in a jeep to get you. "There's a guy in a dell near where the boys are on manoeuvres. Will you pop out and pick him up! Understand he's busted a shoulder." That was all. I got some guys and we go after you. And here you are.'

He led the way downstairs. My shoulder was giving me socks now. A stabbing pain had me pulling faces.

'Along here,' Red said, after greeting a couple of his buddies who passed by. 'And don't forget what I tell you. This Jones, he's the swellest guy in this man's Army. And I don't mean maybe.'

We crossed the foyer. Red straightened his battle-dress. Then he said, 'You've got nothing to worry about. Just talk to him as you talked to me.' He knocked on the door. Somebody yelled, 'Come in.' We entered what had once apparently been a dining room—a square room with oak-panelled walls. The captain sat at a desk. Anna, who was sitting with a nurse, jumped up and ran to me, her eyes shining with joy.

'You look wonderful, Mister Harry,' she said.

And brother did she look wonderful! What a transformation! What glowing radiant beauty! I was so overwhelmed I forgot all about the captain and the nurse.

'I hate to break this up,' Captain Jones said, 'but it's only because I happen to be the officer in charge here and I feel sort of shy with people I've not been introduced to. My name's Jones. . . .'

We grinned and shook hands. He introduced the nurse, a sturdy Teutonic type, with small blue eyes. Then he suggested it might be as well if I got the old shoulder strapped up at once.

'I know how painful they can be,' he said.

Jones was built like me but he had a crew-cut hair style and was blond with smiling blue eyes and a big, sloppy mouth.

'You've probably heard all about me,' I said, after the nurse had strapped me up with a figure of eight bandage.

'No, sir,' Jones said. 'I don't read newspapers.'

'Will it be all right if I go now?' the nurse said.

'Sure—sure. Go ahead,' Jones said, jumping up.

'I suppose I can contact my friends,' I asked Jones later, after he'd taken my particulars.

'There's just one thing.' He looked worried about something. 'Two German police are here. They want to see you and the girl.'

'There must be a mistake,' I smiled.

'They say, no. They say you answer the descriptions of a couple wanted by the Plauen police.'

'How could we! We've just come from behind the Iron Curtain.'

'They said you'd escaped from prison.'

'Me?' He was staring at my head. 'Yes, I know. But they cut——'

Jones threw up his hands.

'Look. It's not my show, feller.'

'But I mean to say——'

'They crazy,' Anna cut in.

'I'm not particularly interested,' Jones said. 'It's like I said. It's not my show. It's the Krauts that want you. It's nothing to do with me. O.K. so you're not the guy they want So. . . . After a couple of minutes they say, "Sorry." '

I didn't like it. It stank—stank to High Heaven.

'See what I mean? A couple of minutes and you're cleared,' Jones went on. 'Then you can see our security. . . .'

Anna had gone pale.

'You all right?' I asked her.

'I no like it, Mister Harry,' she said.

I didn't either. Why should I have to see the German police? O.K. so they were now a Sovereign Power. . . . 'Look, Captain Jones,' I said. 'I don't want to appear awkward, but there's no point in seeing these Germans. I'm an Englishman. That can be proved by giving our Consul in Plauen a tinkle.'

'Now you're making me feel that maybe the Krauts have got something. . . . After all it's not an unreasonable request, is it? What I mean is they are entitled to quiz you. It is their country, you know. We've been allies since the Paris Treaty. See what I mean, feller?'

There was no valid argument against that.

'Tell him, Mister Harry.'

'What?'

Anna shrugged.

'It is the big trick.'

'Big trick?' Jones drawled.

'Yes, a very very big trick.'

'I wouldn't know about that, Ma'am. I'm military.' He looked sideways at Red. 'Tell them to come in. They're outside some place.'

'Yes, sir,' Red saluted.

Anna looked at me.

'It's O.K.,' I said. 'It's as the Captain said. They'll see us. They'll talk to us. When we tell them who we are, they'll know we're not the people they're looking for, so——'

'Me no like,' Anna said.

26

I SMELT the old rat as soon as I saw them. They were both hefty blokes, red-faced, bull-necked and thick, very very very thick. The one with the moustache—the Groucho Marx moustache, looked at me like an optimistic hunter looks at a promising specimen of game. They came to attention in the German manner and clicked their heels

'It is him mein Captain,' said the taller of the two. 'And the girl—she is the one who got the car.'

'Inspector Kline,' Jones said. 'He claims he's English—that he's just come from Czecho-Slovakia.'

'Hear that, Hans?' Kline said to his colleague.

'Yes, I hear it. It is the same with all of them these days, Captain Jones. All the crooks claim to be displaced persons or refugees.'

A horrible feeling that they were Red agents took hold of me. But this was no time to panic.

'What's my name?' I asked Kline.

'Wardell—John Wardell.'

'And her?' I indicated Anna.

'Please don't be funny,' he jeered. 'Why play games? You

153

know she's Fräulein Weiss. She hired the car from Schmidt's and when you dropped over the prison wall, she picked you up. . . . Now please——'

There was no doubt about their identity. Jones looked at me grimly.

'My name's Hammond—Harry Hammond,' I said.

'So you're Harry Hammond,' Kline said. 'All right. If that's so, you can no doubt prove it.'

'Well?' Jones looked at me. I was thinking of their audacity —what nerve they had to come this side of the border dressed as German cops and armed with phoney papers. How did they hope to get away with it? My goodness, if Jones stands for this, I thought, he'll stand for the three-card trick.

'My passport's in Paris,' I explained to Jones.

It all seemed so easy—I mean my convincing Jones who I was. You know how it is. Having been through what I had, this looked like a pushover. But I didn't know what I was up against—just how tenacious those Germans were.

'Passport's in Paris,' Kline pooh-poohed. 'Oh, dear. What next?'

The one with the moustache threw up his hands.

'We're wasting time,' he said.

'Leave it to me, Hans,' Kline said. 'First let us establish who we are.' They took out their papers and showed them to Anna and me.

'Well?' Jones said, looking at me. 'You were saying?'

'Oh, yes. My passport's in Paris. . . .' I looked at Anna. 'Being a refugee, she wouldn't have one.' Then I gave Kline and Hans their identity cards. 'They could be phoney,' I said, looking at them each in turn and still feeling as safe as houses.

'Ja,' Kline snapped sarcastically. 'And me—know what I could be—from one of those flying saucers?'

'There's no doubt,' Hans said. 'Our information was correct. These are the two we want.'

'I don't want to argue,' I said to Jones. 'But it's a simple matter to prove who I am. Give our Consul in Plauen a tinkle. Tell him you have Harry Hammond, the boxer here.'

Jones looked at Kline. Kline looked at me and Anna stared at the other German.

154

'How can you be sure?' Jones said to Kline.

'I know this man personally,' Kline said.

I glared at him.

'Me! You bloody liar!'

'We're just wasting time, Captain,' Hans said, clicking his heels. 'If there's any doubt in your mind, why don't you come with us to Plauen? We don't mind. Do we?'

'Not at all,' Kline said. 'Come by all means, mein Captain.'

Jones looked at me, his forehead corrugated.

'You're not falling for that one, are you, Captain!' I cut in, squeezing Anna's hand. 'Look at them. What would be easier? We get in their car and—Bob's your uncle. We'll be over the border in no time.'

'What nonsense!' Kline scoffed.

'Excuse me,' Jones said, with admirable Yankee patience. 'What was the Englishman charged with?'

'The papers, Hans,' Kline snapped his fingers at his colleague.

'Here they are. Do you read German?' Hans asked.

'Yes,' said Jones, taking the papers and reading them. The Germans stared at me, looking so bloody sure of themselves. 'They say you were jailed for robbery with violence.'

'Bosh,' I said.

'Captain,' Kline said, 'I think I'd better contact the Commanding General of the U.S. Forces. It will save time. I don't haggle. I have my duty to perform. That is all.'

'I know that one,' Anna said, pointing to Kline. 'He Secret Police. Me see him in our village. He and others in car.'

'Look,' Jones said to Kline. 'You'd have no objection if I spoke to the British Consul in Plauen?'

'Why should I?' Kline gestured. 'Speak to Sir Winston Churchill for all I care.' He glanced hastily at his watch. 'But hurry.'

'I'm not impressed by histrionics,' Jones said after he'd asked his operator to get our Consul in Plauen. He was five minutes getting through.

He told the bloke at the other end all about me. Then he listened. 'No,' he said after a pause. 'I understand it's in Paris.' He glanced up at me. 'Whereabouts in Paris is your passport?'

I didn't have Lamond's address or telephone number.

I was stumped. Poor Anna looked frantic.

'Well?' Jones said sternly.

'Tell you what—let me talk to him.'

'Sure,' Kline said. 'Go ahead, Captain. Let him talk. We don't mind.'

'O.K., it's all yours,' Jones said, handing me the receiver.

'Who's that?' I asked.

'Reeves.' It was a la-de-dah accent

'But you're not the British Consul?'

'This is the British Consulate's office in Plauen,' he said.

'But I'd like to speak to the Consul personally.'

'Sorry, sir. But he's not here just now. Popped over to Nuremberg. Can I help you? I'm his secretary.'

I told my story as briefly as possible—why I didn't have my passport. I said he'd understand why I couldn't take a British passport with me through the Iron Curtain.

'But my dear fellow,' he said. 'What a yarn. You don't seriously expect me to swallow that one, do you? Hammond you say your name is? I'm an ardent boxing fan, but I've never heard of you.'

'Have you heard of——'

'Look, old man,' he said. 'Why try to bluff? You're obviously Wardell. I recognise your voice.'

Hell! I thought. He could be a phoney too. But what's he doing in our Consulate! It didn't add up. I dropped the receiver into its cradle, stared at Jones and said, 'It can't be the British Consul.'

'You crazy?' Jones snapped. 'Our operator got the number. I asked for it myself—you heard me.'

My neck was sweating.

'You're sure it was your operator?'

'What's he saying?' Hans asked Kline.

'It's all done to delay,' Kline said.

'This bloke said he's never heard of Harry Hammond,' I said to Jones. 'I'm not a world champ, but I'm well known in England.'

'Enough of this!' Kline exclaimed.

'Now listen, Hammond,' Jones said. 'Hasn't this gone far enough? I don't know who you are. But I can soon settle it.'

He glanced at Kline. 'Would the man at the British Consulate know of this prison break?'

'It's in all the papers,' Kline said.

What's to stop them cutting a wire connecting this office from the outside world and linking it up with their H.Q.? I thought.

'I thought you had women operators,' I said to Jones.

'So we have.'

'Who put you through to the British Consul?'

He never had a chance to answer. They took out their Lugers and Kline barked, 'Put your hands up!'

Jones sprang to his feet.

'Look, Captain,' Kline added, 'for the sake of the international situation we don't want any killing. Do as you're told.' He glared at me. 'You too.' This was no joy-ride. They meant business.

Our hands were up and how. . . .

'What's the meaning of this!' Jones exploded. 'You know what you're doing—that you're on United States property——'

'Reds invade U.S.A.,' Kline jeered. 'Now, Captain. This is the set-up. We're going out of here. All of us. So put on your cap. Try to be a hero and you join your ancestors. We want this thief.' He glared at me. 'You've just been dragged into it. Don't worry. Just as soon as we get to the border, you're free.'

Hans gave Jones his cap.

'You won't get away with it,' Jones said.

'That remains to be seen,' Kline said. 'According to our reckoning we shall. It's been well planned. When we heard you'd got the girl, we got cracking. Now this is what you do. You come with us. I shall be near you. If you try anything, you'll get it. When we pass the sentry you salute in the ordinary way. If we're stopped, you'll tell whoever you talk to, that we're going to Plauen.'

Jones glanced at his blotter. While all this had been in progress, I noticed that he'd been doodling on it. At least, that's what I thought.

We went out—Kline first. Jones next. Anna and I followed with Hans behind us.

I daren't look at Anna. I was scared she might lose her nerve and start screaming.

'Keep your hands in your pockets,' Kline whispered, as we trooped through the foyer. There wasn't a soul in sight—only the sentry at the door. What luck! As we drew level with him, the sentry jumped to attention. Jones saluted him. But the clot never even looked at us—just stared intently ahead like a Buckingham Palace sentry. A big Mercedes was parked in the drive. A tall, skinny bloke in police uniform, jumped out and opened the doors.

'We've got an extra passenger,' Kline said in German. 'We drop the Captain off at Trayborg.'

They put Anna and me in the back seat. The driver pulled out two folding seats. Kline sat in one; Hans in the other. Jones got in next to the driver. The car roared away from the house. Rounding a bend, I thought the driver was going to run into two G.I.'s walking to the gate.

'You crazy bastard,' one of them yelled, as they jumped out of the way.

Anna was petrified with fear. She sat there staring into space, pale, trembling. What now? How were we going to get out of this one?

'This could cause a war,' I said to Kline.

'You think so?' he sneered. 'Don't be stupid. Nothing short of an A-bomb on New York would do that.'

'That's what you think.'

'Ja,' he muttered in German. 'That is what I think. And don't forget. What I think is what goes around here.'

27

TRAVELLING at high speed and squealing round bends, the Mercedes jumped and shuddered like a bebop addict. Suddenly crinkling, narrowing, the lane flowed like a ribbon downhill. I sat like Anna, hands behind my head, staring at Kline's Luger. Hans had his gun partly concealed and trained on the ack of Jones' neck. We slowed. The driver wasn't liking the narrowness of the lane. The nearside wheel kept bouncing off the chalky bank.

Whither now, big man? I thought, as we bumped and rolled over the scarred and stony road. It would have been easy to have grabbed Kline—as easy as committing suicide. I thought of doing it a couple of times. Then I began to reflect on all the things I had to do before my death and then cogitated on less impulsive and dangerous alternatives.

Jones sat as rigidly as the Empire State Building. He hadn't expected this. Things like this were as alien to his world as they had been to mine before I'd ventured into this Alice's Wonderland.

Anna? She seemed more relaxed now. It was the gypsy in her. They're more adaptable to radical changes of environment than we are. Perhaps she was psychic or blessed with precognition. My only hope of getting out of this was a primitive belief in miracles.

The width of the lane was reminiscent of a wasp's waist.

'You won't get away with it,' I said to Kline, just for something to say.

'Shut up, thief!'

'Shut up yourself, clot,' I snarled and then got a backhander across the face.

Anna suddenly kicked Kline's shins. He could scarcely believe it. When he did, he smacked her with his gun—a nasty, vicious blow across the face.

'You great big gentle bastard,' I said.

He punched my chest with his Luger and growled, 'Keep your hands behind your neck.'

'You too, Captain,' Hans said, as Jones swung round to see what was going on.

I was learning quickly. It was Kline's face. Tiny sweat bubbles on his upper lip told me he was as windy as the East Coast. Why? It was obvious. If he bumped me off he'd be killing the goose that laid the golden egg. Without me, they'd have nobody to give the treatment to—nobody to tell them where the film was. What an inspiration! What a morale builder that thought was! So there *was* a chance. I'd grab him

and when Hans turned round to assist Kline, Jones coul[d]
grab him. I noticed Anna's face then, that worm of bloo[d]
wriggling from her mouth to her chin. I entered that on[e]
against Kline. When the time came for me to be the governor
it would be repaid with interest.

Jones was still the solid imperturbable Jones. What a
monument of discipline! He sat there next to the driver stiffly
his hands behind his neck, his wide shoulders slightly hunched.
Good old Jones, I thought, as the driver suddenly braked. [I]
peered through the windscreen and there it was—the steep hill
curling like a lasso down to the valley. Just beyond that haze
down there was the Iron Curtain.

It was when we were halfway down the hill that I thought my
miracle had materialsed. There were a dozen solid cows in the
roadway—a more bewildered, apathetic bunch you never saw.

Kline grew anxious and trigger-happy.

'One word from you,' he said to me, 'and she gets it right
through the eyes.'

'Why not me? I'd welcome it.'

He moved the Luger towards Anna.

'Don't mind me, Mister Harry,' she said in a slow, hoarse
voice. 'Let them kill me. Let them kill me. I don't mind. It is
better than going to the salt mines.'

Hans head was out of the window.

'Drive those blasted things back,' he roared.

'Ja,' the drover said. He ran in front of the cows, waving his
stick and for some inexplicable reason, he would insist upon
us all seeing that solitary tooth in the middle of his upper gum.
One cow with a black eye kept trying to squeeze past us. Once
it mounted the bank. But the man drove it back.

Jones was laughing. I wondered why. Had he got an idea to
get us out of this or was the drover's clumsy efforts to turn the
cows back amusing him? There was only one danger as far as
I could see—Anna. If we started something it was almost
certain, that she would get it first.

'Get those damn things out of here,' Kline yelled to the drover.

'Ja, ja,' the drover called, as he cracked his stick across the
cows' haunches. Now they all were doing the wrong things.
The one with the black eye was the worst. It kept turning around

...d running towards us, its swollen udder, swaying grotes-
quely, as if it were intent on annoying Kline and Hans.

At last they were running down the lane. A hundred yards
farther on, they were driven along a track on the right.

Our captors relaxed. The Mercedes ran ahead, purring like
the thoroughbred she was. Well, I thought, as we neared the
bottom, I'm through vacillating.

Kline was staring at me, his face set, his jaw muscles
fidgeting. I thought of his feet. They were close to mine, I
could have stamped on them—What for? I thought, as that huge
American Army truck appeared round a bend in the lane. I
could have whooped with joy.

Kline swung round. I could easily have socked him, but what
was the point? This was the end of the road. This was as far as
we were going. This was the Anglo-Saxon miracle my instinct
had been promising for so long.

Kline turned and faced me. I laughed out loud.

'O.K.' I said. 'Now get yourselves out of this one, you
bastards.'

A sergeant sitting next to the truck-driver, jumped down to
the lane. As he did so, two G.I.'s with Tommy-guns held at the
ready, appeared on each side of the truck. The three of them
were staring at us.

Hans was nonplussed. Kline looked like a sinner suddenly
faced with the prospect of meeting his Maker.

What now? Hans told Jones to put his hands down. 'Tell
them to give way,' he added.

'You tell them,' Kline said. 'Get out and tell them we're on
urgent business.'

'What about the captain?'

'I'll look after him.'

'Where's your officer?' Hans said, walking to the sergeant.

'There ain't none, Bub. Just me,' the sergeant said. The
G.I.'s looked taut and business-like.

'We're police on urgent business,' Hans explained. 'Will you
please give way?'

The sergeant wagged his head.

'Sorry. We're American personnel on manoeuvres,' he said.
'So I'm afraid you'll have to give way.' He sounded like a

New York Irishman—a huge, raw-boned, hangdog of a man with a warty nose and cold blue eyes.

I saw Jones edging towards the door. Never had I been quite so tense, quite so excited as I was now.

'Sergeant,' Kline yelled, 'we have a U.S. Intelligence officer with us. He's——'

Jones did his stuff then. What speed! One minute he was sitting like something in Madam Tussaud's. The next he'd grabbed the driver, wrapped his arm round his neck and pulled him down to the seat. 'Get 'em boys,' he yelled. 'We're being abducted.'

Hans suddenly lost his head. The sergeant had scarcely heard Jones. He couldn't have done. I saw Hans raise his Luger. It spat fire, kicked in his hand—all in the matter of a second. Then there was that awful look on the sergeant's face—the infinite sadness as if in that brief second which elapsed before the bullet actually entered his brain, he realised this was the end of him. . . . He staggered, groping the air with clawed hands. Suddenly his body folded like a jack-knife. Then it dropped face down like a hunk of cement.

The next second Han's body began to contort. I just heard that ferocious stutter from the G.I's Tommy-gun. The bullets from it had already thumped their way into the German's heart.

'Take my gun,' Kline said, pushing the Luger into my hand. My goodness! You should have seen his face—the manifest terror, the realisation that he was about to be no more. . . .

I must have been slow on the up-take. I remember deciding to take the gun—turning and actually reaching for it. But Kline wasn't there. He'd lost his head and had jumped out of the car. I saw him struggling on the bank.

'Don't look!' I said putting my hand over Anna's eyes.

I heard Kline fall against the car, the metallic thump as his body fell against the fender. Sitting up, I saw Jones slide out of the car, pale, tense, and salute the G.I's who were standing in a crowd in front of us.

'Stay here,' I said to Anna.

I got up and joined Jones. There was a lot of excited talking.

'They told us what to expect, sir,' a corporal explained to Jones. 'Too bad about Sergeant Dawes.'

I'll say it was. He was as dead as the stone ground he'd fallen on. So were the others.

'I wrote a code message on my blotter,' Jones said, while the G.I's dragged Kline's body from the bank. 'Did you know that?'

I gestured.

'No,' I said.

'We got it on short-wave,' the corporal said.

'Good.' Jones stared at the bodies. 'Put them in the lorry.'

'Yes, sir.' The corporal detailed some men for the job.

'Girl O.K.?' Jones said.

'I guess so.'

'I'll get a guy to drive you back.'

He asked a black-headed boy if he drove a Mercedes.

'Anything, sir,' the boy said, saluting.

'O.K. Get that tub back to H.Q.' He looked at Anna's face —at the black worm on her chin, squinting. 'Who did that?'

'Kline,' I said.

They dragged the choked driver out and dropped him on top of Hans. The dark boy got in and pressed the starter-button.

'Sonofabitch.' Jones glanced back at the G.I's who'd jumped down and had joined the others in the lane. 'I had no idea they were phoneys—not till you—well actually not until I was peeping down the barrels of their Lugers. It just shows you. You never know what those sonofabitches are up to.'

Colour had returned to Anna's face.

'Feeling all right?' I said, rejoining her.

She nodded.

'Me all right. . . . You all right, Mister Harry?'

'Yes. . . . Fine. Did it scare you?'

She looked at Jones and nodded.

'See you,' Jones said, as the Mercedes went back. A hundred yards along the lane we ran down the track where the cows had returned to. Then we drove back to H.Q.

'These Mercedes sure got power,' the driver said. 'Real honeys, aren't they, sir?'

'So they say,' I said.

He sat and stared at the twisting road. I expected to see the cows, but they were nowhere in sight.

'What excitement?' he said later. 'Know something, sir? An hour before it happened, I was playing poker. For the first time since I've been in this Kraut country, I was winning. Believe it or not, when we got the call, I was holding an ace full. There was fifty bucks in the kitty. How's that for luck?'

'You could have got shot like the sergeant.'

'Poor old Blabber-Mouth Dawes.' He shook his head disconsolately. 'He wasn't a bad guy. He was always bitching. But there was no harm in him. The irony of it is the poor sonofabitch had a date tonight with a big blonde, a glamorous Kraut number he'd met the day before yesterday.'

Anna tugged my sleeve. She was looking puzzled.

'What is it?' I asked.

She linked my arm affectionately.

'I just think—I say to myself, I like the English best, so I must disappoint my father who say you marry American.'

'What's wrong with the Yanks?' I said.

'They call me baby. I told the fat man who take me to Captain Jones. He say, "How do, baby," and I say, "Me no baby. Me eighteen." Then he laughed and call me "cute kid." What's that, Mister Harry—"cute kid"?'

'It means you're O.K.'

'O.K. What does that mean?'

'Hey, driver,' I said. 'Help us out. What does O.K. mean?'

'O'Keefe.'

Anna was more perplexed than ever.

'That's a guy's name,' the driver explained. 'O'Keefe was a good guy. Everybody loved him. That's how the story goes. So when you want to give a guy a good character, you say he's O.K.'

'What is this "good guy" mean, Mister Harry?' Anna asked.

I wasn't listening. I was wondering how soon we could get out of this place. I'd seen all I wanted to see here. I didn't trust it. The sooner we were in England the better.

'I speak to you Mister Harry.'

I explained what the G.I. had meant. Then she told me what a wonderful bath she had had. Pushing out her legs she showed me the shoes and stockings the American girls had given her.

'You like?'

'Nylons! They look wonderful on you. You'll have more when we get to England and a bath every day. You like that?'

'Not me,' she said, shaking her head, pouting. 'I no like bath every day. Once week, yes. But every day. . . . I soon wash myself away.'

As the road straightened out, the driver increased speed. Then we came to the old mansion. At the entrance to the H.Q. a bunch of G.I's waved to us. The driver swung the Mercedes into the drive. Then glanced at us over his shoulder.

'She's kind of cute isn't she, sir?' he said.

'Who?'

'The doll with you, sir. What is she—a gypsy?'

'I no doll,' Anna flared. 'Me grown-up girl.'

'It's like I said, sir. She's kind of cute.'

'You're telling me,' I said.

The sun was now at the height of its glory. There was no breeze—just sticky heat.

We stopped near the entrance. As we got out, an American colonel hurried into the foyer, saluting the guard without looking at him. I helped Anna out. We stood on the lawn and watched the truck come to a standstill behind the Mercedes. Jones jumped down and hurried to us. He looked at Anna, smiled and said, 'How you feeling?'

'Me fine, Captain Jones,' she said. 'You fine too?'

'I guess so.'

'What about your 'phone?' I said. 'Do you think it's O.K. now?'

'I'll have to find that out,' he said. 'I guess they've already attended to it.'

'What's the drill now?'

He shrugged.

'There'll be an enquiry, of course.'

'Does that mean I'll have to stay here?'

'Yeh. . . . And she'll have to be vetted.'

I explained the drill to Anna—that refugees from behind the Iron Curtain had to be checked by security.

'Why?'

'Because they might be spies.'

'Me no spy,' she said.

Jones laughed. We all walked to the foyer. The same clot of a guard who'd seen us leave, jumped to attention. Jones saluted him.

'I'll see what's cooking,' Jones said. 'Would you like to take her to the mess?'

'Thanks.'

'I'll get someone to hustle up some food. . . . O.K.?'

28

THE whole telephonic system at H.Q. had been out of order. A party of engineers sent out to trace the trouble had found what I expected—the wires cut. They were in the process of mending them when Jones saw Anna and me in the mess later.

He asked a WAAC to take Anna to the women's quarters where she was given a room. He said the colonel I'd seen when we returned to H.Q. belonged to Intelligence. He was here to question Anna and me. When G.H.Q. heard Jones was being abducted with me, they'd sent the colonel over to investigate.

When Anna left Jones took me to see the colonel, but he was not ready for us. I waited half an hour, then he sent for me.

'Colonel Brandon sends his compliments and would like to see you, sir,' an orderly said.

The colonel was in Jones' office—sitting at his desk in fact. His white hair glinted in the light streaming in the window. He had a pleasant, young, pink face, arched, black brows, hooded, blue eyes.

'Sit down,' he smiled, indicating a chair on the left of the desk. I sat down. 'Tell me,' he added, staring at the blotter. 'What's this I hear about your being behind the Iron Curtain?' He looked up suddenly, as if he expected to catch me on the hop or to see some betraying expression. His stenographer, a blonde, was sitting at another table. And when I started to speak she switched on a recording machine and opened a notebook.

'You're recording what I'm saying?'

'Yeh,' he said, fingering the silver eagle on his shoulder.

'You want the whole story—just how it happened?'

'Yeh. . . . Everything. Take your time.'

I gave him the lot.

'This will have to be checked,' he said, when I'd finished.

'What will?'

'What you say about your brother.'

'But it's true.'

He lit a cigar and afterwards nodded.

'Sure,' he said. 'But it's a matter of routine. . . .'

That was the Army. Everything had to be checked and re-checked. Red Tape? Maybe. But that's how it was. I understood? Yes. That appeased him. He relaxed. Then he buzzed for Jones who came in smiling.

'What about those communications?' he said.

'They've found the break, sir—about half a mile from here.'

'How long will it take to mend?'

'Not long, sir.'

'Good. By the way would you arrange for Mr. Hammond here to have a room of some sort. We shall need him around for a day or two.'

'We can fix him up,' Jones said.

An orderly came in and said Jones was wanted outside. Jones excused himself and left.

The colonel looked at me.

'I was appalled to learn what happened,' he said. 'The shooting I mean.' We discussed this in detail for about ten minutes. Then Brandon wanted the gen on Anna. What did I know about her?

'I've told you all I know,' I said.

'Which is precisely nil,' Brandon said. 'You don't even know her full name. She may be as good as gold. But you know how it is. We have to be sure. We've got people whose job it is to check refugees. If she's a phoney, they'll soon know.'

Jones came in and saluted.

'Begging your pardon,' he said.

'Yeh?'

'About the dead Germans. We've just got a report from Plauen. It was brought in by messenger. It seems they belonged

167

to a gang operating along the border—a gang specialising in snatching personnel.'

He gave Brandon the dispatch.

'Red Kruger's mob, yes,' he said after he'd read the dispatch. 'I know all about them. Moscow disowns them. They have no status whatsoever. They're just killers and snatchers. They would cut their mother's throat for a hundred bucks. This Kline and the other guy—we're not concerned with them. They're just hoodlums. You'll report that they tried to stick-up the lorry. That will take care of it. The civil C.I.D. will sew the case up for us. So there'll be no political repercussions. There'll have to be a Coroner's enquiry, of course.' He looked at me. 'It won't affect you. We shan't bother about you and the girl. It's apt to complicate things. You understand?'

'Yes.'

He told Jones to sit down. The girl was re-reading her notes.

'This Kruger mob,' the colonel went on, 'we've got to watch out for them. . . . They don't like casualties any more than we do. But judging from their audacity I should say that this guy here,' he stared at me, 'is wanted pretty badly by Moscow. It's his brother they're really after, of course.'

'Shall I double the guard?' Jones asked.

'That's up to you. If I were in your place I would.'

Jones took me to a room at the end of the corridor, one with a window facing the front lawn. On the way there, he said, 'Soon as we get the O.K. from the engineers, you can contact your people in London.'

He opened the door and I walked through to the room, furnished with a single bed, wardrobe, chairs and a carpet. A washbasin was to the left of the window. It had probably been a writing room when the baron was resident here.

'Keep this closed,' Jones said, pointing to the window. 'You heard what Colonel Brandon said about that gang. He knows this cloak and dagger stuff inside out. I wouldn't like anything to happen to you while you're in my charge.'

'I'll be O.K.,' I said. 'I'm not worried. As soon as I'm cleared from here, I'm returning to old England and sanity. Believe me, I've had my bellyful of this cloak and dagger stuff.'

'It's my first contact with it,' Jones said. 'Everything's been so goddam normal since we've been here.' He looked at the washbasin. 'You'll want soap and towels. I don't know about pyjamas. I'll try and rustle you up some.'

'How about Anna?'

'She's having a swell time trying on our girls' civvies. They're all crazy about her—a quaint kid.'

I wanted to tell Jones about the tramp I'd had to kill. But the more I thought of it the less of a good idea it seemed. Let sleeping dogs lie, I thought. The world was better off for the brute's death, anyway. And I was devoid of remorse.

'Is the colonel seeing Anna?' I asked Jones.

'Sure. Right away I should think.'

'What's the drill?'

'Concerning her? I really don't know. It's a security job. These guys have their own routine.'

A G.I. came in and told Jones the 'phones were working again.

'Thanks,' he said saluting the soldier. Then turning to me. 'I'll get you London as soon as possible. . . . O.K.?'

'O.K.,' I said.

He returned to say there'd be a delay up to an hour. I asked if I could see Anna.

'As a matter of fact,' he said, 'Colonel Brandon's talking to her. He's very interested in her. It's on the cards they'll want to quiz her at General Headquarters.'

'What will that mean?'

'We'll run her over there,' he said. 'She'll be well looked after. What the routine is, I don't know. It shouldn't take long. We've a pretty efficient set-up now. You'd be surprised. Our security people have all sorts of irons in the fire. . . . Anyway, I'll let you know.'

My call came through at about 3 p.m. I'd given Jones Motty's number. I wondered what to say to Motty. It was pretty dicey saying anything important until I'd been in contact with Rick. I took the call in Jones' office. It was a joy just to hear old Motty's voice again.

'Who's that?' he snapped.

'Harry—Harry Hammond,' I said. 'Don't you remember me? I'm the boy who was scheduled to win——'

'Harry!' he yelled. 'You mean our Harry?'

'Yes, old boy. How are you?'

'Where you been? We've been worried to death. What happened? You with Rick?'

'No. . . . Where is Rick?'

'You mean you've not seen him? My God! Know what he told me—that you were probably dead.'

'So he didn't say what I was doing?'

'Not a word. That's what I couldn't make out, Harry. . . . Just said you'd got mixed up in something. Not a blind word what it was. It's a bit much, you know. After all I *did* let you go. You might have kept in touch with us.'

'I couldn't very well.'

'Well, what's it all about? Why all the mystery?'

'I can't tell you yet. I've got to contact Rick. Where is he?'

'Paris.' He gave me the number which I scribbled on Jones' blotter. 'Why can't you tell me what you've been up to?'

'I can't on the 'phone.'

'You're in trouble?'

'I'll tell you everything as soon as Anna's cleared. We'll come straight to England.'

'Anna,' he almost screamed. 'Who's she?'

'A girl I met.'

'Oh, no,' Motty drawled. 'It's not that kind of mix-up. Don't tell me you're mixed up with broads, Harry?'

'She's O.K.,' I said.

'Well, I know that, Harry boy, but—oh, no, it's not true. Not you, Harry. Rick, yes. I could understand Rick——'

'It's not what you think,' I said. 'The whole thing is simply explained. But I can't do it now. I'll contact Rick. Then I'll be home.'

'When?'

'That depends. I'll let you know as soon as I get the O.K. How's everybody?'

'Fine. . . . Can't you give me some idea when to expect you?'

'Not now. Later.'

'I don't get it.'

'It's a security job.'

'Security job!'

He'd have gone on all day had I let him. Finally, I had to get tough.

'I've got to hang up,' I said.

Motty sounded very cheesed off.

'Well, I think it's a pretty poor show,' he said, and then dropped his receiver. I felt pretty bad about it. But I had to talk to Rick—to get the lowdown on what had happened. I wasn't even sure he was through the Iron Curtain. Jones tried to get Rick on the blower. But there was no reply to the number Motty had given me.

'We'll try later,' he said. 'And by the way, they've taken Anna to G.H.Q.'

'What! They might have let me have a word with her,' I said, feeling pretty peeved.

'There wasn't time,' Jones said. 'You were on the 'phone. The colonel couldn't wait—he had an appointment. But don't worry, she'll be O.K.'

He tried the Paris number again. A woman answered.

'Who's that?' she asked.

'Harry Hammond,' I said. 'I want to speak to my brother Rick.'

'Harry Hammond?' she repeated loudly.

'Yes. Is Rick there?'

She never answered. There was a motley assortment of noises.

'Hello, hello, hello,' I shouted, thinking they'd cut me off.

'Wait a minute,' the woman said. 'Won't keep you a tick.'

The voice was familiar.

'O.K?' Jones said. I nodded. He said so long and left me alone.

'Rick's just popped out,' the woman said. 'Where are you?'

'Who are you?' I asked.

'Don't you recognise my voice, brave man?'

'Mrs. Lamond.'

'Kathie to you. My God, are we glad to hear from you! Look. Where are you?'

I gave her the address.

'Rick's demented. He'll be dying to see you. We'll probably pop over. What's your 'phone number?'

I looked at the instrument and then gave the number to her.

171

'Good,' she said. 'Rick and I will——' She suddenly stopped. There was an infuriating noise going on.

'Hello,' I said. 'Hello.' There was no reply. I hello-ed a couple of times more. Then I got through to the operator.

'They've disconnected,' she said. 'Do they have your number?'

'Yes.'

'They'll probably ring you back.'

There was no point in my ringing Kathie again. Rick was out. When he returned she'd give him the number and he'd ring me here.

I waited all evening for Rick to call. At ten o'clock I asked Jones if I could ring Paris again.

'By all means,' he said. He tried to get the number. 'They say it's temporarily out of order.'

I was puzzled and annoyed. Rick could have rung me from elsewhere. What was cooking? Something was radically wrong. That stood out a mile. I knew Rick—knew that once he'd heard I was on this side of the Curtain, he'd go through hell to contact me. I finally decided he was probably on his way here. Even so, I thought, he'd have tried to contact me. . . .

In the mess later, Jones bought me a Scotch. That's how bad my nerves were that day. He had the same. We sat at the horse-shoe bar on high chromium stools and discussed the shooting.

After a couple of doubles, Jones trotted out his main belly-ache—a disastrous love affair he'd had back home. An old story about his best friend double-crossing him.

Poor Jones. He was an eldest child and had suffered all sorts of dethronements in his twenty-five years of life. The last and most humiliating was that of being emulated by his alleged best friend.

'So he and Maria were married,' he said bitterly. What did I think of that? I wasn't helpful. I said that it was a good thing for Jones that she had married his best friend. How did I make that out? I told him that she obviously loved the guy and that being so, she didn't love Jones.

'Yeh, I know that argument,' he said. 'But it doesn't help a guy. How do you get rid of that choking feeling?' he sighed.

I couldn't help him there. I'd never had that feeling.

172

'Well?' he said.

'Time cures everything,' I said.

'Yeh. . . . How right you are. . . . It even cures you of the desire to live.'

He drank up and looked at his watch.

'I'll see you to your room,' he said thickly, as he slid from the stool. 'You're my responsibility while you're here. Another thing. Didn't tell you this, did I? I—I've detailed a guard to watch over you tonight just in case. . . . Know something? The colonel was real worried about that Kruger gang. Before he left he warned me to keep a sharp look-out. I'm not saying this to scare you. But that's how it is.'

We left the mess and walked along the deserted hall, passing Jones' office on the way. A sentry posted outside my room jumped to attention and saluted.

'Carry on, soldier,' Jones said, then went in and checked the window. 'Everything's O.K. feller,' he added. 'Sorry about the girl. Wasn't my fault. The colonel was in a hurry. Had a date like I told you.' He looked around the room. 'You've got everything—pyjamas, shaving-kit.'

'I'm very grateful,' I said.

'You're O.K.,' he said, patting my back. 'Sleep well.'

In bed later, I suddenly realised that Rick was supposed to have gone to Washington with Lamond—that Lamond had told me he was saying nothing about me to Rick until after he'd got that film safely on the other side of the Atlantic. What had misfired? If Rick was still in Paris something had obviously gone wrong. Perhaps Rick had discovered about me? Perhaps he'd refused to play ball until he'd heard from me?

I yawned. My eyes grew heavy. It was too complicated to figure out. Pulling the piece of string which switched off the light, I slid down in bed and then rolled over on my side. In the dark my brain grew active again. Perhaps the story wasn't yet ended? Perhaps there'd be a lot of other things to complicate my life? Outside the wind sighed and moaned. Sometimes an owl hooted. Then I'd hear the sentry in the corridor cough and put down his rifle. It must have been after midnight before I finally dropped off. . . .

29

DESPITE my anxiety about Anna and Rick, I had a good night's sleep. A G.I. woke me next morning with a pot of coffee.

'With Captain Jones' compliments, sir,' he said, putting the tray on the table beside the bed.

'What is it?' I asked, after thanking him.

'Coffee, sir.'

'What time is it?'

'Eight-thirty.' He pulled the curtains aside. 'When you're ready, breakfast will be awaiting you in the mess, sir.'

'Thanks a million.'

He went out. I poured a cup of coffee. When I'd drank it, I got up and stared through the window at the neglected lawn. Everything out there was bright. While listening to the singing birds, I felt that something was radically wrong with Rick. It stood to reason. . . . He'd have rung me had he been able. Of that much I was certain.

Then there was Anna. Despite Jones' explanation, I thought it was odd that she'd been whisked off so quickly—that she hadn't been allowed to say good-bye to me.

When I'd shaved, I went to the mess where Jones was looking less and less like the embittered and disillusioned Jones, of the night before. A pale slightly yellow Jones, with a lean and liverish look, greeted me as I joined him at the long table.

'I feel goddam awful,' he moaned.

The steward poured me out a cup of coffee.

'Any news?' I asked Jones.

'Not so far,' he said, helping himself to some marmalade.

The steward asked me what I wanted to eat.

I fancied a stack of hot cakes which you plastered with butter and maple syrup.

'No news from Paris?' I said to Jones.

'No. But don't worry. We'll put a call in just as soon as you're through eating.'

A patch of yellow light lay on the floor beneath the french

windows which stared across the gravel path at the back of the mansion.

After breakfast Jones tried to get through to Paris. Lamond's 'phone was out of order.

'It's damn funny,' I said.

'Well, there it is. It's the best we can do, I'm afraid.'

'What about Anna? I hate to bother you. . . .'

'No bother at all.' Jones reached for the blower and asked for General Headquarters. He spoke to somebody and was afterwards put through to the colonel.

'It's O.K.,' he said, when he'd finished talking. 'She's quite happy. Looking forward to seeing you,' he said. 'They're just waiting for a report. Should be through tomorrow. He said you could talk to her this afternoon. She'll be free then.'

I thanked him and then went outside for a breath of air. Five minutes later, a G.I. told me I was wanted on the 'phone. I ran back to Jones' office.

'It's a woman,' he said, handing me the receiver. 'Didn't give a name.'

'Thanks.' It was Kathie Lamond.

'Are you free?' she asked.

'Why, of course. . . . What's up?'

'I've got to see you.'

'Where are you?'

'In the village.'

'What village?'

'A little place about two miles from you. I took the night plane to Nuremberg. Then a car here.'

'Anything wrong?'

'I can't tell you on the 'phone. Can you meet me?'

'Where?'

'Outside your place.'

'But can't you come here?'

'I could, but I'd rather not.'

'Is there anything wrong?'

'Look. . . . It's pretty urgent.'

'Can't you give me——'

'It's about Rick and my husband,' she said. 'I can't tell you any more.'

'How long will you be?'

'Say half an hour. What's the time now?' She paused. 'Say about noon. Where will you be?'

'Just outside the gate. You can't miss it. It's a big white gate.'

'Could you make it—could you walk say two or three hundred yards to the east of it. There's a special reason for this. I'll tell you all about it when I see you. Do you understand?'

'O.K.'

'Be on the right of the road. I'm travelling in a black Buick tourer.'

'O.K.' I dropped the receiver in its coffin and looked at Jones.

'Well?' he said.

I shrugged.

'I don't get it.'

'What did she say?'

I told him.

'She could have seen you here.'

'I told her that.'

'Why didn't she want to come here?'

'She never said.'

Jones walked to the window deep in thought.

'What do you think?'

He turned and shrugged.

'Where's she picking you up?'

I told him.

'You'd better keep the date. . . . Who is she by the way?'

I explained the little I knew about Kathie.

I had coffee laced with brandy with Jones in the mess.

He walked with me as far as the lane which ran past the white gate at the end of the drive. What a lovely day! The wind had dropped. A haze hung over the wood opposite. I said so long to Jones and crossed the road. On the grass verge I watched a flock of birds fly overhead. I was still uneasy about Rick. What had Kathie Lamond to tell me about him—that he'd been shot or kidnapped again?

Stopping about 200 yards from the gate, I stood with my face to the sun. It was good to feel its warmth. Five minutes later a big black Buick swept round a bend. Kathie was driving. I saw her plainly through the windscreen. Nobody else was

176

visible. She wore a gay little white hat, and seeing me she smiled and slowed down. Stepping from the grass verge into the road, I raised my hand.

Then it happened! A shot rang out. Kathie's face blanched. I'll never forget it. Then to my horror, she stepped on the gas. There was no escape. The car roared at me like a mad monster. The last I remember was that look of horror on Kathie's face as I was knocked down. . . . It seemed as if she'd lost control of the car, as if she'd been suddenly paralysed by something she saw behind me. . . .

30

OPENING my eyes I thought it was blood smearing the windows. I blinked a couple of times and thought, I wiped it off surely. . . . Then I saw what it was—red curtains drawn together. Beyond them the sun throbbed in the sky. And I was in bed surrounded by a pleated red silk screen. Something was wrong with me! Pain flooded my limbs and head. A feeling of infinite weariness pervaded my body. Breathing was difficult and panting didn't seem to be any use at all. . . . Then my heart! Why was it tapping my ribs like a pneumatic drill. . .?

How bewildering it all was! Why couldn't I remember what had happened? Suddenly it returned—Kathie Lamond's terror-stricken face, the leaping car and that shot. . . . I don't remember struggling to rise . . . just the stabbing pain. I yelled out involuntarily as I collapsed on the bed. Was this dying? I had no weight—just an awareness of pain and that whirligig of confused thoughts.

I was back with Dr. Klaus. Kathie Lamond had betrayed me. Was I naked and in a cell? Was I being stared at? Were they jeering? No, no, I was merely thinking all this. Actually I was in bed and wet with perspiration and feeling so unbearably hot. . . . Who was I anyway? Somebody. Silly—silly wasn't it? Not knowing who you were—knowing other people but not knowing yourself. Downright stupid.

If only I didn't have to pant. Hark at me. I saw myself as an engine panting up a gradient. Puffing Billy. Who called me that?

A door squeaked open. . . . Something clicked. Feet pattered over polished lino. How exciting! Here at last was the sinister Dr. Klaus. But I wasn't scared anymore. . . . Because only his name was real. No other associations existed.

'He's come round,' said an American.

Suddenly everything cleared and I saw the blonde nurse and the dark young doctor in their white gowns staring down at me from way up above.

I blinked a few times. Then focused them. I regained my substance. Pain was very real now. My limbs seemed to have sunk into the mattress.

'How you feeling?' the doctor whispered, bending down.

'Not too bad,' I managed to say between pants.

'Good. . . . Good.' He looked sideways at the nurse, his face grave, eyes troubled.

'Where am I?' I whispered.

'American hospital at Plauen. You had an accident—a car knocked you down. Remember?'

He had hold of my wrist.

'You don't remember?'

'Not yet,' I said.

Nurse opened my pyjama top and the doctor checked my heart with stethoscopes. Something on my forehead felt cold—so cold and so soothing. Glancing up, I saw the nurse's hand resting there.

'You're a pretty sick guy.'

'Who?'

'You.'

'Me?'

'Yes, you,' the doctor said.

The nurse tucked the covers under the mattress.

Somebody was singing. Or were they? I cocked my ear. Yes, it was a boy's voice—a sweet alto. And he was singing a hymn.

'Isn't it sweet?' I said.

The doctor frowned at the nurse. They were talking to each other but I couldn't hear what they said. It was like watching a movie when the sound track packs up.

'He's the nicest guy in this man's Army,' I said.

'Who—who?'

'Jones.'

'Jones?' said the doctor.

'Captain Kelloway Jones.'

Then everything started to boil and mix—mix and boil. I was surely round the bend. Yet how could a bloke be round the bend when he was aware that that's where he probably was? Who was it that was aware that he was aware that he was probably round the bend? . . . Oh, hell, hell. Who cares? It didn't make sense. Nothing made sense. The hell with Jones. The hell with the doctor. The hell with everything. Blow out the light and let's get some sleep—all this nonsense. Somewhere out there in the world a voice was echoing in a huge hall. 'Go to sleep.' It sounded a million miles away. Next I knew I was riding in a perambulator. The nurse I'd seen when I regained consciousness, wheeled it. She kept saying, 'Now go to sleep like a good boy.'

Next I was playing with Rick—we were in a field of emerald green. The sun was shining. A lark was singing as it soared up to the deep blue sky. A wasp attacked Rick. I picked up a bat and drove it off. Rick was furious. He said, 'I can fight my own battles, if you don't mind.'

I felt terrible. I wanted to explain that I loved him; that I'd do anything in the world for him, but I couldn't speak, my throat was paralysed. It was terrible. Rick kept nagging me—telling me I was always poking my nose into his business.

I came to for a few minutes. I remember seeing a sea of faces above me—grave faces. They were all concerned about me—about my being misunderstood by Rick. They told me not to brood about it, that things were like that in this world. All of us were born to be misunderstood. I mustn't blame Rick for his not understanding my motives. How could he when he wasn't me. 'But he is,' I said. They shook their heads and said, 'No.' We looked exactly alike but we were separate and distinct personalities. His attitudes were obviously different. He disliked me playing the protector to him. It all seemed so unfair to me. I'd only done what I had to help him. I had no hope of reward. I'd done it out of the goodness of my heart and it deeply grieved me to know my actions weren't appreciated.

179

That's how it went. I lived in so many worlds—some sane and rational; others were crazy. This went on for a week. . . .

'It was just a toss-up whether you'd survive,' the doctor said. I had a multiple fracture of the left thigh; a fractured skull and of course the fractured clavicle which I'd collected before Kathie Lamond ran me over.

It was curious. . . . How I came to, I mean. Suddenly everything was normal. It was like descending from another universe to a world in which everything made sense—the window, the screen round the bed, the trolley. These were real things. And I was back in the real world.

I had no idea how ill I'd been. Nor for some time did I know what had happened to me. It didn't matter just then. It was enough to know I was alive.

The nurse came in. What a sweet smile she gave me! She fetched the doctor. He looked as pleased as Punch. But I wasn't strong enough to take much notice of reality. He gave me a shot in the arm and I went off to sleep again. There were more dreams—fantastic, beautiful, crazy. . . .

One day I woke up and found that I didn't have to lie still any more. . . . that I was eager to see my brother Rick, eager to know what had happened to Kathie Lamond and Anna—Anna whom I'd almost forgotten.

31

THE day Rick and I were reunited rain came down, grey, solid, slow, slanting across the window. The curtains were drawn and there was a background of traffic noises; a symphony of gear-changing, acceleration and vague clattering and roaring. Red and white carnations, my favourite flowers, sprouted from a vase on the white pedestal beside my bed.

I'd just been washed. The nurse on this shift, a round-faced girl with dark flabby skin under expressive brown eyes, was less for me than the blonde. Her favourites were elsewhere, I presumed. 'Your brother Rick's coming today,' she said.

'Really!' I said. It seemed scarcely credible. I don't know why but he seemed to have become an illusive character—

a-not-quite-true personality in my mind. I'd reached a point where I wondered if he'd ever really existed. . . . I'd lived too long in fantasy. Perhaps I was still partly round the bend.

'Don't excite yourself too much,' she said, picking up the basin and towel. 'You're not as well as you probably think you are.'

Now I had to get things straight—in their logical order. Begin at the beginning. I was like a kid. I went back to my childhood with Rick. I saw my father die again. Then my mother. After this I was married. And Joan was looking after me—saying, 'You'll win the championship and then we'll retire and lie around in the sun in the South of France.' Suddenly Joan went out like a light.

'It's no good kid,' Motty said. 'You've got to forget it. There's nothing you can do about it. Death is final—horribly final. So snap out of it and remember this fight with Hanslip will put you in the running. . . .'

Then the cable, 'Rick dead believed murdered.' That was the last of sanity. The rest had been a crazy nightmare. . . . Who would believe it? What had it done to me? I wasn't the same anymore. Never would be.

Rick came at 3 p.m. Rain had stopped but iron-grey clouds smeared the sky. I remember how I tingled with excitement. It was always the same when we met. Rick was like that too. I think it was because when we met it was like looking at ourselves in a mirror.

I heard the screen move and looking round, I saw Rick staring, his eyes full of concern for me. He came round and stood at the foot of the cot, palpably tongue-tied and over-emotional.

'Rick!' I said, when I found my voice.

He came over and took my hand.

'You all right?' he whispered.

I nodded.

'You sure you're all right, boy?'

'I think so.'

Although I hadn't visualised any embracing or other violent emotional demonstrations, I did expect something more than this jerky dry-as-dust dialogue. For my part I had so much to say I was at a loss how to begin. And Rick was apparently the same. Then it went on like this:

'Why did you do it, boy?' he said, frowning at me.

'What?'

'You know what.'

I hesitated. Then I said how much I liked his new grey suit and how brown and handsome he looked. 'Is that a nylon shirt?' I said.

He nodded and grinned.

'But why did you do it?' he said at last.

'There was a cable,' I said.

'Yeh, yeh, I know,' he said. 'I know the lot now. They told me the whole thing—Nina did. You know what's got me down, Harry? It's that you—you had to get mixed-up in my—my lousy life. You, of all people. And to think—think that there you were in that bathroom—actually in there when they were getting me out. When I heard that—what I didn't call Lamond is nobody's business. Even old Rumbold never gave me a clue that you were in there. Nobody did. Why did you do it, Harry?'

'You were in a spot,' I said.

'Even so. . . . Motty should never have let you come alone. . . . How did you get out of that place?'

'I'm more interested in you, Rick.' I glanced at the carnations. 'It was nice of you to remember.'

'I never thought you'd live long enough to see them,' he said. 'God Almighty! You don't know what I've been through during the last three or four weeks. Ask Nina. I've almost been round the bend.'

'Did you see a little gypsy girl—Anna?'

'No,' he said.

'What!'

He looked puzzled.

'But—she—oh, never mind. Did you see Captain Jones?'

He nodded.

'The American? Yes. A nice fellow.

'Isn't he?'

'Look, boy,' he said, sitting on the one and only white chair and crossing his long legs, 'I owe you a full explanation. Here it is.'

He gave me the lot—exactly how he'd become involved in that cloak and dagger business. It wasn't Rick's racket. He'd only become mixed up in it fortuitously. He confessed to being

182

a grafter; to being involved with shady characters and indulging in doubtful enterprises. He wasn't ashamed of this. He held the view that all big business these days is 'a bit of a swindle.'

'There's nothing very noble about me, Harry,' he said. 'Never has been. I haven't got your honesty or your integrity. I mention this because had I been like you, you wouldn't be lying here now.'

The nurse appeared and Rick dried up. She looked at me and smiled. 'Are you quite comfortable?' she asked.

'Fine—fine,' I said.

She checked my pulse and looked at Rick.

'Don't excite him too much.'

He jumped up and said, 'Look, perhaps I ought to go. . . .'

'Don't go, Rick,' I said. 'Please don't go.'

'Will it be all right?' he asked the nurse.

'Yes, but don't let him talk any more than is necessary.' She went out and Rick and I looked at each other. He still wore that sheepish—almost guilty expression he'd had when he first saw me.

'I'm trying to find a lead in,' he said.

'How did it all begin for you?'

He shrugged and then dropped his arms.

'I'm to blame,' he said. 'It was all my fault, Harry. I mean that sincerely. I should have got the kidney punch, not you. You see I'd planned to double-cross Kathie Lamond. The story they told you about me, Pierre and Nina was practically fiction. There was a film. There was a bloke named Pierre. But he wasn't Nina's brother. They never even met. He was a free-lance agent. He came to Paris to deliver the film to Kathie Lamond. He got this film out of Moscow. It was given to him by another free-lance agent. It was pictures of secret Russian equipment. That's all I know about it. Somehow the Reds traced Pierre to Paris. Don't ask me how. Anyway, the poor devil was tipped-off by Kathie that the Reds knew he was in Paris and to lie low in the Latin Quarter until he heard from her again.

'This is where I come in. I met Nina in Monte Carlo. She introduced me to Lamond, her step-father. We grew very fond of one another. She told me how her mother had died two years before, how Lamond had since married Kathie—the notorious

Kathie Harrington, who controlled a big espionage syndicate from West Berlin. I didn't know this till afterwards.

'Anyway, I was well in with the family when Kathie was looking for somebody to collect the film from Pierre. She couldn't send any of her regulars to him because they were all well known to the Russian Secret Police. She was scared that they'd be picked up by an agent in Paris and followed to the Latin Quarter, in which event Pierre's life wouldn't be worth tuppence.'

Rick paused and then went on.

It was eventually decided that Rick should go to Paris, collect the film from Pierre and fly back to Monte Carlo.

'It was as simple as that,' Rick said.

What Kathie didn't know was that Rick had been knocking around in various rackets and wasn't strictly speaking as honest as he might have been.

'But what happened,' Rick said, 'was partly her fault. You see, old boy, she wasn't a hundred per cent honest with me. Had she told me what the set-up was at the outset things might have been different. Kathie tried to bluff me. But don't get her wrong. She was a brilliant woman. One of the best, too. But she had a blind spot. I was asked if I'd like to earn a monkey. Now that's a lot of potatoes in any language. All I had to do was to deliver a letter to Pierre in the Latin Quarter in Paris and bring one back to her. I thought she was kidding. Why couldn't it be sent by post? "Never you mind," she said. I didn't argue. Five hundred quid was always worth while picking up. My instructions were to go to an address in which a room had been reserved for me and wait until I was approached. I knew then that it was crooked. It didn't shock me, mark you, I was a bit of a fiddler myself.'

Although the letter Kathie Lamond gave Rick was sealed, he opened it and then put the contents into another envelope, which he sealed. He apparently had no difficulty in forging Kathie's handwriting. There was a cheque for £10,000 and a letter. This told Pierre that he could cash the cheque just as soon as the Americans were convinced that the goods he'd brought from Moscow were the real McCoy.

Rick realised then that he was being used by spies. He didn't mind that. All that really interested him was the cash.

'I had no intention of two-timing Kathie,' he said, 'after I'd tumbled the nature of her racket. The job looked easy. I couldn't see any risks in it.'

After reading Kathie's note to Pierre, Rick noticed that he was an object of interest to a character travelling in the train.

'I didn't pay a great deal of attention,' Rick said. 'But I was always conscious of him. Anyway, I went to the address in the Latin Quarter and the concierge showed me to the room. Nothing was said about Pierre. All I had to do was to await developments.

'About eleven o'clock that night Pierre came to my room, scared stiff. Kathie was crazy to send me, he said. She knew he'd been traced to Paris. And she must have known that agents would have her under observation since they knew she was the person to whom he had to deliver the film.

'"So I'm not giving it to you," he said. I asked what made him so sure I'd been followed there. "Take a look out there," he said, pointing to the window.

'There were two of them—both wearing grey velour hats and grey raincoats. "In case anything happens to me," Pierre said, "return to your room and switch on your reading lamp." I didn't get it. "What's the idea?" I asked. He told me not to ask questions—I'd see what it was all about later.'

Rick 'phoned Kathie the next day and told her what the strength was. She told him to stay there and look after Pierre. If there was trouble, he was to 'phone the police. When he returned to the house, he saw a crowd surrounding an ambulance outside. Pierre had been found hanging from the banister.

The concierge was demented. She'd just returned from shopping and had found Pierre. There was a note pinned to his jacket apologising for what he'd done. Rick was pretty certain that it was suicide—that Pierre suddenly lost his nerve, probably because he feared being kidnapped.

'Now comes the fireworks,' he said. 'Both Pierre's room and mine were turned upside down. You never saw such a mess. They'd ripped chairs, sofas, mattresses—even the wainscoting. The concierge went nearly barmy. Returning to my room, I suddenly thought of the light. Switching on the reading lamp, I saw that it was dimmed. Then I found it—the film in an envelope, the flap of which had been stuck to the bulb. What to do now? Should I ring Kathie? No. Her line was probably tapped. Then I had an idea. Running downstairs, I called the concierge. She wasn't there. I saw her bag on the table. Dashing back upstairs, I got a safety razor blade. Then I returned and slit the lining in the old girl's bag and slipped the film in it. After this, I contacted Kathie. It was then that the idea of double-crossing her came to me. Pierre was dead. Would she come to Paris?

"'What about the other?" she asked.

"'Search me," I said.

"'Stay there. . . . I'll contact you later. I've got to make a call —somebody with whom Pierre was in contact." She hung up. And I went back to my room wondering if Pierre had perhaps told this fellow Kathie was going to contact what he had done with the film. It looked dicey. I was worried. I didn't want to fall out with her because of Nina. But I needn't have worried.

'As I opened my door and walked through into the room, I was grabbed, handcuffed and thrown on the bed. There were three of them.

"'O.K.," one of them said. "The film."

"'What film?" I said.

'They searched me then. After stripping me of all my clothes, the man in charge said, "We know you've got it. We heard the dead man tell somebody just before he killed himself that he'd given it to you and for him to tell Kathie Lamond that."

"'He's a liar," I said. "You've searched the room. You must have tailed me when I made that call. You know I saw nobody."

"'O.K.," this fellow said, "give him the works." I was held down and one of them gave me an injection. That's all I remember till I woke up in that hospital.'

He paused and sighed.

'Kathie must have guessed what happened to me,' he went on. 'So she got cracking and her organisation behind the Iron Curtain finally located me. She's told me since that she spoke to Big Francis, who told her there wasn't a hope in hell of getting me out of the country. He explained the set-up—the Q-plan and all that. It was then that she remembered you—that I had an identical twin. You know the rest.'

186

He said getting me from London to Paris was carefully planned—the cable, the Hotel Sylvia's 'phone being out of order, the Nina interview, the snatch outside the mortuary. . . .

'The whole success of the switch depended entirely on your wholehearted co-operation,' he said. 'That's why the plan had to include a body and Nina acting as a Red agent. Had they put the proposition to you coldly, they were afraid you wouldn't believe them. They thought you'd probably go to the police. Then the Foreign Office would have been involved and that in turn would have meant my having to take the treatment. You see, boy, it was *time*. Had Klaus not been detained in Moscow it would have been hopeless. But that gave them time to get you to the hospital.

'I hadn't a clue what was cooking. The first I knew I was being rescued was when Jan took me to the bathroom. I thought I was going to have a bath. Then as we were level with it, he pushed me in the linen room and told me I was being got out of there. There was no time for questions. I just got in that basket you came in and hoped for the best.'

Kathie met Rick at the farmhouse where I first saw Rumbold. They flew to Paris. Then Kathie told him that the man to whom Pierre had spoken just before he died had told her Rick had the film. He denied it.

While Kathie was 'phoning her husband, Rick rang me at the gym. His idea was to get the film from the concierge's bag and send it to me for safe-keeping.

'Then Motty told me about the cable you got from Nina,' he said. 'I gave him Kathie's 'phone number and asked him to tell you to ring me there if he heard from you. Then I had a showdown with Kathie. "O.K." I said. "So I know where the film is. You can have it if you get Harry out."

'She took me to the Hotel Sylvia in Montmartre. Here I met Big Francis who'd just flown in from Plauen. Kathie introduced us. He told me that you were out of the hospital but whether you'd succeed in getting here was anybody's guess.'

Rick laid low in Kathie's house on the hill. 'I did a lot of thinking there,' he said. 'I saw I was to blame. So I told Kathie where the film was. She got it from the concierge and Lamond took it to his American contacts. Then you rang. Kathie took the call. I was in fact out. She said nothing to me about it—nothing to anybody. She just vanished. Lamond was worried to death. He thought she'd been kidnapped. Then we heard from Captain Jones about you. He'd found Kathie's number you'd written on his blotter and 'phoned. He told me how you'd been knocked down by a car and taken here. I saw him the day after you were injured.'

Jones had been worried. He thought Kathie's call was a ruse on Red Kruger's part to get me out of the H.Q. so he sent two men to keep an eye on me. When I stepped into the road to stop Kathie's car, two men dashed out of the wood. Kathie must have seen them.

'Jones said that she seemed to lose control of the car,' Rick said. 'There was no need for her to panic, because Jones' men fired and the men ran away. Kathie's car zig-zagged across the road and crashed into a tree. They found her slumped over the steering wheel. Her neck was broken.'

Rick didn't tell me that day what was wrong with me—that I was doomed to be a cripple for life. He softened the blow by saying that Lamond had deposited £25,000 to my account—that being my share of the price the Americans paid for the film.

But I was more interested at this time in Anna than in money. I told Rick about her—how I'd killed a man for her; how she was the only person I'd ever been really at peace with.

'And that includes Joan,' I said.

He looked at me in that doubtful quizzical way of his and shook his head.

'O.K.' he said. 'Leave it to me, boy. I'll find her.'

I thought he would too. That's why I didn't brood about her. I thought of Kathie Lamond. Why she had lost her head and run me down. Did she perhaps think that by doing so she'd save me from the men who were about to grab me? Or did something happen to the car—something that made her lose control of it?

I still have a soft spot for Kathie. What a wonderful woman she was! Rick told me all about her. How during the war the Gestapo had sentenced her to death, how she escaped and returned to her job of sending hundreds of British airmen through France and Spain. Since the war she'd been one of the most colourful characters in West Berlin and she was supposed to have a wonderful underground organisation behind the Iron Curtain.

It was strange how meeting me indirectly killed her. And how my meeting her had indirectly resulted in my being a cripple for life. But there it is. That's life. . . .

32

I WISH I could have ended this story on a happy note—to have told you how Anna and I were reunited, how we found a great love, married, settled down and had lots of kids. But that wasn't so. Anna disappeared into the blue. Rick searched for her all over Europe practically. He got her full name from NATO Security, who'd given her papers and money.

He discovered how she had come to the hospital every day the first week I was there. All the porters and sisters remembered her. Then she'd apparently given me up as a bad job. I'd been critically ill at that time. Even the specialist had given me up.

Poor Anna. How was she expected to have faith in my survival when everybody else had virtually written me off as dead?

The last person to see her was the tall blue-nosed porter on duty in the front hall. I had a long chat with him. He remembered Anna well—'Such a whimsical little child,' he said, 'with big sad brown eyes which seemed to look right through you.'

'I must see poor Mister Harry,' she told him.

But nobody except the medical staff was seeing me then—not even Rick. I was watched night and day. A slight move of my fractured head might well have proved fatal, they said.

So Anna looked very sad, the porter went on.

She'd sighed and staring up at the big man with troubled eyes, she said, 'I hope where he goes he'll have something more solid than memories.' Then she turned and ran out of the doorway. Outside she stared up at my window and saw the red curtains drawn. Just then a big grey car drew into the kerb.

'A low-slung job,' the porter said it was. 'Like the Americans drive.'

He saw Anna duck and get in beside the driver. Then there was only the lingering blue exhaust smoke out there. . . .

We advertised for Anna in all countries. I even told the story of how she got me through the Iron Curtain to all the newspapers. It was splashed all over the front pages of papers in Berlin, Nuremberg, Paris, London and New York. With it was a picture of me—the man who was waiting for 'just a word to say that she's happy and O.K. . . .'

That was two years ago. Since then I've wandered halfway round the world on the off-chance of bumping into her—a forlorn hope, maybe, but one that might have come off.

Only the other day I thought I saw her in Regent Street. I was in a cab on my way to meet Rick and Nina, who were married in June.

'Stop,' I called to the driver.

This girl was with a tall American officer, dressed like a Paris model, in pearl grey, and smiling in the sun. The brief glimpse I had of her convinced me it was Anna. The cab stopped fifty yards past where I'd seen her. Jumping out, I hobbled back, searching the hurrying faces of anonymous pedestrians. But neither she nor her escort was in sight.

I searched nearby shops. I stayed in the vicinity for over an hour. But she had vanished completely.

It probably wasn't Anna—just another girl with a face on which my mind had printed Anna's image.

So there it is. . . . I'm still looking for her. Sometimes I dream she's with her father, slaving in some Russian salt mine. I see those lynx-eyed Commies grinning at me. Sometimes they say, 'He who laughs last laughs the best.'

I can't believe this dream. I think rather that she probably took her father's advice and married a rich American. . . . If she has, I hope she's happy and that she occasionally remembers 'Mister Harry.' . . .

THE END

Museum Street Thrillers

DEAR DEAD DAYS   *by Jay Barbette*

This is the story of a murderer and blackmailer caught in the sinister trap he set for somebody else. A spine-tingling tale of the ugly, twisted ways of a murder that hurt everyone it touched. This thriller re-introduces some of the characters we met in *Final Copy*.

9s. 6d.

FINAL COPY   *by Jay Barbette*

A thriller with a newspaper office as a background. A young reporter covers a routine murder and stumbles on to a clue—he doesn't know what—that makes him dangerous to the killer. Already crippled for life by this unknown assailant, he waits helplessly in a wheelchair for the second attack which he knows must come and, while he waits, his mind is grappling with the mystery trying to recall the clue.

3s. 6d.

DEAD PIGEON   *by Robert P. Hansen*

Tim Lanigan exchanges plane tickets and finds he has also exchanged identities, and he collects all the trouble that was awaiting the stranger he met at the Airport. But he also collects a beautiful brunette and $3,000, so he had some compensation for being a scapegoat.

3s. 6d.

TROUBLE COMES DOUBLE   *by Robert P. Hansen*

When Ebon Sickel went into Jake Devers' office to pay the final instalment on his fishing boat he did not expect trouble but he found it and his partner was killed in the process. When Ebon decided to go after the killer himself his troubles really did come double—and then some! A fascinating story of smuggling, dope running, and all the assorted mayhem of the waterfront.

9s. 6d.

ALONE IN THE GRASS
by Conrad Phillips

A fast-moving story of crime in Mayfair and the three young men, who are not habitual crooks, who become involved in it. By the author of THE BARBER'S WIFE.

9s. 6d.

SHADOW PLAY
by Conrad Phillips

An exciting story based on the recent mail-bag robberies. Joe Hemingway worked on the inside and it was his information that helped the crooks select the right post-office van to hold up, but once the job was done it was his evidence that could send them all to prison. Hunted by the police, hunted by his fellow crooks, this is a tale full of suspense right to the last sentence.

9s. 6d.

GLASS ON THE STAIRS
by Margaret Scherf

The delightfully mad interior-decorator sleuths—the Bryces—plumped for murder when Mrs. Otis Carver was found shot in Link Simpson's gun and antique shop. Everybody else said "suicide," but by the time they had unearthed such wildly improbable clues as a pink glove, poisoned toothpaste, glass on the stairs, and several motives—including a luscious TV actress who was an intimate friend of Mr. Carver—the plot had thickened considerably, and they were right in the centre of one of the craziest cases of homicide on record.

9s. 6d.

PRELUDE TO MURDER
by Norman Leslie

A missing heiress and an escaped convict—two completely different news items, but they intrigued Red Shannahan who began an investigation of his own, and finally uncovered the connection between the two.

9s. 6d.

THE JUDAS GOAT
by Leslie Edgley

How would you like to attend your own funeral? Dix Latham did, and discovered that he would be held responsible for his own murder if he didn't think fast. How the irresponsible Mr. Latham extricates himself shows us the author of THE ANGRY HEART and DIAMONDS SPELL DEATH at his best.

9s. 6d.